The Bloody Book of Law

Sara Woods was born in Bradford in Yorkshire, but moved with her husband to Canada in the 1950s. Before she started writing full-time she did many varied jobs including breeding pigs and working in a bank. However, it was her experience of working in a solicitor's office in London, together with her great interest in the law which led to Sara Woods writing her most successful crime novels – those featuring the lawyer and sleuth, Antony Maitland.

Maitland, his wife and his uncle, Sir Nicholas, have gathered a huge following on both sides of the Atlantic and Sara Woods' many readers felt a great loss when she died in 1985.

SARA WOODS

THE BLOODY BOOK OF LAW

...the bloody book of law
You shall yourself read in the bitter letter
After your own sense...
> *Othello*, Act I, scene iii

M
PAPERMAC

First published in the United Kingdom 1984 by
Macmillan London Ltd

First published in paperback 1988 by
PAPERMAC
a division of Macmillan Publishers Limited
4 Little Essex Street London WC2R 3LF
and Basingstoke

Associated companies in Auckland, Delhi, Dublin, Gaborone, Hamburg, Harare, Hong Kong, Johannesburg, Kuala Lumpur, Lagos, Manzini, Melbourne, Mexico City, Nairobi, New York, Singapore and Tokyo

British Library Cataloguing in Publication Data

Woods, Sara
   The bloody book of law
   Rn: Sara Bowen-Judd
   I. Title
   823'.914[F]

   ISBN 0-333-46626-8
Printed in Hong Kong

Any work of fiction whose characters were of uniform excellence could rightly be condemned – by that fact if by no other – as being incredibly dull. Therefore no excuse can be considered necessary for the villainy or folly of the people appearing in this book. It seems extremely unlikely that any one of them should resemble a real person, alive or dead. Any such resemblance is completely unintentional and without malice.

S.W.

THE LONG VACATION, 1974

Wednesday, September 25th

I

Even in the City of London, that hotbed of crime where scandals are two a penny, fraud cases abound, and all the juiciest murder trials (and England, as we know, is the envy of the world, not for the quantity but for the quality of her murders) seem to end up, there is room for a certain number of firms of solicitors conducting a practice as peaceful as any that might occupy them in the quietest of country towns.

The landed gentry, up for a little amusement – or, more likely nowadays, on business – think perhaps that here they will get more sophisticated advice. Matthew Barlow didn't actually number any noble earls among his clients, but the county were well represented and he undertook on their behalf a great many of life's more mundane duties, as had his father and grandfather before him. But if ever there was a living proof that residence in the metropolis does not necessarily qualify one as an expert in the wickedness of this world, that proof could well have centred on Matthew's rather innocent outlook on life; so that his initial pleasure in receiving a visit from his old friends and clients, Arthur Gilchrist and his widowed mother, Mrs Helen Gilchrist, was quickly turned to dismay when he heard why they had come to him.

His first instinct was sheer disbelief that such a thing could have happened to clients of his, but presently he fell back upon the comforting idea that the police had made a terrible mistake. It is true that he knew very little of Vincent, Arthur's younger brother, except by hearsay. In fact, he hadn't seen him since he was a boy. But surely no member of that respectable family . . .

'You can rest assured,' he told his visitors as he showed them out some time later, 'that I shall do everything in my power to see that this dreadful error is put right.'

But it was a criminal matter, there was no doubt about that, and his experience in such cases was not merely negligible it was non-

7

existent. Still, there was his old friend Mr Bellerby who had chosen to steer his practice in quite a different direction from his own, and who would no doubt be glad to advise him. He reached for the telephone with a sense of relief, and was lucky enough to find his fellow solicitor in his office and at liberty.

'You see my difficulty,' he concluded after he had explained the situation. 'There's no question that I must act in the matter myself, though I should be only too glad to turn it over to somebody with your experience. The Gilchrists are friends as well as clients. I must certainly do my best for them.'

'Have you seen the young man yet?'

'Vincent Gilchrist? No, though of course I explained to them that I must do so as soon as possible. But the trouble is, you see . . . well, to tell you the truth, I find myself quite out of my depth.'

'And you want me to recommend counsel to you,' said Mr Bellerby thoughtfully. 'Well, that shouldn't be difficult,' he added more cheerfully. He was a naturally ebullient man, and a good many barristers of his acquaintance were inclined to think that he overdid his encouragement to their mutual clients, giving them a confidence which it was not always easy to justify.

'Someone,' said Matthew Barlow, feeling that the point could not be made too often, 'who won't despise me for my lack of – of know-how in these matters.'

'Yes, I gathered as much,' said Mr Bellerby jovially. 'If you want my advice you'll try to get Antony Maitland. He's an independent-minded chap, only too glad to take his own line. He'll look after you.'

'I've heard of him,' said Mr Barlow, rather as if this presented an insuperable difficulty.

'Yes, I daresay you have. Unorthodox, they say, and has a knack of getting himself talked about. But I'll tell you this much, there's no one I'd rather trust with a difficult matter, as this sounds to be if your belief in young Gilchrist's innocence is justified.'

'A terrible mistake,' said Matthew Barlow firmly, and then, 'I'll take your advice, of course.'

If there was a little hesitation in his friend's tone over this last statement, Mr Bellerby chose to ignore it. 'Mr Maitland is in his uncle's chambers,' he said. 'Sir Nicholas Harding, you've heard of him too, I expect. The chap you want to get hold of is Mallory, Sir Nicholas's clerk. He'll look after you.'

And so it was that Antony Maitland, returning to town with his wife Jenny a few days before the beginning of the Michaelmas term, found the case of Regina *versus* Gilchrist among the matters that had accumulated during his absence, and was told by old Mr Mallory in tones that brooked no argument that a conference had been arranged with solicitor and lay clients that very afternoon.

Sir Nicholas's chambers were in the Inner Temple, up one rather ill-lit flight of stairs. When Maitland had exchanged suitable greetings in the clerks' office – not altogether sincere on Mallory's part as he knew – he made his way down the corridor to his own room, only discovering when he turned to close the door that Willett had followed closely on his heels.

John Willett had been in chambers a long time, and was now junior only to Mr Mallory. Of all the clerks he was the one who identified himself most nearly with Maitland's interests, and he had realized early in his career that Mallory had never become completely reconciled to Antony's slightly eccentric ways which could, admittedly, be disruptive of a peaceful, well-ordered existence. This was apt to result in the dullest cases being accepted, while matters which would have been of real interest were turned down on the grounds of overwork, but Willett was not without ingenuity, and had discovered over the years ways of circumventing this deliberate perversity.

'This Mr Barlow,' he said now, when Antony had invited him in and closed the door, 'we've never had any work from him before.'

'No, I've never even heard of him,' Maitland agreed.

'High society stuff,' said Willett rather scornfully. 'Shouldn't think you'll find it interesting myself, but Mr Mallory got it into his head that where one brief came another might follow, especially as Mr Bellerby had recommended him. There didn't seem to be anything I could do to head him off, but now when I've asked around I find that Barlow & Mecks is strictly a family firm. Nothing in our line at all, this must be an exception. One of a kind,' he added in case the other man might have missed his meaning.

'I've never heard of Mr Meeks either,' said Maitland, looking with disfavour at the pile of papers on his desk. It was a long, narrow room, inclined to darkness even on the brightest day, and now he leaned forward to switch on the desk lamp. Always when he did this he thought of Jenny's offer to come in one weekend and re-decorate in some cheerful colour, her enthusiasm for the project dampened almost before it was born by Sir Nicholas's outraged stare.

'How the devil are we going to cope with all this?' he asked.

Willett took this question as it was probably intended, as purely rhetorical. 'Mr Meeks is dead,' he said.

'So are a good many other people,' said Maitland, not particularly interested in this piece of information. 'Still, some civil cases can be interesting.'

'This is a criminal matter all right,' said Willett. 'I only meant there'd probably be nothing more to come from the same source.'

Antony looked up and smiled at him. 'Don't be so mercenary,' he adjured him. 'A firm of family solicitors with a criminal client, that might be amusing.'

'The thing is,' Willett told him earnestly, 'I don't think so. Some younger son got himself into trouble, and not the first time either. So what you can be expected to do about it, I can't imagine.'

'Make as good a showing as I can in court,' said Maitland, opening the desk drawer and removing a foolscap pad and a pencil. There were in fact six pencils there, each sharpened to perfection, though he, as well as everyone else in chambers, knew well enough that the day wouldn't have passed in note making – it was important to get a list of priorities on paper – before each point was broken and reduced to bluntness. 'If I find it as dull as ditch water, I won't blame you,' he promised. 'What else is there in store for me in this pile?'

'The usual,' said Willett. 'Ned Bates has been at it again, and Mr Horton says he wants to plead Not Guilty. And there's a chap been in for a spot of arson, so the insurance company say. Nothing special.'

'Ah well, that's something we can leave to the experts,' said Maitland comfortably. 'Sir Nicholas will be in tomorrow by the way, I forgot to tell Mallory. Jenny's meeting them at the airport this afternoon.'

After that he was left in peace until the three o'clock conference, interrupted only by a telephone call from Geoffrey Horton, a solicitor who was a very old friend of his, besides being Mr Bellerby's son-in-law. Geoffrey was anxious to discuss Ned Bates, who kept recurring in both their schedules like the proverbial bad penny. 'I've been trying to talk sense into him,' he said, 'with no success at all. Perhaps you'll do better.'

'Well, I'll try,' said Antony doubtfully, 'but it'll have to wait until I've waded through the pile of stuff here. It isn't urgent, is it?'

'No, a couple of weeks won't make much difference,' Geoffrey agreed. It was typical of him that he didn't waste time on inquiries after the Maitlands' well-being and enjoyment of the summer vacation. Social engagements and social chit-chat were a matter for the women-folk, and not to be allowed to impinge on the working day. He rang off a few moments later, leaving Maitland not too concerned about the fate of Mr Bates, who might be innocent, as he apparently insisted, but was far more likely on previous form to have done exactly what was alleged of him, whatever that might be.

Mr Barlow and Vincent Gilchrist arrived promptly, at a few minutes to three, in fact, and were announced apologetically over the inter-office phone by Hill, who might by his tone have been announcing the arrival of a gang of thugs intent on mayhem. Antony invited him to send the two men in, in as reassuring a tone as he could manage, and a moment later Willett threw the door of his office open and stood back to allow them to pass.

Matthew Barlow turned out to be a short man with a round amiable face, probably in his early fifties. Maitland, who had risen to his feet to greet the newcomers, took in so much at a glance, but it never occurred to him for one moment to doubt which was the solicitor and which the client – Mr Barlow, as he told Jenny afterwards, positively exuded an aura of respectability – so he naturally eyed the younger man who followed the solicitor into the room with more interest. Vincent Gilchrist seemed to tower over his companion, but a moment later Antony realized that his and his new client's eyes were level. At first glance, Gilchrist was rather startlingly good-looking which, perversely, didn't prejudice counsel in his favour, but on closer acquaintance Maitland was to find redeeming features in a chin a little too square and determined for perfection, and in a very straightforward look. For the rest, he had light brown hair and a very fair complexion.

In their turn the two newcomers studied Maitland. Matthew Barlow saw a tall man with dark, rather untidy hair – Antony had been running his fingers through it as he worked, but the solicitor couldn't know that – a manner that was a little too casual for his taste, and a humorous look that he instinctively distrusted. Gilchrist noted the humour too, and an intelligence that couldn't be discounted; but also, hearteningly, a man who wouldn't hesitate to take an unconventional course of action if it suited him. It is perhaps odd that neither of them saw the sensitivity that was perhaps the most dominant characteristic of the man they were

11

studying and which, combined with compassion and an instinctive distrust for his own judgement (uncomfortable bedfellows indeed) contributed, each in its own way, to the unconventional behaviour that some of his acquaintances were so ready to condemn.

The introductions took but a moment; getting his visitors settled with as much comfort as the room could afford, a little longer, and Maitland added the word fussy to his mental description of the solicitor. At last they were settled, tea was offered and accepted with some eagerness by Matthew Barlow and rather less readily by Gilchrist, who exchanged a look with counsel that probably meant, by all means let's do the right thing, but I know quite well we'd both prefer a scotch. Maitland smiled back at him non-committally enough. If he were indeed correct in his estimate of his new client's meaning, the man couldn't have been more wrong. But when he asked for the tea it appeared so quickly that Willett had obviously been expecting the request, and they were at last ready to get down to the business of the day.

'This is a very unfortunate business,' said Matthew Barlow earnestly. 'I've already explained to Mr Gilchrist that I find myself quite without experience in this sort of thing, but the family were very anxious that I should deal with the matter myself. Our connection goes back for many years, to my grandfather's day in fact, so naturally I did not wish to disoblige them. But I should start by telling you, Mr Maitland, as I've already explained to our client, that I took the best advice I could before getting in touch with your clerk.'

Maitland couldn't help smiling. 'And who was the kind friend who recommended me to you?' he asked, apparently forgetting that Willett had told him.

'My old friend, James Bellerby. He assured me that you would not find it too wearisome to guide me through these unknown waters' – a phrase which Antony found revealing, as showing more imagination than he would have expected – 'and also that in the particular circumstances that have arisen, your special talents might be of use.'

It was at this point that Maitland ceased to find any humour at all in the situation. He had worked many times with Mr Bellerby as his instructing solicitor, and knew quite well what was meant when that particular phrase was used. It meant that, rightly or wrongly, Mr Bellerby thought there might be some matter for investigation here, some activity which his uncle would condemn

12

roundly as meddling, which Geoffrey Horton would be inclined to dismiss as 'one of your damned crusades', and which even the more charitable of his friends would describe as being beyond the normal scope of his professional duties. 'I think,' he said warily, 'you'd better tell me exactly what all this is about.'

'But surely–' Mr Barlow waved a hand which seemed to comprehend the entire spread of papers on Maitland's desk.

'If you're thinking I've had time to read my brief–'

'A preliminary survey of the matter only,' said Matthew apologetically.

'–I'm afraid I haven't done so yet. I only got back from the country today, and all my time so far has been spent in deciding which of the matters Mallory has lined up for me is the most urgent.'

'But this is very urgent! I'm given to understand that the case will be heard quite early in this session.'

'Yes, I had gathered that at least. But in any case, Mr Barlow, I have a weakness for hearing things at first hand, which my clerk knows perfectly well, and which I'm sure is why he arranged this conference so promptly. Pretend I know nothing about it, not even the small details he's been able to give me, and start at the beginning and give me the full story.'

'Oh dear!' Matthew Barlow looked rather helplessly from one of his companions to the other. 'It's a very distressing business,' he said, 'and I'm afraid the most dreadful mistake has been made. Mr Gilchrist has been accused of–' (his voice dropped at least an octave, as though what he was about to say was too frightful for words) '–of burglary. Fortunately I was able to arrange for bail–'

'Come now,' said Maitland, his natural humour reasserting itself, 'I thought at the very least you were going to tell me he'd murdered his grandmother. At least . . . which of the particular offences that the Theft Act lumps together are you referring to?'

'Why, to theft, of course.'

'There isn't any of course about it,' Maitland assured him. If he was going to have to explain every aspect of the law to this innocent their meeting might well take all day. 'Our client is said to have entered enclosed premises and stolen something?'

'I'm afraid so.'

'No need to sound so worried, Mr Barlow,' Vincent Gilchrist broke in cheerfully. 'I didn't do it, and even if I had nobody could blame you. I think perhaps I'd better explain matters to Mr

Maitland myself. But before I do,' he went on, turning to Antony, 'if I'm being charged under the Theft Act – is it what you're implying? – what on earth could it cover besides pinching something?'

'A number of things which apparently needn't concern us.'

'No, but I'd like to know.'

At this insistence Matthew Barlow made a sort of clucking noise, obviously intended to be deprecating. Maitland, however, smiled at his client with a benevolence he did not at that moment feel and said gently, 'If you intended to inflict grievous bodily harm on any person in the building entered, or to rape any woman there, or to do unlawful damage to the building or its contents –'

'But that's just stupid.'

'It may be, but that's how the law stands at present.'

'I wasn't even there!'

'I understand from Mr Barlow that you're pleading Not Guilty. In any event let me remind you, Mr Gilchrist, that I said none of these things need concern us. The fact that you're being charged under the Theft Act doesn't mean that you're being charged with every possible offence it covers. Let's go into the question of what you're actually supposed to have done.'

'I thought you'd know all about that,' said Vincent Gilchrist with a hesitancy that Antony was pretty sure wasn't his usual manner.

'I'm sure the papers Mr Barlow has sent me are very complete, but you must remember I only got back from the long vacation this morning, as I told you; and even if I'd had more time to go into the matter I would still want to hear your version of events. Unless Mr Barlow – ?'

Matthew Barlow glanced rather helplessly at his client. 'I think perhaps –' he began, but did not attempt to complete the sentence.

'Yes, perhaps it would be the best thing to follow Mr Gilchrist's suggestion,' Maitland agreed, hoping that he had interpreted the solicitor's meaning correctly. 'Before you tell me exactly what happened, Mr Gilchrist, perhaps you would give me some details about yourself and your family.'

'There's very little to tell. I'm not married and I've lived in London since I graduated, working as a freelance journalist. Our family place is at Hollyhurst near Haslemere, but when my father died about eight years ago my mother preferred to take a flat in town, rather than stay on with my elder brother Arthur and his

14

wife, or move to a house in the village. I was –'

'The Gilchrists are a very old family,' Mr Barlow interrupted him, obviously a little put out by this summary dismissal of his client's family connections. 'My firm have had the privilege of being connected with them for many years, since my grandfather's day in fact. That's what makes it so incredible –' He broke off, noting perhaps Maitland's faintly satiric look. 'Not the fact that they're an old family, of course,' he said with a touch of impatience, 'but because they have always been very prudent in their financial dealings so that, unlike so many of their contemporaries who are similarly situated, they are still people of some substance.'

'I see. But it is our client's own financial circumstances that we should be considering,' Antony pointed out.

'I have an allowance from my brother Arthur,' Vincent explained. 'I know what you're thinking, Mr Maitland, that freelance work isn't a very easy way to establish yourself as a journalist, and I admit it doesn't bring in very much in the way of cash, and that only spasmodically. But I have a home with my mother too; I moved in with her when she came to London and was glad enough to do so – the lodgings I had previously were damned uncomfortable. My father settled a considerable sum on her some time before he died, I don't know how much but I expect Mr Barlow could tell you, so she won't hear of accepting a penny from me. One way and another I do very well.'

'If you want details –' Matthew Barlow began.

'Not at the moment.' Maitland smiled again. 'I'm sure I shall find them in this mountain of papers you want me to read. Go on Mr Gilchrist. You live with your mother in town, and your brother Arthur and his wife are still residents of Hollyhurst.'

'That's right. They don't even keep a place in town, though they could well afford to, they crowd in with my mother and myself when they have to come up on business,' said Vincent rather resentfully. 'My father was just the same, no time for anything but country life, but I think Mother always missed the bright lights and was glad enough to get back to town, though of course she justifies her decision by talking a lot about not being a burden on anyone and things like that.'

'Very well then. Let's come to the alleged offence.'

'Some friends of Mother's were dining with her that night. It was the third of September, a Tuesday. Someone broke into their place . . . do you want addresses and all that?'

15

'No, I'm sure I shall find what I need when I get down to my reading.'

'Well then, it's no more than a few minutes walk away from Mother's flat. Someone broke in while they were out and made off with most of Denise Thurlow's jewellery. The police think it was me.'

'Come now, Mr Gilchrist, there must be more to it than that.'

'I was seen in the vicinity.' His intonation gave the phrase the effect of a quotation. 'By a couple who apparently are neighbours of the Thurlows, and then by two men in the lane at the back of the house who say they saw me turn into the yard of number 113.'

'I think we must go back a bit. First of all, who were this couple who were dining with your mother, and were they the only guests?'

'Yes, they were. David Thurlow, you may have heard of him, he's an actor. Not one of the great names, but somebody who's good enough never to be out of work unless he wants to be. But Denise, his wife, is wealthy in her own right – her father was a successful maker of off-the-peg clothing up north. She never speaks of him now, but she's quite ready to use his money, and she has a weakness for jewellery. That's something I knew perfectly well, of course.'

'So there were just the three of them dining together. Wouldn't it have been more usual for you to have stayed in and made a fourth?'

'No, Mother never expects me to get involved in things she knows will bore me. I meant to visit the Johnsons, Colin Johnson and his wife, he's a reporter on the *Evening Chronicle*, where I place most of the work I manage to sell. That's why I was walking down Chesham Street. It isn't the quickest way to the bus stop from my mother's flat in Halkin Place but it's the route I prefer. I didn't stop at the Thurlows, of course, or set foot in the lane at the back. I went straight on and caught the bus, but when we stopped once at a traffic light there was a cinema advertising one of those science fiction things I hadn't seen, so I got off on an impulse and went to see that instead of going on to see Colin.'

That of course, with a detailed description of the film, would be in the papers too, thought Maitland sardonically. 'These people who saw you,' he said aloud. 'Who were they?'

'Mark and Celia Landon. They're friends of Mother's, too.'

'Do you know them?'

'Oh yes, I've met them a number of times.'

'I asked because you said they are apparently neighbours. That

16

sounds as though they were strangers to you.'

'I didn't know where they live. I met them at Mother's.'

'In any case, Mr Maitland,' Matthew Barlow put in, 'Mr Gilchrist doesn't deny that he was in Chesham Street at the time in question.'

'What time was that exactly?'

'About eight o'clock I should think, perhaps a little earlier. I stayed with Mother till the Thurlows arrived and had a drink with them just to be polite. Then I pleaded a previous engagement and left.'

'Yes, I see, that's all very clear as far as it goes. As the Landons know you there is probably no doubt they identified you correctly, but in any case walking past the house is hardly incriminating. But the two men in the lane . . . number 113 is the Thurlows' house I take it?'

'Yes, it is. I don't know them, but the police got me to stand up with a lot of other chaps, and they both said I was the man they'd seen.'

'That's all very well, but I don't see what made the police think of an identification parade in the first place.'

'You see,' said Vincent, 'it wasn't the first time it had happened. They think I'm a hardened criminal, and they think they detected my – what do you call it? – my *modus operandi*.'

'I see,' said Maitland again, this time very thoughtfully. 'When did this previous incident take place?'

'Six months ago, in March to be exact.'

'And how did you plead?'

'Not Guilty, of course.'

'And what was the upshot? You implied that you weren't believed.'

'No, I wasn't. They found me Guilty and gave me eighteen months, suspended for two years because of my previous good character and so on, and also because the only thing I was supposed to have pinched was recovered.'

Maitland turned to look at Matthew Barlow. 'I got the impression this was the first time you had dealt with a criminal matter,' he said.

'And so it is. That previous . . . incident as you call it, took place at Hollyhurst and Mr Arthur Gilchrist employed a local firm to deal with that one matter only.'

'And where does the similarity between the two cases come in?

17

And what was the evidence in the first one?'

This time it was Vincent Gilchrist who answered. 'I was staying with Arthur and Judy at the time, and the couple who were robbed, Mervin and Karen Chalmers, were dining with them. Again I wasn't present, actually I left just before they arrived – I can't pretend Mervin and I are exactly compatible – and took myself for a drive. Nothing I could prove, but of course I knew quite well they were coming, and that their house would be empty.'

'And the evidence?'

'Karen doesn't have much jewellery, just costume stuff. Except for one rather valuable bracelet, which was her grandmother's I think, anyway it was so old-fashioned she never wore it. It was found in my room in Mother's flat.'

'I admit I find this rather baffling, Mr Gilchrist. How did it come to be found there?'

'I think Mervin tipped them off to look. He's a jealous sort of chap.'

'And had he cause?'

'Yes, I suppose so, but he's an awfully dull stick and you can't blame Karen for wanting a bit of fun on the side. All the same he couldn't have *known* there was anything between us, though I'm pretty sure he suspected.'

'I find it difficult to visualize the issuing of a search warrant on his word alone.'

'Oh, there wasn't one. Two men came to the flat when I was out, and gave some sort of explanation to Mother as to why they wanted to interview me. Of course she said there must be some mistake but they were welcome to satisfy themselves by looking round the flat. And the first place they looked was my room, and there it was!'

'If you had been at home – ?'

'I'd have put them off somehow and got rid of the thing.'

'Mr Gilchrist, you say you pleaded Not Guilty. Are you now admitting – ?'

'I'm not admitting I stole the thing. Karen gave it to me.'

'And later denied it?'

'There was no question of that,' Matthew Barlow interposed eagerly. 'Mr Gilchrist has explained the whole thing to me, that it was a story that as a gentleman he couldn't tell in his own defence.'

'Very commendable,' said Maitland dryly. All the same, it could be true. 'The case was at the local Crown Court, I presume.

18

What happened?'

'I pleaded Not Guilty, because it was true. But I hadn't any explanation to offer, as Mr Barlow says, so nobody believed me.'

'Nobody?'

'Oh, the family, because I explained to them. Arthur and Judy understood all right, because they know Mervin and Karen, you see. Mother expressed a good deal of horror, but she was so relieved there wasn't any dishonesty involved – well, I suppose you could call deceiving Mervin dishonest, but you know what I mean – that she didn't really say very much about it.'

'I'm still not altogether clear about this, Mr Gilchrist. A woman's bracelet, even if unwearable, seems an odd gift to have passed between Mrs Chalmers and you.'

'It wasn't a gift. I know I said she gave it to me, and so she did, but it was because she was hard up and thought I'd be able to sell it for her without Mervin knowing anything about it.'

'Surely in those circumstances she would have been willing to admit what she had done. There is nothing particularly incriminating about being short of money after all.'

'You don't know Mervin,' said Vincent Gilchrist simply.

'It might have led to a dispute between them, certainly, but compared with the result to you of her silence –'

'You don't understand. I told you Mervin was only too ready to suspect the worst, and it so happened we couldn't deny it. What it would have led to was divorce. Karen couldn't afford to let that happen, she's no money of her own. And I couldn't afford to take her on if Mervin ditched her.'

'So you preferred to let the matter run its course?'

'There was nothing else I could do. Besides –' He broke off, and for the first time glanced rather uncertainly at his solicitor.

'There was also the matter of the fingerprints,' Mr Barlow prompted him. 'In both cases,' he added, with a rather apologetic look in counsel's direction.

'Heaven and earth! You don't make it very easy for me do you? And have you an explanation for the fingerprints too, Mr Gilchrist?'

'I have as a matter of fact.'

'You'd better tell me.' He sounded resigned rather than eager. 'Let's take the robbery in Hollyhurst, shall we? Where were your fingerprints found?'

'I'm afraid . . . on the drawer where Karen kept her jewellery.

19

You see now why I couldn't speak up without incriminating her as far as Mervin was concerned. He goes up to town each day, and I'd been with her only a couple of days before in the afternoon. That was when she asked me to sell the thing for her, and when I got dressed she told me where it was and I went to the drawer and slipped it in my pocket. And you know if Mervin had divorced her, naming me, I'd have had to marry her. I thought I'd rather take my chances with the court.' It was obvious that to him at least this seemed a perfectly natural point of view.

'Then to come to the matter which is now our concern–'

'They found my prints on the bedroom door. I'd visited the Thurlows with Mother about ten days before, that was why I knew they were a dead bore and didn't want to stay in the night they were burgled.'

'In ten days it seems odd that the prints hadn't been cleaned away.' He felt rather than saw that Matthew Barlow glanced at him sharply but he kept his eyes on Vincent Gilchrist's face, waiting for his reply.

'The thing is, I was looking for the bathroom,' said Vincent. 'I did open the door of Denise Thurlow's room a foot or so, and then shut it again quickly when I saw I wasn't where I wanted to be. There was nothing, apparently, but a blur on the knob, but I must have pressed the fingers of my left hand against the panel of the door when I tried it, and I suppose their cleaning lady isn't very thorough.'

'And that really is all?' This time Maitland looked directly at the solicitor.

'And quite enough, I'm afraid.' Barlow sounded worried. 'I'm just hoping, Mr Maitland, that you can tell us how to go on.'

'I take it there'll be no difficulty about character witnesses and evidence as to Mr Gilchrist's financial position.'

'No difficulty there at all.'

'No, I thought not, as his previous record was sufficient to get him a suspended sentence the first time. The trouble is, as I'm sure you know Mr Barlow, we can't exclude that conviction from the prosecution's case.'

'I thought–' Vincent began impulsively.

'It's a complicated matter.' It was quite obvious that solicitor and client were in equal need of enlightenment. 'Section 1 of the Criminal Evidence Act contains two rather contradictory clauses, but it was made quite clear in the court of appeal about ten years ago I think – I shall have to look it up for the details – that a question asked in cross-examination concerning a previous conviction that would tend to connect the accused with the offence charged would be allowed; whereas a question concerning a previous conviction for some other type of offence, or a question tending to show he was of bad character, would certainly be prohibited. So I'm afraid what you called the *modus operandi*, Mr Gilchrist, would make the matter admissible.'

'Not my *modus operandi*,' said Vincent, rather huffily.

'I'm sorry, I merely meant that you have referred to the similarity between the two cases in that way.'

'Well, it's simple, isn't it? I don't have to give evidence, and if I don't they can't cross-examine me.'

'That's true, but it would only put the prosecution to the bother of proving the matter, which could be done quite easily, and the fact that you refused to take the witness stand would certainly be regarded as suspicious, even though it is in no way compulsory for you to do so.'

'They've got me all ways, haven't they? But I suppose you know best. Does that mean you think I shall be convicted again?'

'We shall have to do our best to see that that doesn't happen. The fact that you have been identified as the man seen going into the back yard of the Thurlow's house is not necessarily an insuperable difficulty: everyone knows how unreliable even the most honest of witnesses can be in such a matter. But the similarity between the two cases . . . that I see as the worst stumbling block.'

'Supposing you get me off?'

'The previous suspended sentence would remain suspended.'

'But if I'm convicted again?'

'That would be at the discretion of the court. As it's precisely the same type of offence I'm afraid they wouldn't be inclined to be lenient. The jewellery in the second case . . . how much was involved?'

'I haven't the faintest idea, lots I should think, but I don't know Denise Thurlow well enough to know.'

'There is a list of the missing items with your brief, Mr Maitland,' Matthew Barlow put in. 'According to the insurance evaluation there is something like £100,000 involved.'

For a moment Maitland studied him. 'You mean this Mrs Thurlow kept that amount of stuff in the house?'

'She's a strong-minded lady apparently,' said Matthew Barlow.

'Mr Gilchrist tells me she says it's no use owning the things unless she has them handy to wear when the impulse takes her.'

'There's a sort of logic about that,' Maitland admitted. 'All the same . . . I don't suppose the bracelet in the previous case was of comparable value?'

'The prosecution had had it appraised,' said Vincent. 'It was a great heavy thing you know, at least two inches wide, and apparently the stones were quite good ones. They said about £20,000 if it had been broken up.'

'That too was a considerable sum to leave lying in a drawer in your bedroom.'

'Yes, but Karen always said nobody'd recognize it as being of any value among her other stuff. Some of the costume jewellery she had looked a lot more expensive.'

That also might be asking for trouble, but there was a weird sort of logic about it too. 'Then – this is something you can tell me, Mr Barlow – how was entry effected into the Thurlows' house?'

'Through the kitchen window. A pane had been broken so that the latch could be reached, and the criminal climbed in over the sink.'

'The back of the house is not overlooked?'

'It would have been possible from one of the neighbouring houses to see somebody walk up the path to the back door, but short of a witness leaning right out of the window nobody could have been seen when standing close to the house.'

'I see. And in the previous case, Mr Gilchrist. I quite appreciate that you pleaded Not Guilty, but I'm sure you took good note of the prosecution's evidence.'

'They said the thief went in through the back door. A very similar method, I suppose, because the top half is made up of small leaded panes of glass, and one of those had been broken just above the latch.'

'And again nobody had seen anything?'

'Apparently not. Mervin and Karen live a little way outside Hollyhurst, and no one seems to have been about.'

This time Maitland smiled. 'That surprises me,' he said. 'In my experience one is much more likely to be overlooked in the country than in the town. Well, I think you must leave me to study my brief, Mr Barlow, and if I've any more questions for either you or Mr Gilchrist I'll be in touch. As you will be with me, I'm sure, when you get some idea of when the case is coming on.'

Both the visitors got up, but Vincent made no move towards the door. 'Yes, but can you do anything for me?' he asked.

'That's something I can't possibly tell you at this stage, Mr Gilchrist.' Privately he thought it sounded pretty hopeless. 'When I've had the opportunity of going through the papers—'

'Yes, but . . . I've heard Colin talk of you. I thought perhaps there was something you could do.'

'Colin?'

'Colin Johnson. I told you he was the one I was meaning to go to see that night, he and his wife Rosanna. Only then I got sidetracked by the film. He works for the *Evening Chronicle*,' he added and didn't seem to notice Maitland's change of expression at the reminder.

'The newspapers are apt to have a somewhat distorted view of a barrister's functions,' said Antony with a marked lack of cordiality. 'In any case, Mr Gilchrist, what do you think I could do for you? For instance, have you thought better of these chivalrous notions of yours about not asking for Mrs Chalmers's evidence in the first case?'

'No, I haven't. There's no question of that. Besides that's all over, and the people who matter believe me when I say I didn't do it.'

'You're taking too narrow a view. It will matter very much when we get into court this time. You haven't really answered my question, but I think you're suggesting that I should conduct some kind of an investigation into this present incident.'

'Well, I thought—'

'I was afraid of that. But you see—Mr Barlow will understand this if you don't—I have no facilities for anything of the kind. With the whole of London to choose from . . . I'm sure you can see the difficulty.'

'Yes, I suppose so,' said Vincent grudgingly. 'Then you think it's hopeless?'

'Nothing of the sort.' Maitland was brisker now. 'It's a difficult position, I wouldn't have you think otherwise, but a great deal can be done by pointing out the sheer unlikelihood of a man in your situation doing such a thing. I shall be talking to Mr Barlow again, of course, as I think I said, after I've had the chance to look at the matter from every angle.'

Five minutes later he thought he had seen the last of them, but he had reckoned without Matthew Barlow who appeared again, rather apologetically, to have a final few words in the absence of his client. However he didn't stay long, and after that Maitland was able to put in another couple of hours of steady work before leaving to go home.

II

Home was the top two floors of Sir Nicholas Harding's house in Kempenfeldt Square, a far from self-contained conversion that had been made at a time when accommodation was difficult to come by. It was hard to remember now that it had once been regarded as a temporary measure; Sir Nicholas, besides being Antony's uncle, was also head of the chambers to which he belonged, and it had to be admitted that the convenience of the arrangement far out-weighed its disadvantages. Jenny, Antony's wife, had long since become reconciled, not to say fascinated by legal shop, so that even when the professional content of the household was added to by Sir Nicholas's marriage to Miss Vera Langhorne, barrister-at-law, she had been able to take the change with equanimity.

In the event it had turned out to be a great success, and Vera a decided acquisition. For one thing she was able to exercise a modicum of influence over Sir Nicholas's small staff, who had previously done exactly as they liked and bullied him unmercifully into the bargain. This new forbearance did not extend as far as Antony, at least on the part of Gibbs, the ancient butler, a disagreeable old man whom Sir Nicholas had been trying to pension off for years, but who enjoyed making a martyr of himself too much to agree to any such action. Antony himself sometimes wondered what exactly he had done when he had joined the household on his father's death at the age of thirteen to generate such lasting disapproval; he couldn't think what his fault could have been, probably no more than that his arrival had disturbed the household's routine, but there it was and there was no changing it now.

In almost every other way life went on exactly as it had before Vera's advent and all the familiar traditions that had grown up over the years were still observed. Sir Nicholas had always been in the habit of taking his summer vacation in Switzerland, not far from the Italian border, and this practice had continued, with the small change this year that – at Vera's insistence – they had spent some of their time at the Salzburg Festival. Their plane had been due early in the afternoon, and by this time Antony was confident that they would be well settled into their own quarters again, and probably by now drinking sherry with Jenny before she gave them dinner.

The Maitlands had spent their vacation as they usually did, on a friend's farm in Yorkshire, where Jenny was able to throw herself unreservedly into all the activities about the place. Antony had long since resigned himself to the fact that the injury to his shoulder made anything like that impossible for him, at least unless anyone presumed to comment on the fact; and though by now he thought he knew every stick and stone of the neighbourhood by heart he was never tired of the long solitary walks he took, or of chatting to the men who came to help with the harvest while they were having their drinkings, or of the leisurely evenings he and Jenny spent with their friend Bill Cleveland after the day's work was done. But as he made his way home that evening he was thinking how very compartmentalized one's life becomes. Here they were, just back from the depths of the country, and already it was as if those quiet days had never been. The familiar bustle of Fleet Street seemed to be the only world he had ever known, the familiar routine between home and the Inner Temple and the Law Courts a pattern that had never been broken.

As he had expected, Gibbs was hovering in the hall when he let himself in. This was the old man's invariable habit in the evening until all the members of the household were at home; unless of course if it was after 10 o'clock, when, equally invariably, he retired. As usual, too, there was a faint note of disapproval in his greeting, 'You're late tonight, Mr Maitland,' but this was too familiar to cause Antony any qualms and he answered cheerfully.

'Did Sir Nicholas and Lady Harding get back all right, Gibbs?'

'Oh yes, Mr Maitland. An excellent flight they said and a very enjoyable break from routine.' From which Antony felt that it was safe to deduce that Gibbs was glad to see Vera home again. 'They joined Mrs Maitland some time ago,' the butler added, and this too was in its way a rebuke, though Antony reflected as he made his way upstairs that any other attitude would have caused him extreme disquiet.

So he let himself in by his own front door, which had been installed at Sir Nicholas's insistence as a token of his nephew and niece's independence, but which had only once in all the years it had stood there had a key turned in the lock. The familiar squeak as the door swung on its hinges had obviously alerted Jenny, so that by the time he had reached the door of the living-room she was already standing in the corner by the writing-table pouring sherry. 'You see they got home safely, Antony,' she said, not turning round but concentrating on her task as though the exact level of the pale, straw-coloured liquid was a matter of life and death.

'Yes, love, I see. They even survived your driving them back from the airport.' He stood a moment in the doorway, as he so often did, enjoying the moment of homecoming which for some reason that evening seemed to him particularly perfect. The big room that had been furnished from the overflow from both their homes, where no piece of furniture matched another except for the pair of wing chairs that flanked the fireplace, was after all for him the centre of his universe. It might be a little shabby except for the curtains that had been Jenny's last job before they went away; shabby because they could never spare more than one of the chairs at a time for re-upholstering. But it was comfortable, and endowed with Jenny's own special brand of serenity which sometimes seemed to him to be the most important thing in life. And then he was going forward to greet their guests.

Sir Nicholas was occupying his usual place, the wing chair facing the window. He was as tall as his nephew, though rather more heavily built, and very fair, so that though there must be some grey hairs now mixed among the others they weren't readily visible. He was something of a favourite with the newspapers, being a man with a style of his own and eminently quotable at times; but they were far too apt to describe him as handsome, a word which had the worst effect on his always uncertain temper, so that when it happened the female members of the household conspired together to keep the offending article from his view. But in spite of the differences between them there was between himself and his nephew a faint, elusive likeness, one of expression mainly, and it must be admitted that Maitland, who had a strong though mostly unconscious gift of mimicry, at times borrowed his uncle's mannerisms. There were times, too, when he lapsed deliberately into the colloquialisms that Sir Nicholas disliked so much, because (as he had explained to Jenny once) 'It isn't good to let him have his own way all the time.' Just at the moment Sir Nicholas was stretched out in his chair very much at his ease, but he smiled up at his nephew and raised a languid hand in greeting.

Vera, Lady Harding, was sitting at the end of the sofa nearest her husband and opposite the fire. There had been changes in her since her marriage three years before—she had acquired a sense of colour, Antony suspected Jenny's hand in that, and to the sack-like garments which she refused to give up some genius had added the impression that they were well-cut—but the essential Vera, he thought with satisfaction, was still the same. A tall, heavily-built woman with dark hair liberally streaked with grey, which she wore in an old-fashioned bun and which was so thick and heavy that it was forever escaping from the pins that were meant to confine it. She had her own way of speaking in a sort of shorthand, and a gruff voice and a grim smile that had frightened Antony to death when he first worked with her, but that he now knew covered the softest of hearts.

She didn't speak at once, either, but picked up her glass and raised it to him in a sort of salutation. Antony crossed to the hearth rug and took up his favourite position a little to one side of the fire, with one shoulder leaning against the high mantel, and looked at his assembled family with satisfaction. His first words however were formal. Neither the three years that had changed her from a colleague with whom he sometimes worked when he took a case on her home circuit to his aunt, nor the affection he felt for her, had yet put him at his ease in the first moments of any meeting. 'Good evening, Vera. Good evening, Uncle Nick. Gibbs tells me you had a good journey and a very pleasant holiday. I hope he was right about that.'

'Quite right,' Vera told him. 'Glorious music, lots of sun. But Roger and Meg didn't join us in Salzburg, after all.'

'I expect, my dear, that they left things too late,' said Sir Nicholas. 'Though that surprises me, I must say: Meg has a habit of getting what she wants.'

'It wasn't that, Uncle Nick.' Jenny joined them then and handed a glass to her husband, who placed it immediately on the mantelpiece beside the clock. 'The play was coming off, so Meg decided to stay with it until it closed. It was too late for the Festival then, so they took the car over to the continent, and are touring there at the moment.' (Meg and Roger Farrell were the Maitlands' closest friends, Roger a stockbroker, and Meg an actress who was better known to the theatre-going public as Margaret Hamilton.)

'Thought that play was set to run for ever,' said Vera.

'So did Roger.' Antony smiled at her. 'He'll be glad it didn't: at

27

least he's got Meg to himself for a few weeks.'

'Don't expect it will be for long. Another part will be coming along quite quickly,' said Vera. 'Thank you, Jenny,'—as Jenny came over with the decanter and refilled their glasses—'but that's enough about us, now you can tell us about your vacation.'

'You haven't told us a thing,' Antony protested. 'Anyway you know what we've been doing: Jenny's been feeding the pigs and the hens and milking the cows—'

'Not the cows, Antony. You know Bill won't let me anywhere near the milking machine, though I understand how it works perfectly well.'

'Not the cows,' Antony amended. 'And she's been helping Mrs Dibb feed the multitudes while the harvest was on . . . how many meals a day do they eat, love? And I've walked for miles and done my bit towards keeping the work force amused and we've seen all our friends in the neighbourhood and talked endlessly to Bill, and if you want particulars of how many piglets and calves have been born since we were last there I can supply them, though I don't know how many eggs have been produced. I lost count.'

Sir Nicholas roused himself. 'Statistics are a thing I've never taken much interest in,' he said rather repressively. 'You've been into chambers today, I understand?'

'Certainly I have. We can't all afford to pick and choose among the briefs offered us,' Antony told him. 'Which I daresay is the kind of thing Gibbs would like to say to me rather than implying it,' he added reflectively.

'I gather he hasn't benefited from his summer vacation,' said Vera, amused.

'Not a bit, so far as I can tell. What do you think, love?' He didn't wait for a reply. 'I've told you before, Vera, your coming to live here has dashed any hope we ever had of getting the old boy to retire.'

'But at least it's made him easier to live with,' said Jenny, though she should have known well enough by now that Vera wasn't likely to be offended by her husband's teasing. She was a gentle soul, on the whole a better listener than a talker, though she could occasionally be moved to quite violent protest by Sir Nicholas's strictures, especially when they were directed against her husband. Now Antony, knowing what was in her mind, glanced at her affectionately; she was as slim as when they were married, with brown-gold hair, an oval face, a short straight nose,

28

and rather wide-set grey eyes. She gave him in return a look in which dignity and amusement were nicely blended. 'Uncle Nick wants to know what kind of list Mr Mallory has lined up for you,' she said.

There was an unspoken corollary to that which was in all their minds, but which Maitland chose to ignore . . . 'and if you're likely to get mixed up in anything that's going to cause trouble.' There had been times in the past when his relationship with the police had not been uniformly pleasant (that description would have aroused indignation in all his hearers as being an understatement and Sir Nicholas would have said flatly that his dealings with the force had been deplorable, and largely through his own fault), but Antony had never been able to agree with his uncle's view that Chief Superintendent Briggs's animosity might some day prove really dangerous. 'As long as I keep on the right side of the law –' he would say, and leave it at that. Perhaps if anyone but Jenny had raised the subject, even by implication, it would have aroused his annoyance. As it was he merely thought that this time at least it would be easy enough to set Uncle Nick's mind at rest. 'Nothing exciting,' he said casually. 'A case of arson from Paul Collingwood. I should say myself that's a matter for the psychiatrists.'

'This from you, Antony?' asked Sir Nicholas. 'I thought you regarded the whole profession with disfavour.'

'That's not to say I won't make use of them on occasion,' said Maitland, and frowned as he spoke as though his words conjured up some disagreeable vision. 'Anyway something's got to be done, the chap's obviously been going round setting fire to everything in sight, and not for gain either. Then Geoffrey has got Ned Bates on his hands again. That's hardly unexpected, but it will take some handling because it's the umpteenth time and I should think they're likely to throw the book at him.' He ignored Sir Nicholas's pained look. 'And Bellerby has referred a fellow solicitor to me who has no experience at all in criminal matters and needs a guiding hand every step of the way. A chap called Matthew Barlow. Have you heard of him, Uncle Nick?'

'I haven't come across him so far as I recall.'

'No, I suppose you wouldn't have done. Anyway his client is accused of stealing about £100,000 worth of jewels from one of his mother's friends. The trouble is he was convicted and given a suspended sentence six months ago for a similar offence, though not on quite so large a scale.'

'That doesn't sound as though it would give you very much scope,' Sir Nicholas observed.

'It doesn't.'

'How is he pleading?'

'Not Guilty.'

'But is he telling the truth? No, I know you didn't ask him,' Sir Nicholas added impatiently, 'but what do you think about him?'

'The trouble is, it could be true. He has a very specious explanation of the evidence in both cases.' He proceeded to give them a brief outline of the conference that afternoon. 'Mr Barlow's quite convinced of his innocence. The Gilchrist family are somehow sacrosanct in his eyes and he came back again after young Gilchrist had gone to assure me that it was quite out of the question that he could be mixed up in anything like that. The chap's a bit of a tomcat by his own admission' – this time Sir Nicholas appeared to swoon – 'but Barlow (who I'm sure is himself the soul of rectitude) assures me that's nothing out of the way in these wealthy families, which I think myself is little short of slander, whereas dishonesty in money matters, or taking to burglary, is quite out of the question.'

'Obviously not a man of cynical disposition,' said Sir Nicholas, reviving.

'The trouble is, of course, there's no way of keeping the first case out of the evidence, and my client won't hear of our trying to defend him by asking Mrs Chalmers to back up his story. I think myself that's carrying chivalry a little too far, but of course it may be that he knows the lady would deny everything if she were tackled.'

'What is he like?' asked Jenny.

'Good-looking chap . . . firm chin . . . direct way of looking at you,' said Antony, thinking it out as he spoke. 'I don't think we've got a hope of getting him off, though to my mind the fingerprints are a point in his favour. As he said himself, any fool nowadays knows enough to wear gloves, and the fact that they were found might mean that they got there just as he said.'

'That's a rather convoluted argument, Antony, even for you,' said Sir Nicholas idly.

'I shall use it, of course, but I'm not relying on anyone swallowing it,' Antony assured him. 'The other argument is that he was obviously in no need of money, even though his journalistic efforts were bringing in hardly anything, because his brother is generous and he lives with his mother. And even that can be taken two ways: he may resent the fact intensely. And it *is* odd when you come to think of it that his father didn't leave him provided for.'

But enough had been said, it appeared, to set Sir Nicholas's mind at rest, for the moment at least. 'I think you should stop looming over us and finish your sherry, Antony,' he said. And added unfairly, 'Your aunt is only waiting for the opportunity of telling you about our adventures.'

MICHAELMAS TERM, 1974

Friday, September 27th

I

Maitland spent the next two days in chambers and began to feel as though he were getting a grip on the various matters that had been lined up for him. With Roger and Meg still away he expected they would be alone on Friday evening, but when he arrived home and Jenny came into the hall to greet him he had the immediate feeling that she had some information for him. She didn't say anything, however, until they were both settled in front of the fire, when she announced in a half-defiant tone, 'I had a visitor today.'

'Did you, love? Someone I know?'

'Not yet, but it's someone you ought to know,' said Jenny. 'In fact, I asked her to come back this evening.'

'Why on earth—? Jenny love, here am I thinking Thank God it's Friday and you're loading us up with visitors.'

'One visitor,' she corrected him. 'And she's an awfully nice girl, Antony, I'm sure you'll like her. But she's so upset about this Vincent Gilchrist—Vince she called him—you were talking about the other night that I'm sure you ought to try to help him if you can.'

'There's nothing I can do, I explained that to you, Jenny. And if you're going to tell me she said—'

'He wouldn't do a thing like that.' Jenny smiled and completed the sentence for him. 'No, I know how you hate that phrase, so I wasn't going to use it, but I admit there was something like that in my mind, because she's such a—such a sincere person that I can't imagine her falling for someone she couldn't trust.'

'No really, love, by his own admission he can't trust him an inch where other women are concerned.'

'I expect the *affaire* he admitted to you was before he met her so it doesn't count,' said Jenny firmly. 'Anyway—'

'Anyway, a woman in love is the last person whose word you

35

should take in a matter like this. Or a man in love either,' he amended.

'I know, Antony, but there's something about her, I can't quite describe it. Yes, I can though, something about her reminded me.' Jenny got up and walked purposefully towards the bookshelves. 'Here it is,' she said after a moment's study of the volume she had taken down. 'It's Matthew Arnold, the *Forsaken Merman . . . the cold, strange eyes of a little mermaiden, and the gleam of her golden hair*. That describes her exactly.'

'Too fanciful by half,' said Antony lazily, still not very concerned. 'You'll be telling me next—'

'Don't be silly, Antony.' For once in her life she was inclined to impatience, a thing so un-Jenny-like that it did at least induce him to take more notice of what she was saying. 'I only meant . . . well, there is something uncanny about her. But when you see her, you'll know what I mean and admit I'm right.'

'I'll admit anything you like, love, as long as you don't repeat that to Uncle Nick.'

'Of course I won't.' Jenny came and sat down again. 'But do you really suppose he wouldn't notice it for himself if he ever saw her?'

'He wouldn't recite poetry to me about it,' Antony told her. 'In any case, are you trying to tell me that this—this uncanny quality of hers is what made you believe her?'

'As if she'd looked in her crystal ball and seen exactly what happened,' said Jenny, not looking at him.

'Not another medium!'

'No, nothing of the kind. I'm only trying to tell you the impression she made on me. And Vince—Mr Gilchrist—'

'You'd better stick to Vince, there are already too many Gilchrists about.'

'Well, all right. He'd been talking about you, and told her he didn't think you believed a word he said. I tried to explain you had an open mind, but I don't think it comforted her much. I know you said this was a case where there was nothing you could do, where anyone in London or even in England might be involved, and I think I made her understand that, but she said if you would just talk to some of Vince's family and friends she thought you might get a better idea how impossible it was that he should have done such a thing, and then you'd be able to explain it better when you got into court.'

36

'Mr Barlow sent me a mound of papers,' said Antony rather dejectedly. 'Including the proofs of a number of possible character witnesses.'

'Yes, but I know how you hate wading through all that stuff. Wouldn't it be more fun to talk to them? Then at least Mandy might feel a little happier knowing that everything possible has been done—'

'It's not a thought I find personally comforting, my love,' he reminded her, 'especially when it seems unlikely to do any good.' But Jenny had obviously taken this to heart, and the least he could do was show some interest. 'That's her name is it . . . Mandy?'

'Amanda Barnard.'

'And she's young?'

'Very young I should say. She may be twenty but I don't think she can be any older than that. That's why I felt . . . Antony, don't you remember how dreadful everything seemed when you were that age?'

For a second he closed his eyes, but nothing could shut out the memory her words evoked: of Jenny lying in a white hospital bed, of the feebleness of her grip when she stretched out her hand to him, and she hadn't even been twenty then. 'I remember,' he said opening his eyes again, and finding hers fixed on him anxiously. 'All right, Jenny, I'll see this protégé of yours, but what the devil I'm going to say to her . . .'

II

Amanda Barnard had arranged with Jenny to come round that evening at about nine o'clock, but it was no more than half-past eight and they were still clearing away the dinner things when the house phone announced that there was a young gentleman named Midwinter to see Mr Maitland. It was only under Vera's benign influence that Gibbs had been persuaded at last to make use of the house phone, installed years ago for his convenience, and every time he did so Antony thought what an acquisition his new aunt was. He didn't know anyone called Midwinter but there seemed no reason to deny him admittance, so he said resignedly, 'Send him up,' and went to open the front door.

The young man who was coming up the stairs was slight and

not very tall, as became apparent as soon as he reached the landing. He couldn't, Antony thought, be more than in his mid-twenties, and his look was a nice blend of determination and apprehension which Maitland at first found puzzling. He burst into speech without waiting to introduce himself, saying rather breathlessly, 'I hope you won't think this is an intrusion, but as Mandy said she was coming to see you this evening I thought if I got here first you'd probably be alone.'

'You're a friend of Miss Barnard?' asked Antony, backing away from the door.

'Yes, is she here already?'

'No, I haven't met her yet, my wife told me about her.'

'Yes, she said . . . well, she liked Mrs Maitland very much. But you know she's very young and I don't want to see her get into any sort of trouble. So I thought –' He broke off there looking rather abashed, and this time Maitland smiled, he couldn't help it.

'You thought you'd see for yourself what kind of company she was getting into,' he completed the sentence. 'Well, come along in and meet my wife,' – he was crossing the hall as he spoke – 'I'm sure you'll find her reassuring. Jenny, this is Mr Midwinter. I think that's what Gibbs said,' he added, looking questioningly at the newcomer.

'Nigel Midwinter. Good evening, Mrs Maitland.' He repeated his apologies, this time with a little more assurance. '*You'll* understand,' he said confidently. 'Amanda is so very young.'

'That,' said Jenny, 'is why I wanted my husband to see her.' She sat down in her usual corner of the sofa, not curling up as she might have done if they'd been still alone but folding her hands in her lap, and waved Nigel to the chair that Sir Nicholas generally occupied. 'She's very unhappy, and if we can help in any way –'

'That's just it! I haven't anything against Vince except that he's far too old for Mandy – well over thirty – and though he won't explain how he came to have Karen's bracelet, I'm inclined to believe he didn't actually pinch it. But now it seems almost certain he'll go to prison, at least that's what he told Mandy, and you know what women are. She'll wait for him faithfully and go on thinking she's in love with him, whereas if he were free –'

Again Maitland completed his thought. 'If he were free there's a chance she'd change her mind,' he suggested.

'That's it exactly. It's an infatuation, that's all it is.'

Antony ignored that. 'How do you feel about the second

38

accusation?' he asked, 'I gather you know at least some of the people concerned.'

'I don't really know,' said Nigel rather hesitantly.

'You said you believed him about the first case, so I ought to point out to you that the second one depends very largely on the fact that there are some similarities between the two.'

'Does it?' said Nigel vaguely. 'Then I suppose he didn't do that either. But I've heard of you, Mr Maitland,' (I mustn't let that get to me, it was only a matter of time before he said it), 'and when I heard Mandy was coming to see you–'

'You thought you'd better find out whether I was a proper person for her to know,' said Antony and managed a smile. 'I realize that, and on the whole I find it quite reasonable. My wife has been reminding me what it's like to be twenty, and though I can't promise that your friend Mandy isn't going to get hurt, I can assure you that if she is, it won't be through any doing of mine.'

'No, I can see that now. I suppose you think I was a fool to come.'

'Far from it, I think it was a very natural inclination on your part. Tell me though, Mr Midwinter–'

'You might as well call me Nigel, everybody does.'

'Very well then, Nigel. You said you had nothing against Vincent Gilchrist, but did you really mean that?'

'He's not exactly my type. Mandy says he's sophisticated, by which I suppose she means that I'm not sophisticated enough to appreciate him. And I suppose you think if he went to prison I'd be glad to have a rival out of the way, but–'

'On the contrary, you explained your attitude about that very clearly.'

'Well, it's quite true that Mandy was in love with me once, and she would be still if I hadn't introduced Vince to her, which makes me absolutely furious with myself.'

'And do you think she may be again? In love with you, I mean.'

'If she isn't sitting around waiting for him. Anyway, I'd better go. I only wanted to make sure . . . and I can see now it was stupid of me. You were very kind to Mandy, Mrs Maitland,' he added turning to Jenny, 'and I'm grateful to you for that.'

'Wait a bit! You say you know some of the people involved and perhaps some information about them might be helpful to me. And you haven't told us anything about yourself, either.'

'I'm not really very interesting, but I would look after Mandy if she'd let me.'

'Yes, I'm sure you would,' said Antony vaguely, though obviously on such short acquaintance he couldn't be sure of anything of the sort. Then he smiled again, encouragingly. 'You were going to tell me something about your uninteresting self.'

'I'm trying to be a writer.'

'Not another journalist?' asked Maitland in a rather horrified tone.

'No, nothing like that.' Nigel seemed to take his dismay for granted. 'I'm interested in fiction, as a matter of fact.'

'You said "trying to be",' said Antony with a question in his tone.

'Yes, it's not all that easy to get started. I'm working in a bank at the moment, which I find pretty deadly between you and me, but it keeps the wolf from the door.'

'Doesn't that mean you have to take a lot of exams and things?'

'Yes, but I don't let that worry me. The thing is,' he added confidingly, 'I got in through my uncle's recommendation, he's something pretty high up in Bramley's bank, and when the exams come round I take them but just don't worry too much about the results. It means I don't get promoted, but I don't care about that as I don't mean to make a career in banking.'

'I gather you're familiar with Vincent Gilchrist's problems.'

'Yes, quite familiar. Of course, one always hears things, and it's sometimes difficult to sort out what's true and what isn't, but in this case Mandy told me everything, and as she got it from Vince I expect it's pretty accurate. Only he didn't explain to her how he came to have Karen's bracelet.'

'You know the Gilchrists well?'

'My uncle lives near them. Not in Hollyhurst, but in the next village. He comes up to town every day, there's quite a convenient train service. As a matter of fact'—again there was that confiding tone—'I think he gets on better with Arthur and Judy, though they're a good deal younger than he is, than he does with Vince's mother. She's older, but nearer his generation. You see her husband, Justin, was a stuffy sort of chap, and Arthur takes after him which just suits my uncle's taste. And Mrs Gilchrist—'

'It would be more convenient if you could remember to call them all by their Christian names. So many members of the same family are rather confusing to an outsider.'

'Yes, though I feel a bit awkward calling her Helen. Vince's mother, I mean. I don't think she liked living in the country a bit, even though it's so convenient when you want to come up to town. That's why she came to live in Halkin Place when Justin died, though I daresay by the time that happened she was too old to enjoy herself,' added Nigel with a knowledgeable air that made Antony and Jenny exchange a smile. 'Anyway, Vince takes after her, just as Arthur takes after his father, so it works very well for them to live together.'

'May I ask you a rather personal question, Mr – Nigel?'

'I've told you all about myself.'

'Perhaps personal wasn't quite the right word, but you may think it impertinent.' He hesitated a moment but Nigel made no comment so he went on. 'I gather you'd like to marry Amanda Barnard.'

'Yes, of course I would. Apart from anything else she isn't really fit to be out alone.'

'I rather got the impression that was what you thought. You also said, if I remember rightly, that she is infatuated with Vincent Gilchrist.'

'She'd marry him like a shot if he asked her.'

'That was the point I was leading up to. She wants to marry him, but does he want to marry her?'

'I wish I could tell you. He takes her about quite a bit, well anyone would like to be seen around with Mandy, she's a lovely-looking girl, but I don't know whether – well, whether she's the only one or not.' He glanced at Jenny as he spoke, so that Maitland jumped to the conclusion that the rather coy phrase was for her benefit.

'You've told us about yourself, Nigel. What is Mandy's background?'

'That's what makes it so awkward. She's Denise Thurlow's niece.'

'The woman Vincent Gilchrist is supposed to have robbed? What do the Thurlows think about him?'

'I'm afraid they're quite convinced the police are right and that he's guilty.'

'What about Mandy's parents?'

'She's an orphan. Her mother was Mrs Thurlow's sister, and they both inherited goodness knows how much from their father who made a fortune in trade in the north. Mandy was brought up by an uncle and aunt on her father's side of the family, but he's retired now and they've moved into the country, the Lake District or somewhere quite a long way away. Mandy has a tiny flat of her own in a new block not far from where the Thurlows live. I think the idea was that they can keep an eye on her, but I don't think she sees an awful lot of them. Only it does make it difficult for her now, with their being so set against Vince, and her being just as sure that he's innocent.'

'You're acquainted with the Thurlows then?'

'I know them fairly well. And Mervin and Karen Chalmers, too.'

'What about the Landons, the couple who saw Vincent Gilchrist walking down Chesham Street the night of the robbery?'

'I've met them. And if you're going to ask me whether they might have anything against Vince, I can't see why they should.'

'No, I wasn't. Their evidence isn't particularly significant. Mr Gilchrist doesn't deny that he was in the neighbourhood at that time.'

'Now you're doing it,' said Nigel half-humourously. 'Not using Christian names, I mean.'

'No, you're quite right, I'll have to get used to it if only for my uncle's sake. Sir Nicholas Harding,' he added seeing Nigel's inquiring look. 'He's another lawyer, so it's quite likely I shall consult him about this business. But he has the greatest dislike of cases where all the witnesses have the same surname.'

'I shouldn't think any of the other Gilchrists will be witnesses,' said Nigel, who seemed to have a weakness for exactness.

'They may not be, but we can't divorce them from the story altogether. As to the other people of your acquaintance, perhaps you can tell me –' But at that point the house phone rang again, this time to announce Miss Barnard's arrival.

'I'll go if you like,' Jenny offered, but Antony was already at the door.

'There isn't another way out?' said Nigel rather apprehensively. 'I didn't tell her I was coming.'

'No other way I'm afraid, except through the window,' said Jenny, smiling at him. 'And we're rather high up for you to take that way.'

A moment or two later Mandy preceded Antony into the room. He had thought as soon as he saw her that Jenny's description had been pretty accurate, and now, looking at her in a better

42

light, he realized that above and beyond what his wife had told him, here was an authentic beauty. Her hair, which fell gently to her shoulders in a series of loose waves, was as near gold as made no matter, and almost certainly without the intervention of her hairdresser. She had green eyes, a small straight nose, a really beautiful complexion, and a strangely other-worldly way of looking at things that seemed to penetrate far beyond the surface of what was going on around her. But her first words were human enough. 'Nigel Midwinter, what on earth are you doing here?'

'Well, I thought – ' began Nigel rather weakly.

'Mr Midwinter has been the greatest help to me,' Antony assured her. 'My wife tells me you're concerned for Mr Vincent Gilchrist's well-being, and as Mr Midwinter knows a good many of the people concerned in this sad affair I asked his help in getting them sorted out in my mind.' This was near enough to the truth, and perhaps it would pass muster without her inquiring exactly how the two of them had become acquainted. 'I'm sure you understand how difficult it is for a barrister, being plunged suddenly into the midst of the affairs of people of whom he knows nothing, with only the written word to rely on.'

'That's what Vince said, that you like to hear everything for yourself,' said Mandy. She smiled at Jenny, ignored Nigel, and then turned her attention fully on Antony again. 'But he said you didn't see how you could help him except by trying to put a good complexion on things in court, and he thought that was because you didn't really believe he was innocent. So I thought perhaps I could tell you . . . it's quite impossible that he would ever do a thing like that.'

Maitland, who had heard that phrase more times than he cared to remember, and who disliked it more every time he heard it, valiantly suppressed an inclination to snarl at her and instead said quite amiably, 'Come and sit down, Miss Barnard. We may as well all make ourselves comfortable.'

'Unless you want me to go, Mandy,' Nigel offered, speaking for the first time since she had arrived.

'No, of course not, I'm glad you were able to help,' said Mandy, more graciously this time. 'But I wonder,' she eyed Antony again intently, 'are you a very materialistic man, Mr Maitland?'

'I – I hope not,' said Antony rather blankly.

'I asked because – ' She changed course suddenly. 'No, I can see you aren't,' she said. 'I know Nigel thinks this is nonsense, but I think Mrs Maitland believes me and I hope you will too. I've been told ever so many times I'm psychic – Vince calls it seeing further through a brick wall than most people – but I really do seem to know things sometimes which turn out afterwards to be true.'

'I see,' said Antony, forbearing to add that all Jenny wanted was not to see her hurt. The others were all seated now, and he turned, ostensibly to see if the fire required attention, but really to hide a smile at this rather ingenuous approach. 'And one of the things that has been revealed to you,' he went on, turning to face the company again, 'is that Vincent Gilchrist is innocent of both the offences with which he has been charged.'

'It's true!' she flashed at him. 'And if you'd only look into the matter yourself, as I've heard you do sometimes, you'd find out that I'm quite right.'

'I haven't denied that, Miss Barnard, only I have to tell you, as I told Mr Gilchrist and as I believe my wife explained to you, that I have no facilities for this kind of investigation.'

'But knowing about people is half the battle,' she insisted. 'They call you the man who never loses a case –'

'I'm afraid that's just newspaper talk, Miss Barnard, and nonsense at that.' That was another remark that would normally have brought out the worst in Maitland, but he was finding himself drawn to this ridiculous child, perhaps by the very unexpectedness of her approach. 'I wish it was true, of course, but I'm afraid it isn't.'

'But you do see things that other people don't,' she insisted. 'I'm right, aren't I, Mrs Maitland?' she added, turning quickly to Jenny. 'You must know him better than anybody else.'

'I've heard it said that he has a certain perception where people are concerned,' said Jenny, 'and I've heard people use the same phrase about him that Mr Gilchrist used about you. But I'm afraid you'll never convince him that he has psychic powers, if that's what you mean.'

'Well, I suppose it is. If he would just talk to some of these people –'

'Miss Barnard.' Antony leaned forward the better to empha-size his point. 'If Mr Gilchrist is innocent, and I'm certainly not arguing with you about that, the guilty party is almost certainly some habitual criminal, completely unknown to any of the people

44

involved in the case. Nothing they could tell me would be of any help at all.'

'I don't see that. If my Aunt Denise, for instance, told her charwoman she was going to dinner with Mrs Gilchrist, the charwoman might have a son who got into bad company and he and his friends might have carried out the burglary.'

'And similarly Mrs Chalmers might have mentioned in the village shop that she and her husband were dining with the Arthur Gilchrists?'

'You're laughing at me, Mr Maitland,' said Mandy with dignity. 'I don't think you mean to be unkind, but it's no laughing matter.'

'No, indeed it isn't.' He turned his head to look at Jenny, but Jenny was staring into the fire. 'And you really think, Miss Barnard, that if I take a hand in the matter some evidence will come to light to prove Mr Gilchrist's innocence?'

She met his rather quizzical glance with a direct and rather solemn look. 'Yes, Mr Maitland, I really do think so,' she said.

'I'm not psychic you know,' he assured her. 'I've no gifts whatever except a certain amount of common sense.'

'And I think . . . kindness,' she said. 'And sensitivity. Which perhaps is the same thing as the perception Mrs Maitland was talking about.'

'If that's true it's more likely to be a curse than a blessing,' Antony told her a trifle ruefully. 'Look, Miss Barnard, I'll make a bargain with you. I'll go and see the people concerned in these two dinner engagements as you suggest, though not Mrs Thurlow, as she's one of the prosecution witnesses, but I'm pretty sure nothing will come of it.'

'But you said yourself, Mr Maitland, *you*'re not psychic,' said Mandy quickly.

'*Touché*. There are, however, two sides to a bargain.'

'Yes. What's my part in it?'

'Not to be disappointed when the results don't come up to your expectations.'

He gained no reassurance from her reply. 'I won't be, I promise.' And then she added blithely, 'I can promise that quite safely because you won't fail, I know it!'

Having got her own way Mandy wasn't inclined to linger, even though Jenny offered a choice of refreshment, from a cup of tea to the sweet liqueur they kept for Meg. Nigel went with her and she accepted his escort without demur. Coming back from seeing them out Antony said to Jenny, 'And that'll be a wasted weekend, love. I hope you're satisfied.'

'Was it my doing? I think you're captivated by her,' said Jenny laughing. 'However, I'll forgive you.'

'You know perfectly well you wanted me to agree,' Antony grumbled, going across to the writing-table where the drinks were set out. 'Do you really think – ?'

'I really think she sees more than other people. It's those eyes of hers.'

'That's a trick of nature. You'd better think up some story to tell Uncle Nick and Vera when I'm out at lunch time tomorrow, rather than that you believe in this girl's psychic powers.'

'I shall say what you always do, that you felt there were grounds for an investigation,' said Jenny. 'And I don't *exactly* believe that she's psychic, but there is something there . . . don't you think?'

'No,' said Antony flatly.

'But you believed that Mrs Selden – '

'I didn't think she was psychic, I thought she was a telepath which is something quite different. I do believe some people have powers in that direction, though I don't think they work all the time. But there's nothing like that about what that child was claiming just now. Except perhaps her confidence in Vince Gilchrist, which obviously has no other grounds than the fact she's in love with him.'

'No, I suppose you're right. Are you going to phone Mr Barlow?'

'Of course I am. He'd be frightfully shocked if I tried to do anything on my own. It's one thing with Geoffrey, he's used to my ways, but Matthew Barlow is a respectable family solicitor. I wouldn't want to upset him. Besides, if I'm going into this at all I may as well go the whole way and ask him to put somebody on to finding out whether the two men who identified Gilchrist have any connection with him, or perhaps are of bad character . . . the real thieves looking for a scapegoat.'

'Do you really think it will be a sheer waste of time?'

'Yes, I'm afraid so. The police aren't fools, you know, They'll have thought of that already. There is one thing though,' he added thoughtfully, and turned half way across the room towards the telephone to look down at her in a queerly intent way. 'I might go and see Father William, and see if I can find out exactly what happened to Denise Thurlow's jewellery.'

'Do you really think that would be a good idea?' asked Jenny doubtfully. 'I mean, I adore Father William, but—'

'He's a receiver himself . . . I know. But I'm not wanting his evidence, love, just some information. And he can give me it, if anyone can.'

Tuesday, October 1st

On Tuesdays Mrs Stokes, Sir Nicholas's housekeeper, was in the habit of going to the pictures, having first had what she invariably referred to as a snack in town. She herself was an excellent cook, so they had always wondered where she went for this repast that would live up to her own high standards, but nobody, not even Vera, had ever dared to ask her. So far as was known this was her only dissipation, if you discount the visit she paid with equal regularity to her sister in Fulham every Sunday afternoon. In the days of his bachelorhood Sir Nicholas had fled from the cold collation which was the only life support left to him, to Jenny's hospitality, and though Vera would have been glad enough to have the run, occasionally, of her own kitchen that too, it was felt, would be presuming too far. So the custom had continued, to everyone's satisfaction, and when Antony and his uncle got home together that Tuesday evening Vera was already upstairs with Jenny.

Owing to Antony's activities that weekend the two other traditions – a ceremonious lunch downstairs on Saturday, and tea in the Maitlands quarters on Sunday afternoon – had only been partially observed, and Antony was a little surprised that his uncle hadn't take the opportunity to question him about what he had been doing, which normally he would have done at the first opportunity. However, on this occasion he had held his peace, and it was not until they had finished dinner and were settled round the fire with coffee and cognac and Sir Nicholas was making leisurely preparation for the enjoyment of a cigar, that he looked up from his task and said in a gentle way that might possibly be genuine, but was more likely to be the prelude to something considerably more exciting, 'Jenny tells us, my dear boy, that you have succumbed to the blandishments of a siren.'

Antony, who for once in his life was sitting quietly in the chair

48

opposite his uncle's and sipping his coffee, looked up with a grin. 'It all depends what you mean by a siren,' he said. 'I admit Jenny quoted the *Forsaken Merman* to me, but that's hardly the same thing.'

'Antony, you told me not to tell Uncle Nick that,' said Jenny incautiously, which of course led inevitably to the recitation of the verse she had read to her husband, and her admission that she had a sort of funny feeling about Mandy Barnard, that perhaps it was true that the girl could see a little further than most people.

'Dear me,' said Sir Nicholas mildly. 'And did you subscribe to that opinion, Antony?'

'No, I didn't. And if you ask me, Jenny only put it like that to try to arouse my curiosity.'

'In that case it would be interesting to know what induced you to meddle in this matter, which I understood was quite straightforward. Besides, whether your client is innocent or guilty, there is nothing you can do about it.'

'Know he could never resist an appeal like that,' said Vera.

'Which brings us back to what Jenny was saying,' Sir Nicholas pointed out.

'Well, if you must know,' said Antony, goaded, 'it wasn't Mandy Barnard at all who made me decide to look into the matter, but another caller we had – did Jenny tell you about him too? – a chap called Nigel Midwinter who's in love with her. He thinks she's only infatuated, but if Gilchrist goes to prison she'll remain faithful to his memory and he won't have a chance of changing her mind.' He wasn't surprised to know that Sir Nicholas had got a fairly complete, if rather confused, account from Jenny of their visitors on Friday evening. It had, he knew, been inevitable; so inevitable, in fact, that he hadn't even asked her about it.

'Match-making again?' said Vera.

'Not really, except in the sense that I think those two would be more suited to each other than the girl and my client. And you know, Uncle Nick, Vera's right about one thing: he could be innocent, and if he is I don't want him on my conscience.'

'And has anything come of these inquiries of yours?' Sir Nicholas asked courteously.

Antony was pretty sure now that his uncle regarded the whole expedition with disfavour, and said rather hurriedly, 'Nothing whatever, so you needn't worry about my meddling any further.

There's just a chance that Gilchrist will come across well in court. He's a personable sort of chap, and the jury may believe him. Though as he still categorically refuses to allow us to use his explanation of what happened in the first case, I think it's very unlikely that they will.'

'His unwillingness to do so,' said Sir Nicholas reflectively, 'may have its roots in chivalry, which would be commendable though foolish, or it may simply be that the whole thing is an invention which the lady would deny.'

'Yes, I think you pointed that out to me before. I'm not sure about anything, Uncle Nick. On the whole I think the probability is that he's guilty. In any case there's nothing more to be done, we'll just have to wait and see what happens.'

'Did your new friend, Mr Barlow, mind having his weekend disrupted?'

'He didn't seem to. He's a bit of an old maid, I suppose, but an awfully nice chap for all that. But he's so absolutely convinced that no Gilchrist could never do anything so vulgar as mix himself up in a burglary that it really makes talking to him about the case rather difficult.'

'May as well tell us how you got on,' Vera suggested. Antony sometimes wondered whether she still missed her own days at the bar; in any event she was always keenly interested in everything that went on.

'On Saturday we went down to Hollyhurst to see Arthur Gilchrist and his wife Judy. They live at the Manor House, and as we'd hired a car and driver in Haslemere Mr Barlow was able to concentrate on pointing out to me the numerous farms that formed part of the estate. I'd say Arthur's a good landlord, everything looked in splendid shape, and the home farm too was obviously excellently run. The Manor House is a big place, and what we saw of it is just pleasantly shabby. I know what Nigel meant when he said they were a bit stuffy—something like that, at any rate—but they struck me as being a nice couple, very devoted to each other, and with very few interests beyond their own milieu. Arthur is very unlike his brother, what they'd call in Yorkshire a stiffish sort of chap, and . . . oh well, quite different. As for Judy, she might be a carbon copy of her husband, except that she's a good deal thinner. They have an aged retainer, who was Arthur's and Vince's nurse, I understand. Well, I daresay she's not so ancient really, anyway she seems quite spry and she sees to the running of the house with a series of charwomen when they're available.

'Of course, the housekeeper knew all about the small dinner party, and so did one of the village women who stayed on after her usual time to help with the meal and then with the washing-up. Knowing villages, I'd say from that that every last man, woman and child in Hollyhurst knew what was happening, but that's not to say that any of them had any criminal connections as Mandy seemed to think might be the case. I was more interested to meet the couple who were robbed while they were out, Mervin Chalmers and his wife Karen. Vince was right about one thing: Mervin obviously dislikes him intensely, and just as obviously is jealous of him. Whether he has cause to be is another matter.'

'From what your client admitted to you –'

'Yes, Uncle Nick, but it may or may not be true. He was very anxious to convince Mr Barlow and me of his innocence, and that was an integral part of his explanation. Or it may be true that he had an affair with Karen. On the whole, I think that's the most likely interpretation of how his fingerprints got into her bedroom, but that isn't to say that the story about her giving him the bracelet to sell is true as well, and of course it wasn't something I could ask her about.'

'What were they like?' Vera asked.

'Older than Vince, I'd say about the same age as Arthur and Judy. Mervin is dark and glowering, with very heavy black eyebrows that accentuate that impression. As for Karen, if you described *her* as a siren, Uncle Nick, I'd go along with you all the way, but I could believe the story that she wanted to raise some money without her husband knowing about it. He obviously considered himself very much in control of the family, and I shouldn't be at all surprised if he wasn't the sort of man who never discusses money with his wife.'

'They have expensive tastes and he couldn't afford to give her all she wanted,' Vera suggested.

'No, if she was hard up I should think it was as I say, nothing to do with his financial affairs. Something she wanted to buy without his knowledge, or perhaps just without him knowing exactly how much it cost.'

'Appearances can be deceptive,' said Sir Nicholas.

'I know that very well. I don't know his occupation, Uncle Nick, but somebody – I think it was Arthur – said he was an

51

importer, whatever that may mean, with an office in the City. In any case, he had that indefinable air about him of someone who's never in his life known what it is to be hard up.'

'Guessing again, Antony?'

'Yes, I admit it. Not that either way helps me in the slightest with this very unsatisfactory case. They hadn't made any particular secret of the fact that they were going out, but they only have a daily and though they'd told her they wouldn't be in to dinner, so there was no need for her to get anything ready, Karen couldn't remember whether she'd mentioned where they were going. I thought she was inclined to be sympathetic . . . and that's only an impression,' he added hastily. 'But at that point Mervin more or less threw the pair of us out, which didn't worry me particularly, but upset Mr Barlow rather, saying he couldn't think why we were going to all this trouble for a chap who was obviously guilty. So we put the best face we could on our farewells and came back to town.'

'And yesterday afternoon, I understand, you continued what must by now have obviously been a hopeless task.'

'Yes, Uncle Nick, we did. On my part mainly because I'd promised Mandy and Nigel, though I have a suspicion that Mr Barlow thought I might be about to perform some sort of a miracle before his eyes. I can't think what Bellerby's told him about me.'

'I have a very good idea on the whole,' said Sir Nicholas, his tone leaving no doubt that in his opinion the information must have been derogatory. 'But you may as well tell us –' He broke off, leaving the sentence invitingly open.

'We went to see Vince's mother, Helen Gilchrist. Again Nigel was quite right, she's a frivolous old girl, although at the moment rather upset by all this trouble her son's in.'

'Was that what this Nigel Midwinter told you . . . that she was frivolous?'

'Not in so many words, so far as I remember. He just said that she preferred living in town, and that Vince took after her, and I can't imagine either of them in a country setting. Certainly there's a great likeness between them, only softened, I suppose you'd call it, in her case. What I'm trying to say is that she's not at all masculine-looking, anything but. She said there was nothing at all special about the occasion, the Thurlows often dined with her, both of them when he was resting – you remember he's an actor – and Denise alone if he was in the theatre. She made all the preparations herself, she likes cooking, and the daily would certainly know the next morning when there was an extra large washing-up, but she can't remember mentioning it to her beforehand. And, of course, she simply loathes the Thurlows now, because they don't believe in her precious son's innocence.'

'Helpful,' Sir Nicholas commented.

'Yes, sir, I know what you mean. Anyway to complete matters we went round to see David Thurlow, and as far as whether anyone knew of their plans or not he was no more help than the others. He probably hadn't mentioned it to anyone, because it was such a common occurrence, and he thought it was improbable that Denise had either, for the same reason. Anyway he's violently anti-Vince at the moment, and so, he said, is his wife, mainly I think because Mandy's so keen on him. They're frightened of her getting mixed up with all this unpleasantness. He admitted that Vince had visited them when he said he had, and as it was the first and only time he might well have got lost while looking for the bathroom, though of course he couldn't remember whether he'd actually been upstairs or not. Naturally they're upset about the whole business, even though they were well insured, but he was quite decent to us, and I got the impression he too was devoted to his wife.'

'Insurance?' said Vera, rather like a war horse responding to a bugle. Antony smiled at her.

'No, I'm sure you're wrong, this wasn't an insurance fraud. I've heard Meg speak of David Thurlow, he's well-known in his profession though not in the first rank, and I don't think there's any question of his being hard up. And Denise was an heiress –'

'Money can be spent,' said Sir Nicholas.

'Yes, I know, and I know if it is people don't put on sackcloth and ashes and go around declaiming the fact. All the same I just don't believe it,' said Antony stubbornly. 'Besides, a woman who'd keep that amount of jewellery at home just to have it handy when she felt like wearing it, is obviously crazy about the stuff.'

'So your activities got you precisely nowhere.'

'Precisely nowhere, Uncle Nick. You needn't rub it in.'

'There is, however, one visit you have neglected to mention to us.'

'Yes, I gathered you'd got the whole thing out of Jenny.'

'You mustn't blame Jenny, my dear boy. Your aunt and I naturally take an interest in your well-being.'

'You're talking about the fact that I went to see Father William, of course.'

'What else? And I really don't know which of your habits I find more distressing, Antony: that of getting mixed up with the police, or that of insisting on fraternizing with members of the criminal fraternity.'

'Father William's a perfectly respectable jeweller, Uncle Nick. For all anyone knows,' he added with belated honesty.

'That old sinner!'

'Whom I have a good deal of reason to be grateful to,' Antony pointed out. 'Anyway, I thought perhaps he might be able to find out for me who had sold Denise Thurlow's jewellery.'

'Father William is a receiver of stolen property, my dear,' said Sir Nicholas turning to Vera. 'A fence in common parlance . . . hence that particular nickname.'

'Yes, you've told me about him. Thing is, Antony—'

'Precisely, my dear.' He turned to his nephew again. 'Might not that course of action have been dangerous?' he asked. 'Supposing he had told you that your client had taken his ill-gotten gains to him for disposal?'

'That would have been rather too much of a coincidence, Uncle Nick. In any case you don't think I asked him the question straight out like that. I explained the situation first, and he knows my duty to my client as well as I do. If he finds out anything helpful he'll let me know and if he doesn't he'll keep his own counsel.'

'I see.'

'He wouldn't do anything to hurt me, Uncle Nick.'

'No.' He gave his nephew his sudden companionable smile. 'That's one thing I think we can be reasonably sure of. As for the rest, as you'd say yourself, Antony . . . who lives may learn.'

'Yes, sir, exactly.'

'You're not thinking of taking any further hand in the affair yourself, except when it gets to court?'

'Which won't be very long as a matter of fact. No, I'm not thinking of doing anything else. Even if I wanted to, Uncle Nick, the field's too wide . . . don't you think?'

Wednesday, October 9th

And there the matter rested for a little over a week until, in fact, the day before Vincent Gilchrist's case was due to come up for trial, which happened to be the day on which a conference had been arranged with Geoffrey Horton and his client, Ned Bates.

Geoffrey was a very old friend of Maitland's and had worked with him, and for him in his capacity as his solicitor, many times in the past. Time had done something to dim the vivid red of his hair, and perhaps a generous application of hair oil had had something to do with that too; otherwise Antony at least saw very little difference in him since the day they first met. Off duty he was the most cheerful of companions, but he had a streak of seriousness where his profession was concerned that Antony at times found amusing, especially on those occasions when he was not himself absorbed in the case under consideration. It was quite impossible to convince him that Maitland ever studied a brief with the diligence it deserved, but this didn't discourage him from carrying with him a bulging briefcase, the contents of which he would in due course lay out before his friend.

Today his companion was also well known to Maitland, a man whom he had defended many times on charges of burglary, and never with success. Ned Bates was a little man, with unruly hair of a nondescript colour and a round, cheerful face. And indeed he had generally taken his convictions philosophically, and still wouldn't hear of any other barrister being briefed to defend him, on the grounds, Horton insisted, that in each case the sentence might have been worse. Now he greeted counsel cordially and sat down looking at him in a hopeful way.

'You've read your brief,' said Geoffrey, with no conviction in his tone.

'Every word of it,' Maitland assured him. 'I hope there's no more of it in that case you're carrying.'

'No, not today. Unfortunately,' said Geoffrey who could be trusted to plunge *in media res*, 'it's a perfectly clear case. I wouldn't have bothered bringing Ned to see you, a few words before we got into court would have done quite well, but I want you to talk some sense into him.'

'Now then, guv'nor,' said Ned, 'what sort of a way is that to talk? I don't deny there've been times in the past . . . but now I'm an innocent man and don't you forget it.'

'Are you indeed?' said Antony, who had a pretty good idea what Geoffrey's trouble was. 'It just shows how unreliable witnesses can be. I was under the impression from reading what Mr Horton sent me that you'd actually been found on enclosed premises.'

'But innocently, Mr Maitland. As innocent as a newborn lamb, that's me,' said Ned positively. 'Now what would I be doing in a jeweller's shop?'

'Robbing the till, I daresay,' said Maitland frankly. 'Or more likely, knowing you, looking for any unconsidered trifles that might have been left lying about.'

'I didn't have a thing on me and they can't say I did.'

'Not even a jemmy?' asked Antony sceptically.

'Now you know me, guv'nor, I don't go in for anything violent. Get in quiet and easy, that's my motto,' said Ned, apparently unconscious that he was contradicting his protestations of innocence. 'Who needs to carry a dirty great thing like a jemmy around when if you look about you carefully like, there's always some easier way of getting in?'

'How did you get in in this case?'

'The back door was open and I just walked in. Well, wasn't that my duty as a citizen, to see nothing was going on that shouldn't have been?'

'That's a nice line, Ned, but somehow I don't think the court will buy it. Whoever heard of a jeweller leaving his premises unprotected, anyway?'

'Someone had been before me,' Ned explained. 'Knocked out a pane of glass and opened the door simple-like, couldn't have done a neater job meself.'

'And it was his entry that triggered the burglar alarm, and led to your being found,' Antony suggested.

'That's right, guv, you're getting the idea,' said Ned enthusiastically. 'This chap's an eccentric, see, the owner of the store.

56

Makes it as easy as pie to get in, and then locks everything up in a ruddy great safe.'

'Thus explaining why you hadn't helped yourself,' said Antony.

'Look here, guv, whose side are you on?'

'Yours, for my sins. Look here, Ned, you know the score. I can't—'

'You can't act as judge and jury,' said Ned, who had probably heard this speech from counsel before.

'Exactly what I was going to say. If you want to plead Not Guilty I'll do it for you, I'll even tell that story of yours to the court with a perfectly straight face and do my best to imply that nobody but a simpleton would disbelieve it. You know what'll happen, they'll find you Guilty, and because it's the—how many times is it, Geoffrey?'

'Five,' said Geoffrey non-committally

'Yes, Ned, because it's the fifth time you'll have been convicted for a similar offence, the judge'll come up with the heaviest sentence he can think of.'

'But that's not fair when I didn't take anything.'

'Fair or not, it's what'll happen. Whereas if you plead Guilty—'

'And lie to the court?' said Ned virtuously.

'If you plead Guilty,' Antony insisted, as though the interruption had not taken place, 'you won't get off, of course, but I do think you'll get off more lightly. I'll even do my best to think up some extenuating circumstances,' he added handsomely, 'but to tell you the truth I can't see offhand that there are any.' He paused, and Ned stared back at him woodenly. 'Mr Horton's told you all this before, of course,' Antony said. 'Why won't you listen to him?'

'P'r'aps I wanted to see if you agreed with him,' said Ned. He didn't seem unduly cast down by counsel's opinion. 'This takes a bit of thinking about. You see, guv, I've been feeling lately it's about time I started going straight.'

'If you really mean that . . . does he mean it, Geoffrey?'

'I think perhaps this time he does,' said Geoffrey. 'Not that he's admitted anything to me. His story is it would be a pity to be sent down for something he didn't do just when he was on the verge of turning over a new leaf. There's a little more to the story than that actually . . . tell him, Ned.'

'There's this little widow,' said Ned. 'A comfortable sort of body, husband left her a pub in the country. Just the sort of thing that would suit me down to the ground.'

'Is the lady willing?'

Ned grinned at him. 'I should say she is,' he agreed.

'If you go back to prison will she wait for you?'

'She knows about this bit of trouble. She'll wait,' said Ned confidently. 'Only it's like this, Mr Maitland, I'd rather she didn't have to wait too long.'

'Then take our advice.'

'I said it takes some thinking about. Tell me, Mr Maitland, would that advice include asking for some other things to be taken into consideration, cleaning the slate like?'

Antony looked at him for a long moment. 'Geoffrey?' he said then.

'If he really wants to make a fresh start,' said Geoffrey, 'that should ensure it. As long as you're completely honest about it, Ned. It would also serve to convince the court of his genuine penitence . . . though I'm not quite sure that that's the right word.'

'It'll do as well as another,' said Maitland briskly. 'What about it, Ned?'

'If I do what you say there'll be nothing more against me when I come out?' asked Ned with every appearance of suspicion.

'Nothing whatever, as Mr Horton told you, as long as you're completely honest with us now.'

'It's only two other cases,' said Ned, rather in the tone of the girl who protested that her illegitimate baby was only a little one. 'Five years ago, Mrs Allenby's jewels. Nice little haul that was.'

'And the other?'

'That was only a month or so ago. But it should convince the court that I mean what I say about going straight, Mr Maitland, because they've got someone else for it so there's no real need for me to confess.'

'You mean someone else has been arrested?'

'What else would I mean? A chap called Gilchrist, a bit of a swell from what I hear.'

'Now look here, Ned . . . no wait a bit, Geoffrey, I've got to be sure about this. Who did you rob?'

'Have you heard of David Thurlow, the actor?'

'Yes, I have.'

'Well, his missus is a wealthy woman, fond of jewellery, and isn't the sort to keep her stuff in the bank. I kept an eye on the place for a bit – getting in was a piece of cake – and one night when they came out all dressed up, obviously off for the evening, I just went in and helped meself to what I wanted.'

'How did you get in?'

'Same way as usual. Broke a pane of glass in the kitchen window so that I could reach the latch. It meant climbing down over the sink, but that's no great difficulty.'

'What night was this?'

'That's an easy one. September the third. That's my birthday, you see, and when I saw them coming out all dolled up I thought, here's a nice present for you, Ned Bates.'

Geoffrey was beginning to look puzzled. 'There seems no doubt –' he began.

'No, but I've got to be sure. I'll tell you why later. Can you give me a list of what you took, Ned?'

'That'll take a bit of thinking about, but yes, I could do that.'

'Will you write it out for me now? I'll ask you to look on, Geoffrey, and witness it when he's done.'

'All right then, if you're so keen on it.' Antony pushed the pad on his desk towards him, and Geoffrey produced a ballpoint from his pocket.

'What's all this about, Antony?' he asked as he handed it over.

'The chap who's accused of that particular robbery is a client of mine and is coming up for trial tomorrow.'

'In that case . . . are you willing to give evidence, Ned?' Horton asked.

Ned looked up from his writing, which seemed to be rather a laborious task. 'Prove my sincerity, wouldn't it?' he demanded. 'Would it mean they'd arrest me though, right off?'

'I got you out on bail this time, didn't I?' Geoffrey asked. 'I think in the circumstances I can do the same thing again.'

'All right then.' Ned was writing again. 'Be a bit of a change to see the court from the witness box, instead of the dock,' he said. 'But I hope this client of yours, Mr Maitland, will be properly grateful for what I'm doing for him.'

REGINA *versus* GILCHRIST, 1974

Thursday, the first day of the trial

I

A consultation with Matthew Barlow the evening before had revealed the fact that the solicitor was very much against going to the police with the information Maitland had gleaned and trying to get the charge against Vincent Gilchrist dismissed without ever coming to trial or, more probably, by an announcement that the prosecution did not intend to offer any evidence. 'I don't want anything hole-in-the-corner about this, Mr Maitland, which would leave people still thinking Vincent might be guilty. Let them put on their case without interruption, let them – even encourage them – to talk about the earlier case, and then bring on this witness of yours. Nobody'll think after that that he was guilty in either affair. Sensation in court, that's what we're after.'

On consideration Maitland was inclined to agree with what he considered at the time to be a very un-Barlowish remark, but he didn't yet know that the prosecution were not the only ones who were due for a surprise.

In fact, his one worry was that Ned Bates wouldn't turn up as promised, and before going into court himself he made sure that the little man was actually in the room where the witnesses were sequestered until it was time for them to give their evidence. They had no words together but Ned gave him a wink, which he hoped could be construed as an assurance that the little man wouldn't go back on his proof.

The case was to be heard by Mr Justice Lamb, who had been recently elevated to the bench. Lamb was a man of gloomy aspect, whom Maitland had always compared in his mind to a huge melancholy bird, and his new robes did little to dispel that impression. During his years at the bar he had often appeared for the prosecution in cases in which Antony had also been involved, but this was the first time Maitland had appeared before him in his present capacity. Vincent Gilchrist's case was by no means a *cause célèbre*, however important its outcome might be to himself and to his family and friends, and the prosecution was being handled by Mr Hawthorne, a coming man – so Sir Nicholas said – for whom Antony was already beginning to entertain a good deal of respect. A good fighter, but not one to press his case unduly. The jury were just the usual crowd, seven men and five women in this case but otherwise indistinguishable so far as he could see from any other jury. (This impression, though quite obviously mistaken, is perhaps forgivable in a man who spent most of his time addressing the members of the jury box as one entity.)

For the rest, Vincent Gilchrist, who by now had appeared in the dock, seemed perfectly calm, as he probably would have done anyway if his counsel's impression of him was right, even if he hadn't had a talk with his solicitor that morning. Matthew Barlow, however, was fidgeting nervously, obviously ill-at-ease in these unfamiliar surroundings. Maitland turned his head and grinned at his instructing solicitor reassuringly. 'Like taking candy from a baby,' he said, but hadn't time to wait to see whether his words had any calming effect. The indictment had been read, and Mr Hawthorne was already on his feet making his opening address.

This was brief, and started with a request for the details of Vincent's previous conviction to be admitted in evidence. 'Naturally, my lord, I should not have made this request in open court if I had not already had the agreement of my learned friend, Mr Maitland, who is appearing for the defence, as to its relevance in the present case. When the facts are put before you, you will see that there are certain similarities between the two incidents that cannot be ignored.'

Lamb looked unhappily from Counsel for the Prosecution to Counsel for the Defence. 'So there is a previous matter to be taken into consideration,' he said, rather as though the depths of depravity to which human nature could sink were too much for him. 'Well, Mr Hawthorne, if you have Mr Maitland's agreement I'm sure we can none of us have any objection to hearing what you have to say about it, but I trust that it will not unduly lengthen these proceedings.'

'Certainly not, my lord. It is only a matter of proving this previous conviction, and the investigating officer will outline for us the grounds on which it was obtained. I will not myself go into the matter at this time, except to say that it concerned a theft of jewellery—an old-fashioned but very valuable bracelet, to be exact—which took place while the prisoner was visiting his brother and sister-in-law at Hollyhurst Manor in Surrey. One evening in the second week of his stay friends of his hosts, a Mr and Mrs Chalmers, were dining with them, but Vincent Gilchrist absented himself, and was not later able to give any account of where he had been.'

He paused there, seeing Antony on his feet. 'Yes, Mr Maitland?' sighed Lamb.

'My lord, I believe my friend would be more exact to say that my client could not substantiate his story of where he had been on that evening, rather than that he could give no account of himself.'

'Is that correct, Mr Hawthorne?'

'Yes, my lord, I'm afraid it is. I'm afraid my allusion to the prisoner's lack of an alibi on that occasion was rather loosely worded. But I promised your lordship to be brief, so I will do no more than add that on that evening the home of Mervin Chalmers and his wife Karen was broken into, and a valuable bracelet was stolen. This was later found in the prisoner's possession at his mother's home in London. It was also established that fingerprints found on the drawer where the bracelet was kept belonged to him.'

Lamb was leaning forward as though his interest had been caught. 'And when did these distressing events take place, Mr Hawthorne?' he asked.

'In March of this year, my lord.'

'And you say the prisoner was convicted?'

'He was, my lord. He was sentenced to eighteen months in prison, but in view of the fact this was a first offence and that he'd never been in trouble of any kind before the sentence was suspended for two years.'

'That's all very well, Mr Hawthorne,' said Lamb rather peevishly, 'but where does the similarity to the present case come in?'

'I was about to explain, my lord.'

'Well, I think you had better do so very carefully. We don't want the members of the jury to be confused as to which case they are trying, do we?'

'Indeed no, my lord. The present case,' he added turning a

65

little to face the jury box, 'concerns the theft of jewellery from a Mrs David Thurlow, a friend of Mrs Helen Gilchrist who is the prisoner's mother, and with whom she and her husband were dining on the night the robbery occurred. The accused makes his home with his mother, but again excused himself from dining with the party, though he stayed to have a drink with them before he left, to be polite, he says in his statement to the police. Again, members of the jury, his story of his activities that evening cannot be verified. Entry was made into the Thurlows' house in almost precisely the same way as in the previous incident I have mentioned, the defendant was seen in the vicinity, and again there were fingerprints, this time on the door of Mrs Thurlow's bedroom, where they certainly had no business to be. I think,' he added (quite gratuitously as Antony thought), 'that when my friend Mr Maitland comes to address you for the defence he will stress the unlikelihood of anyone committing such a crime without going to the trouble of providing himself with gloves. Detective fiction has much to answer for, and today we are perhaps all a little over-wise. But it is also a fact that, just as we all do in ordinary life, a man in the course of committing a crime will make mistakes. If you can place yourselves in such a man's place . . . his hands might be sweating perhaps from nervousness, and so a glove removed for a moment only, but long enough to leave some trace of his presence. I will not at the moment labour the point, but I'm sure that, like me, you will find this a particularly distressing case, involving as it does a member of an old family with a previously unblemished record. That, however, cannot be taken into account in your deliberations. When the time comes, his lordship will advise you as to the legal aspects of the matter but I'm sure you will agree with me that there can be one verdict only, that of Guilty as charged.'

Having already got his right to introduce the previous case established, Mr Hawthorne made no delay about calling as his first witness the police inspector from the local CID who had dealt with the theft of Karen Chalmers's bracelet. The detective was a sturdy-looking man, whose down-to-earth manner reminded Maitland vaguely of his old friend Chief Inspector Sykes of Scotland Yard, though his accent, of course, was completely different, Sykes being a north country man. His evidence didn't take long: the defence, as well as allowing it to be introduced without argument, had waived the necessity of sworn proof of the conviction. Antony remembered that Hawthorne had been a little surprised at the readiness with which he had done this, but it had never seemed to him to be any good arguing about the inevitable, or drawing out matters unduly to everyone's annoyance when not the slightest advantage could be gained thereby. But when the evidence was completed and the detective was about to leave the witness box, Counsel for the Defence rose leisurely to his feet.

Lamb gave him a sharp look. 'You wish to cross-examine this witness, Mr Maitland?'

'With your lordship's permission.'

'I don't have to remind you, I hope, that except for showing method this case is really no concern of ours.'

'No, my lord, there's no need to remind me of that. You will recall that I gave my consent to the introduction of this evidence because I did not wish to waste the time of the court unduly.' He paused, giving Lamb – he hoped – a chance to absorb the fact of his magnanimity. 'Two questions only, my lord,' he added persuasively.

'Very well, Mr Maitland, you may ask your two questions. But bear in mind that I shall inform the members of the jury in my closing address that this matter is over and done with and cannot be re-opened except upon the discovery of some fresh evidence. And that even if some such evidence were forthcoming it would not be the concern of this court.'

'Yes, my lord, I appreciate the reminder, and I'm sure the jury will have no difficulty in distinguishing between the two cases.' Truth to tell he had no such conviction, but it sounded well, he hoped. 'Inspector,' he said, turning to the witness, 'did you find anything inherently improbable about the account of his movements that my client gave you?'

'No, I accepted what he said without question. He went for a drive, and stopped at a public house a few miles away, where he wasn't known, for as long as it took him to dispose of a pint of bitter. He didn't see anyone he knew, and inquiries at the public house in question showed that no one remembered him, but I have to admit that I didn't find that surprising.'

'How did it come about then that you suspected him sufficiently to search his home in London?'

'Information received, sir.'

'Yes, so I suppose, but from whom did you receive this information?'

'From the gentleman whose wife was robbed.'

'Who knew my client, but presumably was not a friend of his.'

'Perhaps not.'

'Did he also know Mrs Helen Gilchrist, my client's mother?'

'I took it he did.'

'Thank you, Inspector, that is all I wish to know.'

The next witness was also a detective inspector, this time from Central, as Chesham Street fell within their jurisdiction. He told of being called to the Thurlows' home after they returned from their dinner with Mrs Gilchrist, gave a detailed description of the means of entry apparently used by the thief, and went into some detail about the investigation both at the house and among known receivers in case any of the stolen jewellery appeared. Unfortunately nothing had so far come of this last line of inquiry.

'And during the time you were still at the Chesham Street house, did you have some conversation with the constable who had first been called to the scene of the crime?' asked Hawthorne.

'Yes, sir, I did.'

'Will you tell us what action you took in consequence of this conversation?'

'As soon as I could get away I went to Mrs Helen Gilchrist's flat in Halkin Place, where Mr and Mrs Thurlow had been dining, and asked to see her son Vincent, the accused in this case.'

'Did you find him at home?'

'Yes, I gathered he'd just got in. That was at 11.30. I asked for an account of his evening, and he said he had intended to visit a friend, which was why he had refused his mother's request that he stay and dine with the Thurlows, though he had lingered long enough to have a drink with them when they arrived. As it turned out the friend's name was not material, as the prisoner's story was that he was distracted from his purpose by an advertisement outside a cinema on his way and went there instead.'

'Did he tell you what was the film he wished so much to see?'

'Yes, a return visit of *2001*. He said everyone had told him he must see it.'

'Did you form any judgement as to whether he had indeed done so?' asked Hawthorne with one eye on his opponent. Maitland, however, held his peace.

'He was certainly able to describe the story in some detail. He also said that when he came out from the film he had a snack in the restaurant on the ground floor of the block of flats where he and his mother lived. That I was able to verify.'

'And then?'

'Then I got in touch with the local police who had investigated the burglary from the Chalmers's house.' He paused there and Hawthorne was quick to prompt him.

'It is quite in order for you to continue the story, Inspector. His lordship has given permission, and my learned friend for the defence has agreed that the matter is relevant.'

'Thank you, sir.' He went on to repeat what he had been told, in very much the same words as the previous witness had used. 'Meanwhile, of course, inquiries were going on in Chesham Street, and a Mr and Mrs Landon were found at number 103 who had seen Mr Gilchrist going in the direction of the Thurlows' house on the night in question.'

'Did you put this point to the prisoner?'

'Yes, I did. I warned him before I did so. He admitted having been there, on his way to the bus stop, he said. It didn't seem to me that it was the quickest way, but he told me it was the way he preferred. By this time two other witnesses had come forward, who had seen a report in a newspaper and who claimed to have seen a man entering the back yard of the Chalmers's house at about eight o'clock on the evening in question. Later they both independently picked out the accused in an identification parade.'

'And by then did you have a report from your fingerprint experts?'

'Yes, I did. The accused's fingerprints were found on the panel of the door to Mrs Thurlow's bedroom. They were the prints of his left hand: he said he had made them when pushing the door open looking for the bathroom on a visit some ten days previously. Mrs Thurlow has confirmed that this visit was in fact made, but of course could not speak to the other part of his statement.'

'Then I think that is all, Inspector, though I'm sure my learned friend has some questions for you.'

'No questions,' said Maitland, shaking his head.

'Very well then. You may step down, Inspector.'

Following his superior officer came the constable who had first been on the scene. He was an older man who obviously liked to know exactly what was going on in his manor, and he was quite familiar with both Mrs Helen Gilchrist and her son. Naturally he had followed the case in Surrey rather closely, knowing the accused man so well. He had been able to point out to his superior the points of resemblance between the two affairs, but after that, of course, the matter had been out of his hands.

Again the defence declined to cross-examine. Mr Justice Lamb sighed deeply and glanced at his watch. 'We made a late start, and this seems to be a good time to adjourn for the luncheon recess. We will re-convene at – shall we say? – one-thirty.'

Maitland got up and stretched and turned to look at his instructing solicitor. 'You'll lunch with me, won't you, Mr Barlow?' he asked. 'If we go to Astroff's, with any luck we'll find my uncle there, and I know he'd like to meet you.'

'Sir Nicholas Harding? Yes, indeed I should very much like to meet him.' They began to make their way slowly towards the door. 'You do think we took the right course, don't you, Mr Maitland?' Matthew Barlow went on anxiously. 'You see,' he said again, unnecessarily, 'I'm not at all used to this kind of thing.'

'Don't worry, it'll be perfectly all right. Anyway you'll feel better when you've had some lunch,' said Antony reassuringly, which might or might not have been true but unfortunately they had no immediate chance of finding out.

They had barely reached the corridor outside when a young woman rushed up to them, placing herself firmly in their path. 'You're Mr Maitland,' she said, looking directly at Antony.

'Yes, I am. How did you know?'

'I've seen your picture a hundred times, and Colin's talked about you.'

'I'm sorry, but you have the advantage of me.'

'I'm Rosanna Johnson. Colin's a reporter for the *Evening Chronicle*.'

'And is Colin also your husband?'

'Yes, of course. It was Colin that Vince says he was going to see the night all this happened.'

'Only he went to the pictures instead.' Something about the intenseness of her attitude puzzled Maitland. She was above average height for a woman, very slim, and with dark, straight hair cut short enough to display the contours of a well-shaped head. The rather severe suit she was wearing was probably what she considered suitable for the occasion, and she carried a close-fitting hat in her hand as though she had been uncertain whether

70

it would be correct for her to wear it. Her husband could probably have told her, but almost certainly he knew nothing of her errand.

'No, he didn't, of course he didn't! He came to our place, only Colin wasn't there. We spent the whole evening together.'

'Then why in hell's name didn't he say so?' asked Antony.

'Because . . . don't you see he *knew* Colin would be out, I'd told him so. That's why he said I wasn't to say anything about it, only when it came to the point I just had to.'

Not another jealous husband! Antony thought, but fortunately had the presence of mind to keep the comment to himself. 'Well, of course, Mrs Johnson,' he said aloud, 'we're grateful to you for coming forward, but circumstances have arisen which I believe render your evidence unnecessary.'

'But of course I must say where he was. Then they'll know he couldn't possibly have done it. Look, Mr Maitland, he arrived at our place not later than eight-thirty and he left me in time to get home at 11.30 as he says. Colin was out of town, as it happened, and I'd rung up to tell Vince that.'

'I understand, but I still think the best thing we can do is to keep your evidence in reserve in case his lordship and my learned friend for the prosecution are not quite as receptive to the story I have to offer them as I hope they will be. Yes, Mr Barlow?' he added, feeling the solicitor tugging at his sleeve.

'Has she been in court all morning?' Matthew Barlow asked him in a worried tone.

'Have you, Mrs Johnson?'

'Yes, of course, but when I thought it might be getting near lunchtime I came round here to wait for you.'

'Well, I don't think that need be an insuperable difficulty, if we do in fact need your evidence. If we explain the matter to the court I'm sure his lordship will realize that Mr Gilchrist's prevarication was due to chivalrous motives. Now I agree with Mr Barlow, Mrs Johnson, we'd better keep you in reserve just in case. I don't think you'd better come back into court again; when you've got yourself some lunch, any of the attendants will tell you where the witnesses in this case are waiting.'

'I don't understand at all, I thought you'd be very anxious to have an alibi for him.'

'We shan't call you unless it's absolutely necessary,' said Maitland firmly. He hesitated, glancing round to see that no one

71

was in earshot. 'To begin with, if your association with my client has been a close one –'

'We've been lovers for about two months.'

'Then I'm afraid you'd be in for some rather severe cross-examination. The jury might regard your evidence almost as suspiciously as they would a wife's. Or perhaps even more suspiciously in these cynical days,' he added to Matthew Barlow, when at last they got rid of the rather distraught young woman. 'I must say our client seems to have a knack of spreading sweetness and light among the ladies of his acquaintance wherever he goes.'

'Youth will have its fling,' said Matthew Barlow indulgently, if not particularly originally. Then he glanced at his watch fussily. 'I'm not quite sure how far away this restaurant you mentioned is –'

'No, I'm afraid we shan't have time to make it. There's a place round the corner though, that's rather better than going downstairs to the cafeteria. And they're quite used to people in our profession being in a hurry.'

II

After the luncheon recess the first witness to be called was Denise Thurlow; after the rather definite impression of her that he'd obtained from her husband, Antony looked at her with unusual interest. Ordinarily, of course, he would have been weighing her up just as carefully, though in a rather more disinterested way, looking for a chink in her armour, a weak spot in her evidence, something that could be turned to his client's advantage. She was, he decided, not exactly pretty; but beautifully groomed, expensively dressed, and with a pleasant expression. She took the oath in a clear voice; that was another thing about her, she was completely self-possessed, probably the result of never having had to worry about so mundane a matter as money. Antony wondered vaguely whether the years would turn Mandy into a replica of her aunt, but somehow he doubted it. And if only Hawthorne knew it he should be truly thankful that there had been no occasion to ask for her testimony. A witness given to knowing things positively, but without a shred of evidence, would be a nightmare for any counsel even on direct examination. But there his thoughts brought him up with a jerk. Mandy had told him, hadn't she, that if only he'd take a hand something would

72

turn up to clear Vincent Gilchrist? Well, he had taken a hand, and though what turned up was none of his doing there it was just the same, the perfect defence. For a moment he wished it had been Geoffrey who had briefed him, so that they could have shared the joke together. Matthew Barlow, he was afraid, just wouldn't see any amusement in it.

Not only was Denise Thurlow's evidence very clearly audible, it was given almost without prompting. On the evening in question she and her husband had been invited to dinner by Mrs Helen Gilchrist. They had accepted with pleasure, they were both very fond of Helen, and were only too sorry for the way she must be feeling about this dreadful business. 'I tried to see her, you know,' she went on, completely ignoring Hawthorne's attempts to interrupt her, 'but when she saw who it was she just shut the door in my face. Of course, I don't blame her for that really, I expect I'd feel just the same if it was a son of mine. Only I can't pretend, not about a thing like that.'

Fortunately at this point she paused for breath, and Counsel for the Prosecution was able to get a word in. 'You were describing the evening in question, Mrs Thurlow,' he prompted her.

'Yes, we arrived there about seven-thirty, and Vince was at home which surprised me, only it turned out he had a previous engagement and had to go out which he did about ten to eight. And after that everything was just as usual until we got home. We didn't stay late, because I know Helen likes to go to bed early, so we were home by about half past ten. But that was a bit early for us to go to bed, so we thought we'd like a nightcap and I went out into the kitchen to get it. And that's when I saw the broken window, and some scratches on the window ledge, and some mud on the edge of the sink. So of course I called to David, and he went round the house to make sure there was nobody still there, and then I said, My jewels! and rushed upstairs to see if they were all right.'

'I think perhaps it would be helpful, Mrs Thurlow, if you told us where your jewels were kept.'

'Why, in a hatbox at the back of the wardrobe. I thought it was such a good place, I still can't see how anyone would think of looking there,' said Denise earnestly. 'And there wasn't a sign that anything was out of order, but when I opened the box everything was gone.'

'Everything Mrs Thurlow?'

'Well, I was wearing my pearls. And a rather nice brooch that I got from that very clever jeweller in Bedford Lane.' (Father William? Maitland thought to himself.) 'It isn't really valuable but very pretty, a tiny bunch of snowdrops with the flowers made of pearls. I don't believe in ostentation, that was quite enough for a simple dinner with friends, but I don't see the point either of having jewellery and keeping it locked away in the bank. It would be too much bother keeping track of it, and anyway I like to know all my lovely things are there and to look at them sometimes. I must say the insurance company weren't very understanding about that, I had to pay an absolutely enormous premium, but it was worth it really. I might as well have sold them if I hadn't had them handy to look at when I wanted.'

'Did you give the police the list of the items concerned?'

'I remembered almost everything.' She said this proudly, as though it had involved some tremendous feat of memory. 'But I told them I couldn't be quite sure it was complete, so then they showed me the list the insurance company had, and I put a cross by the pieces I'd been wearing, and everything else was there. Of course they asked me if I'd sold anything, and I never had, I wouldn't for anything. And I told them – the insurance people, I mean – that if I had they'd have been the first to know, because I'm not such a fool as to pay a premium on something I no longer possess.'

And that was really all. Hawthorne wasn't a man, it seemed, to indulge in much repetition. (More faith in the collective intelligence of the jury than some I could name.) Antony, however, found Mr Justice Lamb's sad eyes fixed on him. 'I find it a little odd, Mr Maitland, that the only cross-examination of a witness you have undertaken has been concerning the previous crime, which – except in the one respect which allowed mention of it in evidence – is no concern of ours.'

'I'm obliged to your lordship, but I see no reason to take up the court's time with unnecessary questions.'

'Unnecessary, Mr Maitland?'

'I'm quite sure the witnesses are telling the truth.'

'But you were in some doubt as to the veracity of the evidence of the Detective Inspector who was the prosecution's first witness?'

'No, my lord, not at all. His evidence as to the facts I accept

74

absolutely; it is his interpretation of them that I cannot altogether agree with.'

'Well, Mr Maitland, no doubt you know your own business best,' said Lamb more in sorrow than in anger, so that Antony remembered immediately that he had been better known to his brethren at the bar as Poor Lamb. 'Yes, Mr Hawthorne, you have something you wish to say to the court?'

Hawthorne, who had been watching the exchange between Judge and counsel with a mixture of amusement and curiosity, took the opportunity as the next witness entered the court of introducing the list of jewels and their appraised value into evidence. This proved to be a timely move, as the witness now taking his place and being sworn in was an employee of the Imperial Insurance Company and had been responsible for the valuation. He read from the list, of which he had brought a copy with him, giving the date of each purchase, the value of the item at the time, and the value which he considered should be placed on it today. 'Mrs Thurlow took out the first insurance with us a little over twenty years ago. It happened to be in the month of June, and every five years since then she has made a point of asking for a re-appraisal at current prices. The last such valuation therefore was made last June, and is reflected in this list.'

'And the total at that date was – ?'

'£98,300.' (If Mr Barlow had wanted a sensation in court he got one at this point.) 'Of course, when considering the value of the – ah – haul we must deduct the pearls that Mrs Thurlow was wearing, and the brooch, though this latter was of small value. I may say,' he added rather severely, 'that I have spoken to Mrs Thurlow on a number of occasions about the dangers of keeping such valuable things in the house, but all she would say was, They're very beautiful and I like to have them with me. She is a lady of excellent taste, and I couldn't but sympathize with that point of view. Of course the danger was reflected in the premium she paid.'

'I've no doubt it was,' said Hawthorne rather drily. 'My lord, may I ask a question of this witness which calls for his opinion. In a sense he is here as an expert, so I hope there'll be no objection.'

'None from me, Mr Hawthorne. Unless Mr Maitland has decided to break his silence –'

'I shall be very pleased to hear the answer to whatever question my friend has in mind,' said Antony obligingly.

'Thank you.' Hawthorne divided his gratitude neatly between his opponent and the Judge. 'The question is this: these pieces of jewellery that were stolen, the diamond necklace and the bracelet and ear-rings that match it in particular, would they be well-known? Would the thief, for instance, have any difficulty in disposing of them?'

'Great difficulty, I think, unless he was able to take them out of the country. The diamonds you spoke of, for instance, were made to Mrs Thurlow's order, and the jeweller in question was able, I understand, to supply the police with the original sketch that he did for her to see. This I'm sure was circulated –'

'Yes, we have the evidence of the investigating officer on that point. What I am getting at is whether you think the jewellery is still intact somewhere or whether it will have been broken up.'

'If I were the thief,' said the witness, suddenly becoming human, 'that's what I'd have done. Broken it up, I mean. You wouldn't get the full value for it that way. I'm afraid I can't give you an opinion as to what price you'd get, not being familiar with the ways of the criminal fraternity, but I presume it would be quite sufficient to make the theft very worthwhile.'

'Thank you, I have no further questions. Unless Mr Maitland –'

'No questions,' said Antony cheerfully.

He had been hoping that Ned Bates's evidence might be reached that evening, although it would certainly have meant their sitting late and he had no knowledge yet of Mr Justice Lamb's habits in this direction. But Hawthorne, perhaps unnerved by his adversary's continued silence, kept his last witnesses rather longer than Maitland felt their evidence warranted. They were the rather dull couple, Mark and Celia Landon, who lived at number 103 Chesham Street, and the two men, Herbert Bellamy and Sidney Backhouse who were the other witnesses to Vincent's presence in the neighbourhood. The Landons had been coming out of their house when Vince Gilchrist passed. He hadn't seen them, and by the time they had locked the door and got down the steps to the street he was some distance ahead of them. Both of them knew him slightly and there could be no doubt of the identification. He had preceded them along the street, passed the Thurlows' house which was about half way down, and turned right when he got to the end. A map of the area prepared for the police had already been introduced into

76

evidence, and would no doubt have been sworn to by the surveyor concerned if it had not been for the unusual complaisance of the defence. Neither of the witnesses therefore had any difficulty in demonstrating that this right turn would bring Vince to the entrance to the lane on which all the houses in Chesham Street backed. As far as either of them could say, they had left their house about eight o'clock. At that time and in that area there weren't many people about, but they had turned left themselves at the end of the road, and couldn't say anything further about Vince's movements.

Maitland was thoroughly bored by the time Mark Landon had given his evidence, repeated it, and then been echoed almost word for word by his wife. Mark seemed indifferent to the whole affair, but Celia showed some signs of animosity towards Vince, whom she knew well enough to call by his Christian name except when she recalled herself and spoke of him more formally. And there were still the two other men to come. Their evidence too was straightforward. They had been coming down the back lane in the opposite direction from the man they had seen going into the back yard of number 113, which they now knew to be the Thurlows' house. They had seen his face quite clearly and had later been able to pick him out from a line-up of men of very similar appearance.

Obviously this was where Hawthorne had expected his opponent to make his stand ... perhaps the most damaging evidence against the accused, but at the same time, paradoxically, possibly the most easily discredited. He was obviously bewildered by Maitland's continued silence, but that, thought Antony callously, couldn't be helped. However, it was later than he had expected when Hawthorne at last closed his case, and he wasn't surprised that the adjournment followed immediately.

Friday, the second day of the trial

Matthew Barlow was still decidedly apprehensive when they met the next morning, and Antony had his work cut out to reassure him. 'We'll be out of here in an hour,' he said confidently.

'But supposing the Judge doesn't believe this man Bates, supposing he refuses to dismiss the case when you ask him. What then?'

'I suppose, since our client has never admitted to you that he lied about his movements that night, that we shall have to call Mrs Johnson's evidence.'

'Might it not be better to call it first? After all, she's a respectable woman, and this man Bates is a known criminal.'

'I think, Mr Barlow, if you don't mind, we'll do it my way. You see, I have the gravest doubts myself as to whether she's telling the truth, and it may be that she'll break down on cross-examination. In any case, as I pointed out to her, the evidence of a woman in love – and we must give her the credit for that at least – has perhaps less chance of being believed even than Ned's story, which is extremely circumstantial.'

'Yes, I see your point, of course, but I don't see why you should disbelieve her. After all, what she's admitted to is not very nice.'

'No, but don't you think if it were a true story our client would have told us? He made no bones about admitting his affair with Karen Chalmers. Why should he have more consideration for this woman? Even to the extent of denying it to you when you spoke to him last night, as I gather he did.'

'Well, I suppose . . . I'm in your hands, Mr Maitland. I explained that to you at the beginning. You must do what you feel is best.'

As Antony intended to in any case he wasn't too grateful for this indulgence. A few moments later he was on his feet to open the case for the defence. 'My lord, the circumstances of this case are unusual, in that, purely by accident, I received incontrovertible proof of my client's innocence late in the afternoon of the day before the trial commenced.' He paused a moment to let the hum of surprise that rippled through the court subside, and perhaps also to allow the pencils of the few reporters who were present to catch up with him. 'Therefore I intend, with your lordship's permission, to dispense altogether with an opening address. I have one witness to call, who, as it happens, is also a client of mine, and who is here, as you will see, at a considerable disadvantage to himself. After you have heard his evidence I shall take the opportunity of asking your lordship to instruct the jury that the case against the accused be dismissed. I think, my lord, that when you have heard what this witness has to say you will agree with me that that is the proper course to follow.'

'Well, Mr Maitland, you have of course the privilege of calling whatever witnesses you like, and in whatever order. Let us hear this evidence on which you place so great a reliance.' Lamb sighed as though the thought of listening to what was to come was an ordeal almost too great for him to bear.

'I am obliged to your lordship. Call Edward Bates.'

Ned entered the courtroom cheerfully, took the Bible in his hand reverently as though every word it contained was precious to him, and announced his intention to tell the truth in ringing tones. There was another small stir when he announced his profession as Retired Burglar and Mr Justice Lamb was again moved to intervene, looking as he did so as though he were about to burst into tears.

'Retired burglar, Mr Maitland?' he asked despairingly.

'Retired since the third of September last, my lord,' Maitland told him, as though this were the most natural thing in the world, and barely stopped himself from adding that Ned had abandoned his profession without the presentation of a gold watch *or* a pension.

'I don't think I quite understand,' said Lamb, as though this was the last straw.

'It gets easier as you go along,' Antony assured him, but recollected himself immediately and became more formal. 'May I have your lordship's permission to question the witness?'

'I suppose you must.'

'Then perhaps you will describe to the court, Mr Bates, exactly what led to your being here today.'

'Well, you see, it's like this, me lord,'—Ned looked as if he had settled down for a good long chat—'I seen the error of me ways along of the fact that I'm going to be married. So with this case coming up, see, Mr Horton—that's my solicitor—takes me along to see Mr Maitland who's acted for me before. And they both of them said it would be best to plead Guilty and be done with it, since I was found on enclosed premises and they didn't think much of the story I told the police, and Mr Maitland he gives me the usual speech about going straight in future. So I thinks to myself let's get this one over with, but I don't want the other things coming up afterwards, not when I'm settled down to wedded bliss, as they say. So I said, wouldn't it be best to ask for the other things as I'd done to be taken into consideration, clear the slate like once and for all. And they says, Yes, if I really mean to go straight in future, and I do and so I tells them. And when I comes to September the third, and the jewels I took from that Mrs Thurlow, Mr Maitland he more or less goes off pop.'

Lamb turned sad, inquiring eyes in Antony's direction. 'I think, my lord, he means that I showed some evidence of surprise and excitement,' Antony explained.

'I think perhaps before Mr Bates continues his story,' said Lamb, looking as though he had just heard of the death of a dear friend, 'we should like to hear from you, Mr Maitland, what your reaction was to this statement, besides the surprise and excitement the witness has mentioned.'

'I did my best to ascertain, my lord, not whether he was telling the truth—for I could see no reason why he should be lying—but whether he could prove his story. I should add that Geoffrey Horton, the solicitor who had brought Mr Bates to see me in chambers, was also present and is ready to corroborate the witness's story if you should feel such corroboration is necessary.'

'Thank you, Mr Maitland. I gather, then, that you asked the witness for some details of the crime to which he is now confessing.'

'Yes, my lord, I did. Perhaps if Mr Bates would tell us his story in his own way—'

'Very well.' He turned to the witness. 'Please continue,' he invited.

'Righty-oh, me lord,' said Ned. When he had remarked that it would be a nice change to attend court as a witness he had obviously been telling no more than the truth. 'If I'm to begin at the beginning, that's a wealthy neighbourhood, see. Any of the houses there's likely to have some cash about, but I've always had a weakness for the baubles, and it's not everyone who had so much stuff lying about as this Mrs Thurlow. Good stuff,' he emphasized.

'You're telling us that you knew what you were looking for,' inquired Lamb rather petulantly.

'Oh yes, me lord. There's a pub on the corner, well not on the corner of Chesham Street, of course, but not far away, the Silver Fleece it's called. They knows me there, one way and another I've spent quite a bit of time having a pint and listening to people talk. And I heard . . . rumours.'

'You're telling us that someone told you that Mrs Thurlow had a quantity of jewellery which she was in the habit of keeping at home?' asked the Judge, who seemed to have taken over the questioning of this witness himself, though not to be enjoying it.

'Not exactly told, but there was some talk about it and I thought it was worth looking into. So I hung about the house a bit, she's a nice-looking lady and always gets herself up very nice, so one way and another I could well believe what I'd been told. Anyway it was worth having a look, so one evening when I saw them both go out all dolled up I thought to meself they won't be coming back in a hurry and I started round to the back. Course I'd looked it over before that and getting in was a piece of cake.'

'I think you should tell the court, Mr Bates,' Antony interrupted him, 'exactly what the back of the house was like, and how you effected entrance.'

'Well, there's a narrow lane, and each house has a yard, with a high wall. Someone your height, guv, anyone looking out of the window might have seen the top of your head, but a little chap like me could nip along and nobody the wiser. There was two men in the lane, but once I got into the yard they couldn't know what I was up to. If someone had happened to be looking down from upstairs they could have seen me walking across the yard, but that's hardly a crime anyway. And once I'd got right up against the house, there'd be no way of knowing what was going on.'

'What about the houses across the way, the houses in the next street that also backed on to the lane you mentioned?' said Maitland.

'You asked me that before, and I told you they was too far

82

away to see what I was up to. I had me gloves, of course, and a piece of thick cloth to protect me hand. I just broke the window, and then it was quite easy to undo the catch. And I'm pretty nippy, getting over the sink was no problem. I just scarpered out of the back when I'd finished, it has one of those Yale locks, you just pull it to.'

'But in the meantime,' – that was Lamb, taking over the questioning again – 'according to the evidence we have heard there were no signs of disturbance in the house.'

'Bless you, guv – me lord – I didn't have to turn the place upside down to find what I wanted.'

'Mrs Thurlow didn't keep her jewels in open sight.'

'It's the oldest trick in the world, putting the box they're in at the back of the wardrobe. First place I looked, and there they were in a big round hatbox. Of course, there were other places I'd have looked if I hadn't hit on the right one first off, but there was no need for that.'

'You took the jewels?'

'That was what I was there for, wasn't it?'

'Then I think the next question, Mr Bates, is where they are now?' Mr Justice Lamb still looked as though he were in mourning for the wickedness of mankind, but for the first time since Antony had known him he was beginning to show some signs of animation as his interest in the story grew.

'Mr Maitland asked me that,' said Ned. 'But there, me lord, I couldn't help you or him. I sold them to a man in a pub, and if you ask me they'll be broken up by now. A pity, of course, but there it is.'

'The Silver Fleece?' asked the Judge.

'Oh no, nor anywhere near that. A place I know in the East End.'

'And the man you sold them to?'

'Well, I know him, of course, me lord, we'd met by arrangement before, but never twice in the same place. And he's a fly one, I never knew his name or where he lived.'

'Then how did you get in touch with him?'

'I'd let the word get around that I'd a deal in the making, and after a while he'd phone me. A bit mean I always thought him, but safe as houses, and after all he had to have his profit and the stones wouldn't be worth near as much once the stuff was broken up. Anyway, the 10,000 quid he paid me was good money for an evening's work.'

'You are obviously something of a philosopher, Mr Bates,' the Judge commented. 'Where is this – this 10,000 quid now?'

'Well, me lord, what's money for but to spend?'

'You mean that in the course of no more than six weeks – ?' Mr Justice Lamb broke off there. It was a toss-up whether incredulity or despair predominated in his tone.

'I've blowed the lot,' said Ned cheerfully. 'Easy come, easy go,' he added, as though he felt the Judge might find the thought consoling.

'Indeed?' Lamb turned back to counsel again. 'And is that the whole story, Mr Maitland?'

'Except for this, my lord, which I should like to put into evidence. Here's a list of the jewellery which Mr Bates took from Mrs Thurlow's rather inadequate hiding-place on the third of September, which he made out at my request. You'll see that it is signed and dated last Wednesday, and witnessed by both Mr Horton and myself.'

'Thank you.' Lamb took the list from the usher, who without prompting had added to it the one which the insurance appraiser had made out. 'These appear to be identical,' he said after a moment. 'Perhaps,' he added to the usher, 'you would be kind enough to hand both these lists to the jury.' He turned his head a little, eyeing Counsel for the Defence consideringly. 'The final piece of proof, Mr Maitland?' he asked.

'Unless, my lord, you wish me to call Mr Horton's evidence in corroboration.'

'No, that will not be necessary. I think we have all heard enough. What is your opinion, Mr Hawthorne?'

'I agree with your lordship. If my friend wishes to make application that a verdict of Not Guilty be brought in without further evidence being offered, I for one shall have no objection.'

'Thank you. Do you wish to make such an application, Mr Maitland?'

'Certainly I do, my lord. My learned friend has anticipated my wishes in this respect.' (And thank goodness I shan't have to decide whether to call that Johnson woman, he added to himself. It's perhaps just as well Hawthorne isn't a mind-reader: I've a nasty feeling that he'd have made mincemeat of her.)

Friday, after the verdict

It was a little before 12 o'clock when they came out of court. Matthew Barlow, in high fettle now, declined Antony's invitation to lunch on the grounds of urgent business awaiting him, and hurried back to his office. Antony, after a few words with Geoffrey Horton who was waiting to take Ned Bates in charge and do whatever had to be done on his behalf, strolled round to Astroff's, enjoying for the moment an unexpected feeling of leisure. He hadn't been there five minutes before his uncle joined him.

'I can see from your smug look that everything went as you hoped,' Sir Nicholas announced as he seated himself.

'Well, Uncle Nick, I wasn't sure that Ned Bates would do his stuff, but he seemed positively to enjoy it.'

'And the Judge instructed the jury to find your client Not Guilty without any further evidence being offered?'

'Yes, though he had a question or two for me first,' Antony admitted. 'Why I hadn't gone to the police as soon as Ned made his statement to me, for instance. I was glad I'd talked it over with you, Uncle Nick, because I'd got it all straight in my mind, and I thought if you agreed with what I was doing it was a hundred to one Lamb would too.'

'You are far too inclined to act on impulse,' said Sir Nicholas thoughtfully, 'but in this instance I quite agree with you. Your client's interests were best served by the course you took.'

'Yes, I think so too, and it's amusing that it was Mr Barlow who first pointed it out. It was by far the quickest way of dealing with the matter, and if any of Gilchrist's friends or acquaintances believed him guilty of that first robbery, they must be wondering now.'

'As you are doing yourself, I gather.'

'Yes, I am. You know, I didn't really take to Vince Gilchrist: his morals are his own affair but about the rest of it I had a nasty feeling that he saw himself as a sort of modern-day Raffles. But if there was any doubt about it . . . well, fair's fair.'

'There was besides your damsel in distress,' said Sir Nicholas drily.

'I'm not at all sure that getting Vince off was the best thing for her,' said Antony. 'Anyway, I think she impressed Jenny more than she did me, though I must admit her predictions came true and something did turn up.'

'In the unlikely guise of Ned Bates.'

'Yes, and that wasn't all,' Antony told him. 'You were out last night, and the reason I didn't meet you for lunch yesterday was that an alibi witness turned up.' He went on to tell his uncle how Rosanna Johnson had waylaid him and Matthew Barlow outside the court, and the story she had told them. 'I'm pretty sure she's another of his conquests, willing to sacrifice her reputation for his freedom,' he concluded. 'Of course, I don't *know* that, but I was glad not to have to decide whether to call her, and still more glad not to have to explain to Lamb and Hawthorne why I was introducing an alibi at the last minute without notice.'

'Well, all's well that end's well,' said Sir Nicholas idly. 'By the way, did you ever hear anything from your friend Father William?'

'No, I telephoned him on Wednesday evening after I'd talked to Mr Barlow. He hadn't anything to report – well, it would have been much too soon – and as I was pretty sure everything was going to be all right now I told him not to bother. But I do wonder,' he added thoughtfully, 'whether 10,000 was really all Ned Bates got for his loot, who he actually sold it to, and where he's got the proceeds stashed away.'

MICHAELMAS TERM, 1974

Tuesday, October 22nd

I

For the next ten days life proceeded smoothly for the Kempenfeldt Square household. Meg and Roger Farrell, who though they
lived in Chelsea were practically members of the family, returned
from their trip. Roger was plunged immediately into a backlog of
work, but Meg, though she had accepted a part in a new play,
wasn't due to start rehearsing until January. She tried to make
what capital she could out of this by implying that the
arrangement was of her own making, but Roger, who knew his
wife very well, was having none of this. 'You know as well as I do
you'd have insisted on coming back from the continent if a part
that interested you had turned up earlier,' he said, but he spoke
without too much bitterness. Luckily he had never resented
Meg's success, and though there were occasions when the feeling
that he'd like to have his wife to himself occasionally was
uppermost in his mind, on the whole he had resigned himself
pretty well to her dedication to her profession and the consequent
disruption of their domestic life.

The Gilchrist case being over, Maitland's list for that term
showed no signs of getting out of hand; in other words nothing
arose in which it seemed likely that he would interest himself
beyond the normal scope of his professional duties, a fact upon
which Sir Nicholas and Vera were inclined to congratulate
themselves from time to time when they were alone. In fact Sir
Nicholas's mood grew so mellow during this period that, as
Antony remarked irreverently to Jenny, a child could have played
with him. His only relapse into a sense of outrage was caused not
by any action of his nephew's, but by a client whom Mr Bellerby
brought to chambers for a conference, but who once there,
instead of settling down to a sober discussion of his defence on a
charge of fraud, insisted on falling on his knees in front of the desk
and praying in a loud voice, only pausing occasionally to urge his

companions to join him. But Sir Nicholas got little sympathy from his family when he recounted this story (if you excepted Meg's 'How dreadful for you, darling,' and wide-eyed look of horror), only a good deal of merriment; so that before the evening was over he had come to see the funny side of it for himself.

'Calm before the storm,' said Vera wisely. But that was later.

The first intimation Maitland had of trouble was a telephone call one Tuesday morning from Detective Chief Inspector Sykes of Scotland Yard. 'Something's come up I'd like to discuss with you, Mr Maitland,' he said. 'Is there any chance of your meeting me for lunch?'

Maitland looked rather wistfully at the papers which were spread out before him. 'I'm not in court today,' he said, 'and I suppose there's nothing that can't wait. Could you meet me at Astroff's?'

'Will Sir Nicholas be there?' asked Sykes cautiously.

'He *is* in court, and as he's up against Halloran I'm pretty sure they'll be lunching together. You should be safe enough . . . that is if you're wanting to avoid him.'

'It's not that, Mr Maitland. Just something that's not strictly my business and—'

'Oh well, if I can help in any way—' said Antony quickly. 'Half-past twelve then if that suits you.' It was only after he'd replaced the receiver that a small prickle of anxiety disturbed him. It was almost the first time in his long acquaintance with Sykes that the detective had not started a conversation with detailed inquiries as to the health and well-being of all the members of the family. If he had forgotten his usual punctiliousness, something must be disturbing him seriously. 'But it can't be anything to do with me,' Antony told himself, having examined his conscience briefly and decided that it was as clear as even the sternest of his critics could have wished. It cannot be denied however, that his mood of concentration was lost, and he was relieved when the time came to pack up his work and leave for the restaurant.

Sykes had arrived first at the meeting-place, and he knew their ways well enough to have asked for Sir Nicholas's table which was always kept until one o'clock. Antony paused for a moment in the doorway, taking the opportunity to observe his friend while he himself was unnoticed. It struck him again that anyone who didn't know the detective would be far more likely to take him for a farmer than a police officer . . . a farmer who had done a good deal at that day's market, perhaps, and who had therefore no immediate cause for complaint. He had reason enough, God knew, to be grateful to the detective for many kindnesses and it was characteristic that it had never occurred to him that the other man might feel towards him a similar sense of obligation. But Sykes looked up at that moment and caught his eye across the room, and he went forward hurriedly, hoping that his momentary hesitation hadn't been noticed.

'Well, now, Mr Maitland,' said Sykes, getting to his feet as Antony joined him, 'it seems we're going to have our talk by ourselves after all.' He had a slow way of speaking, and as Antony knew very well there was no hurrying him when there was a decision to be made, or at any other time for that matter. His north-country accent was not as noticeable as once it had been, except when something moved him deeply, or when he wanted to emphasize the fact that he was in sympathy with his companion, but for all the normality of his greeting, which should have been reassuring, Antony sensed immediately some deep disquiet in the other man.

'Yes, I was pretty sure we should be alone,' he said. 'Sit down, Chief Inspector. Have you ordered yourself a drink?' Sykes shook his head at that but the waiter was already at Maitland's elbow. 'What will it be then?' he inquired.

When the order had been given and they were alone together Sykes leaned back in his chair and eyed his companion in silence for a moment. It wasn't long before Antony began to fidget. 'You're looking at me as though you're investigating a murder and I'm the principal suspect,' he complained. 'I'm glad to see you, of course – it was before the long vacation that we last met wasn't it – but what was so urgent that I had to drop everything and come to meet you?'

'I'm usually investigating a murder,' said Sykes in his precise way, 'but this, as I told you, is not strictly my business. Perhaps we'd better wait till the drinks arrive and then I'll tell you what's on my mind.'

'Do you think I shall need a drink to sustain me?' asked Antony, trying to inject a lighter note into proceedings.

'Well, you might, Mr Maitland, and then again you might not,' said Sykes. But the drinks arrived at that moment, so Antony didn't have to contain his impatience for long. 'You see,' said Sykes, eyeing his scotch in an intent way which might have indicated some suspicion of the glass's contents or might merely have been an excuse not to meet Maitland's eye, 'I've a very good idea that you'll be getting a call from Chief Superintendent Briggs in the near future.'

Antony, who had been about to take a fortifying sip, spluttered over his drink. 'B-briggs?' he said. 'What the h-hell can he want with me? I haven't even got a murder case on my list.'

'There's no use losing your temper before I've even started,' said Sykes reprovingly. He knew well enough what the slight angry stammer portended. 'The Chief Superintendent's main concern is the murder squad, of course, but he's senior enough as I'm sure you know to put a finger into any pie he pleases.'

'And which particular p-pie is it this time?' Antony asked him.

'The Gilchrist case.'

'But that's all over and done with d-days ago, and as it turned out there was no mystery about it.' He was making a valiant attempt to control his anger, knowing well enough that it should not, in any case, be directed against Sykes.

'Are you sure of that?'

'Of course I am. Gilchrist was acquitted and that's the end of the matter.'

'So far as he's concerned perhaps.'

'There's no perhaps about it.'

'I was going to add, Mr Maitland, that so far as you are concerned –'

'Now what bee has the Chief Superintendent got in his bonnet? You're becoming as bad as Uncle Nick, Chief Inspector. He's been reading the riot act to me for years about my meddling in cases that might bring me into conflict with Briggs. But there was nothing like that about the Gilchrist case. I admit I asked a few questions about it but they got me nowhere, and Ned Bates turned up out of the blue.'

'I've read a transcript of the case,' said Sykes in his slow way. 'You've been very careful to cover all the points, and to make sure that Mr Horton could corroborate them.'

'Well, of course I was c-careful. First I had to convince myself –'

'Did you take much convincing, Mr Maitland?'

'No, as a matter of fact. What earthly reason could Ned have had for asking for that case to be taken into consideration if he hadn't been afraid it might be brought up against him at some time in the future? As to the rest, I had to make damned certain that his story was water-tight enough to convince the court. But there's absolutely no doubt he was telling the truth: he couldn't possibly have known so much about the detail unless he was really the guilty party.'

'I've heard you say on a number of occasions,' said Sykes, 'that the Chief Superintendent's animosity needn't worry you as long as you keep well within the law.'

'What are you g-getting at now?'

'You've dealt with some difficult cases yourself, Mr Maitland, when it hasn't been all that easy to demonstrate what was actually the truth.'

'You don't need to remind me of that, but in this instance –'

'This case is different,' said Sykes firmly. 'I've warned you before that you were by way of becoming an obsession with the Chief Superintendent, so naturally when he heard what had happened he insisted on dealing with the matter himself.'

'It isn't like you, Chief Inspector,' said Antony, and the stammer was back in his voice again, 'to b-beat about the b-bush like this. What the h-hell do you mean, when he heard what had happened? It was reported in the papers, and for once I was glad of that because I thought it was only fair to Vince Gilchrist –'

'That isn't what I meant,' said Sykes, almost as sombrely as Mr Justice Lamb might have done. 'I'm talking about a statement your friend Ned Bates has made to the police.'

Antony stared at him for a moment. 'I still don't understand you,' he said.

'He says he was able to give so much detail about the crime because you'd supplied him with the particulars,' said Sykes. 'No, hear me out, Mr Maitland,' he added when Antony seemed about to interrupt. 'He says you persuaded him to plead Guilty to whatever it is he's being charged with at the moment, and to ask for anything else he's guilty of to be taken into consideration.'

'The first part of that's true enough.' For the moment Antony was concentrating too hard for the stammer to be in evidence. 'There was no doubt at all he'd be found Guilty, and there seemed no point in antagonizing the court by denying what he'd done. Then he said he meant to go straight in the future – I think that was in answer to a suggestion of mine, too. But it was his own idea to ask for any other outstanding cases to be taken into consideration and that's when he told me about the robbery from Mrs Thurlow. Damn it all, Sykes, Geoffrey was there. He knows what happened.'

'According to Ned Bates's story he'd met with you before that occasion in chambers, when you offered him money to appear as a witness on Gilchrist's behalf and primed him with the facts so that he could tell a convincing story. His first job was to deceive Mr Horton, and then to deceive the court.'

'But that would be s-subornation of p-perjury. Briggs has accused me of that before, along with every other c-crime in the calendar, pretty well, but –'

'But this time he seems to have some evidence.'

'Damn it all, Sykes, d-don't you b-believe me?'

'I believe you, Mr Maitland.' He looked in a rather pointed manner at the glass which stood untouched by Antony's side. 'Sup up, lad,' he invited. 'I think this is a day for you to have another when you've finished that.'

'And I think it's a day for me to stay stone c-cold sober,' said Antony. 'I asked you a question, Chief Inspector. Do *you* think I've been n-nobbling the witnesses?'

'No, I don't. If you'd been listening to me instead of losing your temper, you'd know that I believe everything happened just as you've said. The worst I know of you, Mr Maitland,' he added thoughtfully, 'is that you've not always been completely frank about the things you know. Which is rather a different matter.'

'Sykes, don't you understand I c-can't always be open with you? Indeed, in those earlier cases, which Uncle Nick is always throwing in my teeth because he says I antagonized Briggs from the first, it was a matter of the oath I t-took when I was in Intelligence. There was no way on earth I could tell you everything. And later my d-duty to my clients –'

'I know all about privileged communications, but the fact remains that Briggs has got his knife into you, and this time he's got a witness,' said Sykes. 'And I thought I'd best warn you, Mr Maitland, because there's no doubt he'll be wanting to see you sooner or later, and I don't want you saying the wrong thing when he does. Or losing your temper if you can help it.'

'I appreciate it, Sykes.' Antony smiled faintly. 'I seem to have a whole lot of things to be grateful to you for, and you may be sure I'll be completely dumbfounded when he springs this on me. But I don't understand: what can Ned Bates have against me? I've always done my best for him—in fact I thought he rather liked me.'

'Every man has his price,' said Sykes tritely. 'You'd better start thinking, Mr Maitland. Who else could have prompted him to tell such a story? It would have to be someone who knew all the details of the robbery.'

'Well, as far as that goes, my instructing solicitor I suppose.' He gave a laugh in which there was no amusement at all. 'You don't know Matthew Barlow, of course. He's a nice, respectable family solicitor, who's tolerant enough about the sins of the flesh but recoils in horror at the idea of any of his clients being guilty of an indictable offence. I'd as soon suspect Jenny. Then there's Hawthorne, who took the prosecution, and the chap who instructed him, but that's nonsense, too. That only leaves Vincent Gilchrist, and you could say he had the motive insofar as getting himself acquitted was concerned; but why should he go gunning for me afterwards and stirring up all the doubts that his family must have had about him beforehand, whatever they may say?'

'It's a reet puzzle,' said Sykes. He picked up his glass and sipped thoughtfully, and was glad to see his companion follow his example though in an absent-minded way. 'There's only one consolation that I can see.'

'You mean that more than one witness is needed to convict for perjury, or subornation of perjury,' said Antony. 'I'm grateful to you for trying to sound a hopeful note, as well as for everything else, but it seems to me that this is where we came in.'

'What exactly do you mean by that, Mr Maitland?'

'We've had this conversation, or something very like it, quite a number of times over the last few years. So far as I'm concerned even the suggestion of scandal—'

'I know, and that's what worries me,' said Sykes frankly. 'But it isn't hopeless, lad,' he added encouragingly. 'You're better at pulling chestnuts out of the fire than anyone I know, and this time it just means you've got to put your thinking cap on for yourself.'

The mixture of metaphors made Antony smile with genuine amusement. 'Exactly, Chief Inspector,' he agreed. 'And I'm more grateful than I can say for your warning.'

'Think nowt of it.' Sykes drained his glass and looked again pointedly at Antony's. 'Drink up,' he said again. 'Lunch is on me, and if you'll tell me what to order we'll split a bottle of wine over it.'

'Such recklessness!' said Antony, but he did not mention again the merits of staying sober. The thought of food made him feel vaguely sick, but the wine would be welcome. It is strange to relate, however, that when it came to the point it was the detective who seemed most disinclined to eat.

II

When Maitland got back to chambers he found that Sir Nicholas was still in court and didn't know whether to be glad or sorry. There was no doubt at all that his uncle would have to be told what was happening. Of late years Vera had been able to persuade her husband into a slightly more tolerant attitude towards his nephew's vagaries, but there was no doubt at all that that tolerance would not extend to an attempt to suppress the facts in a case like this. On the contrary, Antony seriously expected his story to be greeted with an unprecedented display of fireworks. Perhaps it was as well that it was Tuesday evening and they would all be dining at home. There was some slight comfort to be derived from fighting the engagement on his own ground.

He was fortunate in having the knack of concentration, but that afternoon he found it perhaps more difficult than ever in his life before. It was fully four o'clock before he lost himself in consideration of the arson case and when he came to with a start he realized that it was long past what Sykes would have called knocking-off time. At least one of the clerks must be waiting to lock up – if they'd all gone they would have let him know – and when he went down the corridor he found the faithful Willett, who greeted him with the information that Sir Nicholas had gone straight home from court.

'There was no need for you to stay on,' Antony told him. 'I could quite well have locked up if you'd let me know.'

'Yes, but there's something I thought perhaps you'd like to know, Mr Maitland,' Willett told him. 'You see, Sir Nicholas phoned Mr Mallory to let him know about tomorrow's arrangements – the case isn't over yet – and Mr Mallory had to go and tell him that Chief Inspector Sykes had rung you this morning. Then as you were so long over lunch we all wondered if you might be meeting him, and Mr Mallory mentioned that possibility too.'

Antony stared at him rather blankly for a moment, wondering how on earth it happened that the clerk should realize that this was a matter of which he might like to have warning. 'Thank you, Willett,' he said at last. 'I ought to have thought of that.' He smiled suddenly. 'Anybody who thinks he can keep a secret around here –' he started, but then he saw Willett's downcast look. 'Don't worry,' he added. 'I'd every intention of telling him that myself.'

On this conspiratorial note they parted, and Antony took a taxi home because he thought there was just a chance he might be able to have a word with Jenny before the others arrived, but Gibbs, hovering in the hall as usual, greeted him with the information that his aunt and uncle had already joined Mrs Maitland. Antony thanked him absently, and went up the stairs rather more slowly than usual.

When he went into the living-room for a moment the familiar scene had a strangeness for him, as though years had passed since the last time the four of them had sat together around the fire enjoying a glass of sherry and talking over the day's events until it was time for Jenny to serve dinner. Then he caught Jenny's eye and she smiled at him – she had scrambled to her feet and was on her way, he knew, to the table where the decanter and glasses were set out – and suddenly everything was normal again. These were his own people and if there was any comfort to be found at the moment, it would be in telling them what had happened. It had taken him years to realize that Jenny could bear anything rather than being excluded from what was going on. In the past she had been inclined to place much more emphasis on any possible physical danger than on the threat of scandal, her attitude being in a way a reflection of her husband's who had always maintained that nothing could happen in that way so long as he kept on the right side of the law; but this was different. There were possibilities that terrified him and which only Jenny, he thought, would understand. As for his uncle, however angry Sir Nicholas might be – and Antony had a feeling that he might be very angry – his advice would be invaluable, as would Vera's gruff good sense.

All these thoughts had passed through his mind in a moment, but his slight hesitation in the doorway had given the three people already in the room time to assess his mood, and when he

97

started across the room they could tell from the stiff way he held himself that he was tired and that the ever-present ache in his shoulder was giving him more trouble than usual. Vera knew the taboos well enough, the subjects that mustn't be mentioned because they were ones to which Antony was unduly sensitive, but this evening something told her that things had gone beyond the need for tact in their dealings with him, that it was time for plain speaking. 'Something troubling you?' she asked bluntly as he took his favourite position on the hearthrug and stood looking down at them.

'There is, as a matter of fact.'

Sir Nicholas put down his glass carefully. 'Something to do with your conversation with Chief Inspector Sykes today?' he queried gently.

'I had lunch with him,' said Antony precisely. 'It was quite a long time since we'd seen each other.'

'Don't prevaricate, Antony. If you've been meddling again in matters that don't concern you, the least you could have done was keep us informed.'

'But I haven't! At least –' He broke off and looked from one to the other of them rather helplessly. Jenny came quietly up to him, and without prompting placed his glass on the mantel-piece beside the clock.

'At least –' prompted Sir Nicholas coldly.

'This is something you know all about, Uncle Nick, I told you at the time. The Gilchrist case.'

'Your intervention there could hardly have been a matter of concern to the police, and even Chief Superintendent Briggs can hardly find fault with you for winning a case on such incontrovertible evidence.'

'I know you've been telling me for years he'd cause trouble sooner or later,' said Antony, 'and in a way that's true insofar as he's taken charge of the affair himself. But this time I can't blame him for his suspicions.' He hesitated, looking down at Jenny who had resumed her place on the sofa. But if there was any way to lessen the impact of what he was going to tell them, he couldn't think of it: the bald statement must suffice. 'Ned Bates has been to the police and made a statement, that I paid him to help get Vince Gilchrist acquitted, and gave him all the details so that his story would be convincing before Geoffrey brought him to chambers.'

Sir Nicholas, who had been leaning back in his chair very much at his ease, sat up suddenly very straight indeed, and for the first time in his life Antony saw a few drops of his uncle's sherry spill over on to the polished surface of the table beside him as he put the glass down. 'What did you say?' he demanded.

Antony repeated his statement. Just for the moment there might have been only the two of them in the room, though later Antony was to remember seeing Jenny's hand groping out blindly, and the fact that Vera took it comfortingly between both her own.

'You don't have to tell me that this new statement is a fabrication,' said Sir Nicholas, 'but how do you explain – ?'

'I don't. I think in this case the *onus probandi* is in their court, don't you?'

'If you must resort to colloquialisms, at least be consistent about it,' Sir Nicholas begged him 'The burden of proof can hardly be considered as a tennis ball.'

'Uncle Nick, you know as well as I do that a second witness is required to get a conviction for subornation of perjury.'

'You will forgive me if I do not at the moment find the thought particularly comforting.' Sir Nicholas leaned back again, but this time without any effect of relaxation. 'Over the years, my dear boy, you have acquired a certain . . . may I use the word notoriety?'

'What are you g-getting at Uncle Nick?' Antony didn't like the reminder and it showed in the stiff way he spoke.

'That this is something that must be taken into account whenever you concern yourself actively in a case. Whenever you choose to meddle in your client's affairs above and beyond the call of duty, as I believe the phrase goes.'

'But in this case I didn't . . . well, in a way I suppose, but my efforts didn't do any good.'

'You may be sure they came to Briggs's attention in some way.'

'But this time he's got a witness.'

'Precisely.'

'Look here, Uncle Nick, don't you t-trust me?'

'I have already intimated that I do.'

'Well then, have a bit of sense,' said Antony incautiously. 'Briggs has accused me in the past of conspiring to make my client appear innocent by having my instructing solicitor hit her over the head, he's accused me of being a Communist of all things, while as for this particular charge of interfering with a witness . . . I've lost count. Even murder's nothing new, don't you remember?'

'I remember that I have never since that time ventured to leave the country while the courts are sitting,' said Sir Nicholas trenchantly. 'But I fail to see why you should consider my concern for your well-being as indicating a lack of intelligence.'

'That wasn't what I meant at all. On all these occasions he couldn't take any action for lack of proof, but this time it's different.'

'He still can't take any action without a second witness,' said Sir Nicholas, 'as you yourself reminded me. But he's distrusted you for years, largely, I may say, owing to your own mishandling of your relationship in the early days of your acquaintance –'

'I thought we should come to that,' Maitland muttered.

'And you may be sure,' Sir Nicholas went on, ignoring the interruption, 'that he'll exploit this situation to the full.'

'Yes, I'm sure he will. But you know, Uncle Nick, I don't understand how it can have happened. I thought Ned Bates liked me rather, certainly he's never shown any sign of feeling any malice towards me.'

'You know this man fairly well?'

'Geoffrey's briefed me on his behalf about four times in the past. I must say we've never succeeded in getting him off, but he couldn't have expected that as he was quite obviously guilty in each case, and he always seemed positively grateful that he didn't get a longer sentence.' He turned his head a little. 'You know the type, Vera. A professional burglar who's never thought of any other way of making a living, and who takes an occasional spell in prison as part of the job.'

'Know the type,' Vera agreed, nodding.

'And he's a likeable little man. Not malicious,' he repeated.

'Then I think we must consider,' said Sir Nicholas, 'who might have persuaded him to this course of action.'

'Sykes and I went over all that together. Thank goodness he believes me too. The trouble is, Ned's story was so detailed that if I didn't give it to him myself it's difficult to think who could have known enough to do so. I think we can discount my instructing solicitor Matthew Barlow – you never met him, Uncle Nick, but I assure you it isn't his line of country at all – and Hawthorne, too: his only motive could be a deep dark plot to discredit me, which is hardly likely. And that leaves us with whoever actually committed the crime – Vincent Gilchrist himself, most likely. In one way he hasn't anything to lose, but if the story gets about he can go on protesting his innocence, but there are sure to be some people who don't believe him. And what could be his motive? He hasn't anything against me either.'

'The police will certainly be interviewing him,' said Sir Nicholas thoughtfully. 'If he's indeed behind Ned Bates's change of heart, for some reason we can't at the moment fathom, he may well tell some story that will further implicate you.'

'Second witness,' said Vera. 'But –'

'But, as you were about to point out, my dear,' her husband interrupted her, 'it would certainly be possible to throw doubt on their evidence. Both would have to admit perjury –'

'Vince Gilchrist didn't give evidence at his trial,' Antony reminded him.

'No, I was forgetting that. Still, I think their evidence would be suspect, not enough for a conviction. I think,' said Sir Nicholas, suddenly brisk, 'we had better stop this profitless discussion and put the whole matter from our minds for the moment.' Which impossible and rather unfair injunction (Jenny hadn't said a word so far, and Vera very little) they all did their best to obey. Antony drank his sherry, Jenny made another round with the decanter, but it cannot be said that the conversation that evening was particularly sparkling.

III

But even this uncomfortable state of affairs was to be subject to interruption, which in the ordinary way they would all have welcomed, but which in the form it took only made matters worse. Dinner was almost over when the house phone rang and when Antony answered it Gibbs's voice, filled with repulsion, announced, 'Two persons from the police who wish to see you, Mr Maitland.'

'Did they give their names?'

'Chief Superintendent Briggs and Inspector Carter,' said Gibbs disdainfully.

'Just hold on a moment.' He turned from the phone and told his uncle what had been said. 'May I use the study, Uncle Nick?'

'Certainly, if you will bear with my company.'

'Yes, of course, I'd like that. Please show them into the study, Gibbs,' he added. 'Sir Nicholas and I will be down in a moment.'

'Are you sure that under the circumstances you shouldn't ask Geoffrey to come here before you talk to them?' Sir Nicholas asked him.

'That would be to give away the fact that Sykes spoke to me. I think Briggs has his suspicions of our friendly relationship already and I'd dislike above all things to make things unnecessarily difficult for him.'

'Yes, of course, you're quite right. I can't imagine,' he added over his shoulder as Antony followed him down the stairs, 'what Briggs is thinking of to be calling here at this time of night. Do you know this Inspector Carter?'

'I saw him in court during Gilchrist's trial. He was the investigating officer, but I didn't bother to cross-examine. His part of the business seemed straightforward enough anyway.'

By the time they went into the study, Sir Nicholas still ahead of his nephew, Chief Superintendent Briggs appeared to be in a state of simmering impatience so that Antony thought immediately that he had probably overheard Gibbs's side of the telephone conversation. Briggs was a tall man and his tendency to stoutness had grown no less with the years. Even when Antony had first encountered him, his reddish hair had grown well back from a bulging forehead; now the colour had faded, and there was really no more than a fringe of it left at the back and sides of his head. He had cold blue eyes that belied his choleric disposition and he would certainly have denied, on oath if necessary, that there was anything at all irrational about his feelings towards Maitland: quite simply, he distrusted him, and his antagonism towards him was therefore completely logical. If there were other causes for his dislike he was most probably unconscious of being swayed by them; true, the younger man's casual air could be annoying, and his sense of the ridiculous even more so. But if he found anything in the present situation to amuse him, Briggs felt himself quite capable of putting a stop to that.

Antony himself was perfectly well aware that his dislike for Briggs, unchanged since their first meeting, was instinctive and therefore unreasonable, and being the man he was, was half inclined to agree with his uncle's often expressed opinion that the other man's antipathy towards himself was in some way his own fault. But he had never before felt himself quite so much at a disadvantage in the detective's presence and was only too grateful that Sir Nicholas seemed prepared to take matters into his own hands.

'Good evening, Chief Superintendent,' he was saying in honeyed tones. 'It seems a long time since we encountered each other. May I ask to what we owe the honour of this visit?'

'It must be something important, Uncle Nick,' said Antony before Briggs had time to reply. 'Chief Superintendents don't usually make house calls.'

But if his intention was to irritate Briggs further, his words misfired. Having got something more than suspicion to go on this time, the Chief Superintendent obviously felt very sure of his ground. 'My business is with Mr Maitland,' he snapped.

'Even so, you will hardly deny me the use of my own study,' said Sir Nicholas in a gentle tone which his nephew felt should have sent the detective running for cover if he had a sense of self preservation. 'And you haven't explained to us yet the precise purpose of this intrusion.'

'Ask your nephew,' said Briggs.

'Can you enlighten me, Antony?'

'Not really, but this gentleman here is Detective Inspector Carter who was the investigating officer when Mrs Thurlow was robbed. I told you about that matter, Uncle Nick. I suppose this visit must have something to do with that, though why when the case is closed – '

'I think you know very well why, Mr Maitland,' said Briggs.

'There seems to be some confusion,' said Sir Nicholas. 'Has murder been done? If not, I really can't understand your interest in the affair, and if it has, why should Inspector Carter have accompanied you instead of one of your own men?'

'I've taken charge of the case because I know something of Mr Maitland's past activities,' said Briggs, still very sure of himself.

Sir Nicholas smiled at him. 'And exactly what accusations have you dreamed up this time?' he asked, in an indulgent tone, rather as though he were humouring a child.

'Your nephew has already admitted that he knows we want to see him about the Gilchrist case.'

'I said I assumed as much from Inspector Carter's presence,' Antony corrected him, 'but like my uncle I fail to see where you come into it. Whatever "it" may be,' he added thoughtfully.

'Let's see if you find anything funny about an accusation of subornation of perjury,' Briggs snapped, answering the tone rather than the words Maitland had used.

'And who am I s-supposed to have suborned?' He glanced at his uncle with a fair assumption of puzzlement. 'It can't be one of the prosecution witnesses,' he said. 'And the only one I called . . . there was nothing wrong with Ned Bates's evidence, Chief Superintendent. Mr Horton was with me when he came out with the story, and can confirm everything that was said.'

'And very cleverly it was arranged,' Briggs admitted. 'I should compliment you, I suppose, on your ingenuity.'

Antony's temper was beginning to slip, though with Sykes's interests in mind he had managed so far to keep a fairly good rein on himself. 'What the h-hell has my ingenuity got to say to anything?' he asked furiously.

Again Sir Nicholas intervened, probably hoping to give his nephew time to cool down. 'I'm still completely in the dark as to what this is about,' he said, 'but an accusation has been made, and should have been preceded, I think, by a warning, and by the opportunity for Mr Maitland to call his solicitor.'

'I'm willing to take the w-warning as read,' said Antony, not allowing the detective the chance to reply, 'and there's no point in g-getting Geoffrey here. Whatever crackpot notion Briggs has got in his h-head I can deal with perfectly w-well myself.' He was aware that his stammer was betraying him, and not only to his uncle, but for the moment he was past caring. 'Well, Chief Superintendent,' he said. 'Tell me the evidence you think you've got to support this charge or get out. Both of you,' he added, turning on Inspector Carter, who had been taking notes with some difficulty as they were all still standing.

'Very well.' The words sounded like a threat. Briggs's colour was normally high, and now almost dangerously so. 'If you insist upon an explanation, I will give you one. Ned Bates has made a statement.'

'Of course he h-has! He made one to me and Mr Horton, and t-then repeated it in c-court.'

'A further statement.' There was a certain smugness about the detective as well as the anger which Maitland's presence always engendered in him. 'He says you paid him to make that admission, pointing out to him that since he was going to be tried

104

in any case, to ask for a further offence to be taken into consideration would make very little difference to his sentence.'

'I can't think what his m-motive can be for telling you this – this –'

'This bare-faced lie,' put in Sir Nicholas, seeing his nephew for once at a loss for words. 'In any case, Chief Superintendent, I think you should be rather more careful. A statement by a known criminal – '

'Which is not unsupported,' said Briggs in a gloating tone. 'Yes, that gets to you, doesn't it, Mr Maitland? I know the law in matters like this quite as well as you do.'

'Who else has been l-lying about me?'

'Naturally the matter had to be investigated.'

'Naturally.'

'The first thing I did was to go to see Vincent Gilchrist. He blustered a little, but eventually he admitted the truth.'

'*What did he say?*'

'He said that you had told him you had a client coming up for trial who would probably be willing to confess to the Thurlow robbery and ask for it to be taken into consideration at the same time as his other offence. He agreed to put up the money, and later you told him it was all arranged. He said that from his point of view he could see no harm in the arrangement, as he wasn't guilty, but I don't have to tell you, Mr Maitland – '

'How much is Ned Bates s-supposed to have g-got out of this?'

'£500.'

'Perjury comes ch-cheap these days, doesn't it?'

'For a man like Bates . . . the sum paid to you was rather larger.'

'You'll have a job p-proving that. Do I have to t-tell you that Vince Gilchrist's story is a pack of lies too?'

'I would hardly expect you to say anything else, though I'd hoped in the circumstances you might be a little more reasonable.'

'Break down and c-confess all, I suppose. I tell you – ' He broke off and looked rather appealingly at his uncle. 'Well, you've g-got your witnesses, though I d-don't think much of them,' he went on turning back to Briggs. 'What now?'

'That is something,' said Sir Nicholas, 'which I think perhaps you haven't taken into consideration, Chief Superintendent . . .

my nephew's estimate of the reliability of your witnesses seems to be reasonable enough. Vincent Gilchrist has one conviction to his name, and if what you tell us is true it seems obvious that there should have been a second as well in spite of his protestation to you. Do you really think the evidence of two such men, one of whom also admits to perjury, would be sufficient to obtain a conviction?'

'As to that, we shall see!' Briggs began to move towards the door followed by his faithful satellite, who was stuffing his notebook into his pocket. 'You haven't heard the last of this yet, Mr Maitland,' he added threateningly. A moment later the front door slammed.

Antony turned a bewildered face to his uncle. 'What did he c-come here for if not to arrest me?' he asked.

'He knew as well as I do he couldn't get a conviction on what he's got,' said Sir Nicholas. 'If he can persuade the DPP to act it will be very unpleasant, but – '

'The only result would be the equivalent of the Scottish Not Proven,' said Antony. 'I suppose I should take comfort from that.'

'I think you should,' said Sir Nicholas seriously. 'As for why he came, he couldn't resist the opportunity of confronting you with some real evidence this time, as opposed to the vague accusations he's made in the past. But I think, Antony, we must consider this matter very carefully. Those two men didn't make their lying statements without some motive.'

'That's what Sykes said.' Suddenly Antony sounded unnaturally weary. 'That this time I had a personal problem to solve, I mean.' He smiled in a half-hearted way. 'I suppose you're going to tell me things would have gone better if I hadn't lost my temper.'

'On the contrary, I think you had every justification,' said Sir Nicholas, surprising him. 'But I think, don't you, that we'd better rejoin the ladies?'

'Need I tell Jenny . . . yet?'

'My dear boy, you know perfectly well that she can bear anything so long as she knows exactly what it is she has to face.'

'That's funny.' Antony sounded anything but amused. 'That's what she always says about you, Uncle Nick – that you can't bear being kept in the dark. All right then, we'll go upstairs, but do you mind awfully if I leave it to you to tell them what's happened instead of doing it myself?'

IV

Much later, when he came back from seeing Sir Nicholas and Vera out, Antony found Jenny standing rather forlornly on the hearth-rug. The fire was dying. 'Shall I make it up?' she asked him. 'Do you want to talk any more?'

'I think everything's been said that can usefully be said,' said Antony. 'Round and round in the same old circle. But yes, let's have a bit of a blaze, love. I've a nasty feeling that none of us are going to get much sleep tonight.'

'Uncle Nick thinks—'

'Yes, I realize you know exactly what's worrying me most,' said Antony. She was on her knees now, seeing to the fire, and he looked down at her affectionately. 'And I think Uncle Nick's right and there's even a chance the DPP will agree with him.'

'Well, then, we needn't worry about *that*,' said Jenny briskly. He put out his left hand to help her to her feet, and then on an impulse slipped his arm round her shoulders and drew her close. 'There may still be the Bar Council to contend with,' he pointed out.

Jenny didn't actually say, Devil take the Bar Council, but she looked as though she would like to. 'So long as you're safe,' she told him. 'Whoever made this plan seems to want to ruin your reputation rather than to kill you. You'll just have to think who it might be.'

He moved then to sit down on the couch and pulled her down beside him. 'There are so few possibilities,' he said in an exhausted voice. 'You didn't hear Ned Bates's story, love, he had the whole thing off pat; if he was really lying someone must have primed him.' He broke off there and a rather startled look crept into his eyes. 'I never thought of that. Perhaps he was telling the truth, and somebody quite outside the whole affair knew it and took advantage of the fact.'

'I don't see how anybody could have known it,' Jenny objected. 'Unless it was some friend of his, and it would have to be a pretty close friend if he confided a thing like that to them. Do you know anything about his associates?'

'No, but I see now it's a pretty unlikely line, worse than the other in fact.' They sat in silence for a few moments and then he said rather diffidently, 'Jenny, what shall we do if I'm disbarred?'

'Uncle Nick won't let that happen,' said Jenny, so confidently that the amusement that was normally never very far from his view of the world surfaced suddenly.

'My dearest love, what should I do without you?' he asked. And then more soberly, 'I'm afraid even Uncle Nick might not have much to say about it. And anyway, once the story gets out who'd want to brief me?'

'There are a hundred things we might do,' said Jenny firmly.

'Such as?'

'Bill said we could build on his land. We could afford that.'

'Just about,' Antony agreed. 'But I can't afford to retire, love.'

'He also offered you a partnership in the farm.'

'I don't want to be anyone's sleeping partner.' That came out rather sharply, and she knew it was as far as he would come to referring to his injured shoulder, which made physical work of any kind impossible for him. 'Besides,' he added, perhaps to show that he wasn't rejecting the suggestion out of hand, 'a partnership would be worth a good deal more today than it was when he started up. He's done pretty well, you know.'

'Then you must take a job as a – perhaps as a company secretary.'

'What on earth put that into your head, love?' For a moment amusement again predominated in his tone.

'Well, I know they don't need a legal qualification, but some knowledge of the law is useful,' she insisted. 'Antony, there must be dozens of people who know you well enough to realize you'd never do anything dishonest. Something will turn up.'

'Yes, Mr Micawber,' he said meekly, and for a while they sat in silence gazing into the fire that was now flickering hopefully. Antony was wondering if her thoughts were keeping pace with his, if she were thinking as he was of the wrench it would be to move from this place after so many years, to leave behind them all the familiar certainties, and the people they loved. 'I never meant to hurt you, Jenny,' he said at last, breaking the silence.

'And you never have.'

'Time after time, from the very beginning,' he said, ignoring her words. Then he turned to look at her. 'That seems to matter now more than anything else.'

'Things have happened to hurt me,' said Jenny carefully, 'things that neither of us could help. But not you, Antony, never you.'

After that there was no more talk between them that night and when at last they went to bed Maitland's prediction proved to have been correct. There was very little sleep for either of them.

V

Going downstairs Sir Nicholas and Vera had ignored the invitation of their beds and had gone straight to the study. There was no fire there that evening, but the room was warm and each had recognized in the other the need for some further talk. 'Vera, my dear,' said Sir Nicholas, settling himself in his usual chair, 'when you first knew Antony–'

'I pursued him because I needed his help,' said Vera with a grim smile.

'Very well, you pursued him. What did you think of him when you got to know him a little?'

'I trusted his integrity. Anyone must who knows him well. But sometimes I was terrified of his way of doing things. He'd win his case, but his way of doing it   the risks he took–'

'I have often felt that myself. But what do you think of him now?' Sir Nicholas persisted.

'I think . . . even before I married you, Nicholas, he and Jenny were as dear to me as my own children might have been. You don't doubt that, do you? That's how you think of them yourself.'

'I suppose it is. I don't think I doubted your opinion really but . . . this is a nasty business, Vera.'

'You've got through some bad situations before.'

'But not quite like this. I've been afraid–lately we've both been afraid–that Briggs's animosity might somehow cause some sort of a scandal. But this is different. Antony lost his temper–I expect you've guessed that–almost at the start of the interview, but he had to admit he couldn't altogether blame the Chief Superintendent for what he thought. But there's the evidence, and even though the men it comes from may not be of the highest character, why should they be lying? *We* know they are, we can deduce that there must be some malice behind their stories, but the whole thing . . . frankly, Vera, I don't know what to do.'

'Not like you to say that,' said Vera.

'I suppose not, but the prospects . . . I don't need to outline them for you, my dear. If Antony and Jenny had to go away I'd miss them terribly, and I think from what you've said that you would, too.'

'Perhaps more than you know. But if the worst comes to the worst, Nicholas, what could Antony do?'

'I hope something will occur to me but it hasn't yet. I'd be willing to give him an allowance, of course, but I doubt if he'd take it. He has a streak of independence . . . did I ever tell you how he came to live with me?'

'It was when his father died. He was thirteen, wasn't he?'

'Yes, but that isn't the whole story. My sister had died when he was too young to have remembered her, and though I was on very good terms with my brother-in-law his job kept him abroad a good deal of the time. He was a foreign correspondent for the *Courier* in the days when stories were followed to their conclusion, not dropped just as you're getting interested in them as journalists seem to do nowadays. I suppose it was lonely for Antony, particularly before he went away to school, but Gerald and I talked it over at the time and he'd have been lonelier still in London because there were friends of his parents in Tilham where he was born and there was some companionship to be had from their children. When he grew old enough he used to join his father abroad during the school holidays. He has an uncanny gift for languages, as you know, and also for mimicry . . . which he may do on purpose, but more often I think it's completely unconscious. Halloran told me once he mimics me in court, and has done ever since his very early appearances there, but I doubt that he knows it himself.'

'Think Halloran's right,' said Vera nodding. 'Not a thing you'd notice yourself, of course.'

'The first time we went abroad together he gave me the surprise of my life by organizing the whole trip,' said Sir Nicholas reminiscently. 'But I'm getting ahead of my story. Gerald died abroad, but that's a story I think I have told you. Antony was at school. I, by mischance, had gone specially to the Liverpool assizes and the trial was half-way through. A murder trial, I didn't feel I could abandon my client at that stage or ask for an adjournment, and it was three days or so before I was able to go south again. By that time Gerald's solicitor, a man called James Winter, had been down to the school and broken the news, including the fact that there was very little money. Gerald had lived right up to his salary.'

'Must have been quite a young man, no reason why he

110

shouldn't,' said Vera.

'No, I agree, and unfortunately he'd let his insurance lapse after Anne died. But I was telling you about what was almost the first meeting Antony and I had had, since he was a small child anyway. I'd taken it for granted, you see, and I hoped he had too, that he'd come to live with me and let me look after things. It was quite a shock to find that he'd mapped out a plan for himself. I don't think he was particularly enamoured of it –'

'What did he mean to do?' asked Vera curiously.

'Leave school and go back to Tilham, where he could get his education free. When the house was sold he thought there'd be enough for him to pay his way as a lodger somewhere. They had a housekeeper, of course, but there was also the cleaning woman. She had a spare room, he said, and he thought she might be glad of the extra money. And – you won't believe this, Vera – I had the devil's own job to persuade the little fool that the plan wouldn't work, that I wanted him to come to me.'

'The question is, did you? Know it worked out all right, but did you then?' asked Vera.

'To tell you the truth, I can't really remember after all this time. But there was obviously nothing else to be done. Only Antony had got some idea into his head, I rather think from Mr Wodehouse's novels, that as a bachelor I lived an extremely exciting life so that I should find him very much of an encumbrance. I had to use every bit of eloquence at my command, I've never had a brief that needed more careful handling, though finally when he began to cry – I think they were the first tears he'd shed for his father, though I know how much he'd grieved for him – and said all right he'd come, I thought I'd won my point.'

'And hadn't you?' asked Vera, obviously fascinated by this saga.

'Only a partial victory. When he came home for his summer holidays – the first time he'd been here – it was very near the beginning of the long vacation, and I didn't take him abroad that year, because I thought it would remind him too much. But I hardly saw him, he was obviously doing his best to keep out of my way, and quite honestly I hadn't the faintest idea how to deal with the situation. Until one evening he didn't get home until nearly ten o'clock, tired and hungry and obviously scared stiff about what I'd have to say about his escapade. Well, I'd had a good fright myself so I wasn't feeling in the best of humours. I told Gibbs to phone the police and tell them the wanderer had returned, and then bring him some supper into the study, and I managed to contain my questions until he'd eaten it. Even then I don't think he'd have told me anything if he hadn't been so worn out, but apparently he'd hardly any of his pocket money left (that was something else I didn't know, how much I should be giving him) but he had enough for the bus fare to Richmond and back, so he went for a walk in the park. It was a nice day and he stayed a bit longer than he intended, and then he dropped his last sixpence down a grating while he was waiting for the bus, and didn't know what to do but walk home.'

'Could have got a cab and asked you or Gibbs to pay the driver when he got here,' said Vera.

'Of course he could! Or he could have gone to the nearest police station and asked them to phone me, or . . . I pointed all that out to him pretty forcibly, and the odd thing is that seemed to be all that was needed to bring us to an understanding. We spent the rest of his holidays sight-seeing, which of course, having been born here, was something quite new for me. As for Antony, I've heard Geoffrey say he'd infuriate a saint, and whether that's true or not there have certainly been occasions . . . all the same, Vera, I'd miss him damnably if he went.'

'Can understand that. But you know, Nicholas, he's shocked out of his wits this evening, but don't you think when he gets used to the idea of what's happened he'll put them to work in finding out who's doing this to him?'

'We can only hope so. I'm completely at a loss myself. And heaven knows,' he added, smiling slightly, 'I never thought I'd live to be grateful for this damnable habit he has of meddling.'

If Vera thought that this last statement was not entirely true she kept her ideas to herself. But the puzzle obsessed both of them, and they went on discussing it far into the night without ever reaching a conclusion.

Wednesday, October 23rd

I

Sir Nicholas was in court again next morning, but he was at his usual table in Astroff's when Antony joined him at lunchtime. 'Have you time to talk, Uncle Nick?' Maitland asked abruptly.

'Conroy likes to take his time over lunch, so I'm at your disposal for the next hour,' Sir Nicholas told him, and signalled to the waiter and ordered a double Black Label without reference to his nephew. Antony pulled out a chair and sat down with his elbows on the table.

'I've been wrestling with myself,' he said.

'And where did this – this sporting event take place?' Sir Nicholas inquired courteously.

'In Hyde Park.'

'I thought perhaps you might have been acquainting Geoffrey with what had happened.'

'I looked in at his office first thing – lord, how I hate explanations – ' he added in parenthesis, ' – and told him what he could do with Ned Bates's brief.'

'I trust you didn't imply that any of this was his fault.'

'No, of course I didn't. I didn't put it quite like that, and by the time I'd finished my story he was in the same mind as myself. Ned can find someone else to represent him. But then I didn't know what to do, so I phoned Mallory to say I wouldn't be in till later and went for a walk to think things out.'

'Did you reach any conclusion? Thank you,' he added as the waiter returned with his order.

'Yes, but I thought I'd better find out if you agree with me.' It had not been unknown for Maitland to assume an air of diffidence for his own purposes, but now Sir Nicholas judged that his lack of confidence was completely genuine.

'It's not like you, Antony, to be so unsure of yourself,' he said.

113

Which was a good way from the truth, but he hoped would provide some encouragement.

'It's different when it's a personal matter,' said Antony. 'Anyway, you know perfectly well, Uncle Nick, that I'm often in two minds what I ought to do.'

'I know you say you are, but I haven't noticed that it made much difference to your actions in the long run. However, what was this knotty point that you were deciding this morning?'

'Whether I should return the briefs I have on hand right away.'

'You say you reached a decision.'

'Yes. If I could think of anything I could possibly do to get to the bottom of this business, I'd be tempted to clear the decks. But I can't, so I needn't let that weigh with me. On the whole I think I should try for business as usual as long as I can. Anything else might seem like an admission that my conscience wasn't completely clear.'

'That seems reasonable.'

'The only thing is, is it fair to my clients? If Briggs gets his way with the DPP –'

'I've been thinking about that, Antony. I don't think he will. Heaven knows you've caused the prosecution trouble enough in your time, but I don't think any of the people concerned hold you any grudge for it. And if the story gets about –'

'But I think it will, Uncle Nick, otherwise what would be the point of the exercise?'

'Precisely what I was going to say. When the story gets about, if you prefer it, I think most of the people in our small legal world know you well enough to discount it, and if the Bar Council eventually decide it is incumbent upon them to take some official notice, I think they'd hold their hand till the end of the term at least. So I think your decision to continue your work for the present is a good one, but perhaps it would be inadvisable to accept any briefs that might carry over into the Hilary term.'

'That means more explanations . . . to Mallory,' Maitland said despondently.

'I'll tell him myself all he needs to know,' said Sir Nicholas. 'And whatever you think of him, Antony, you've never had cause to doubt his discretion.'

'It isn't what I think of him but what he thinks of me,' said Antony still gloomily. 'All right, Uncle Nick, I'll go back to chambers when we've had lunch and face things out as far as I can.'

'In the meantime you might as well have the drink I ordered for you,' his uncle pointed out.

Antony picked up his glass and turned it round thoughtfully in his hand, not attempting for the moment to taste its contents. Suddenly he looked up at Sir Nicholas and smiled. 'Jenny thinks I'd better become a company secretary,' he said.

'What a dismal thought! If it becomes necessary, I'm sure we can do better than that. And don't ask me what,' he added testily, 'because it hasn't come to that yet. It isn't like you either, Antony, to give up without a fight.'

'If I'd the faintest idea how to go about it or even who I was fighting,' said Antony, but he raised his glass to his lips at last. 'Jenny says I never hurt her, only circumstances,' he went on when he put it down again, with rather less than his usual lucidity, but his uncle understood him well enough. Understood, and appreciated the implied compliment, that his nephew, who usually avoided confidences like the plague, should speak even so much of his mind to him.

II

So Maitland went back to the Inner Temple after the light repast that Sir Nicholas had ordered for him, again without reference to his nephew's preference. Old Mr Mallory was inclined to be querulous about his absence that morning: there were several telephone calls of an urgent nature that should have been dealt with immediately.

Maitland looked at him more closely then, but obviously the remark had no hidden meaning. 'I'll deal with them right away,' he offered. 'Are the notes on my desk?'

'Naturally, Mr Maitland.' Antony gave him a rather absent-minded smile and made his way down the corridor to his own room.

Mallory was right: there were a number of phone calls to be made, for which he wasn't altogether sorry, as talking might be easier than trying to concentrate again on the affairs of the arsonist with whom he found himself completely out of sympathy. But first there were the papers Geoffrey had sent him about Ned Bates to parcel up ready for return; not that there was much point to it, as Geoffrey wouldn't be handling the case himself either. Altogether that took him through until nearly half past three, and just as he had replaced the receiver for the last time the phone rang again. 'Chief Superintendent Briggs,' Hill's apologetic voice stated.

'Put him on, Hill.'

'He's here, Mr Maitland.'

Antony gave himself a moment to think. 'Ask him to wait,' he said, 'and then get Mr Horton on the line.'

Geoffrey arrived within a quarter of an hour, grumbling gently to hide his very real anxiety. 'I can't think what you want with my help or anybody else's to deal with that fat bastard,' he said as he came into the room.

'As long as we can we may as well play the game according to the rules,' Antony told him. 'Is Willett sending them in? I suppose he's got that Inspector Carter with him.'

'Not Carter, whoever he may be,' said Geoffrey. 'I caught sight of them as I came past the waiting-room. He's got Sykes with him.'

'I don't understand that. I know Briggs feels himself important enough to take a hand in anything he likes, and he's made the point before that where an officer of the court is concerned the matter is more than usually critical. But Sykes's line is murder: it doesn't make any kind of sense for him to be here.' His words trailed off as the door opened and the two detectives came into the room.

Briggs hadn't liked being kept waiting, and his colour was already alarmingly high. He looked hard at Antony, turned his head a little to take in Geoffrey's presence, and then turned back to his quarry again. 'I see you've decided that discretion is the better part of valour, Mr Maitland,' he said.

'In view of the allegations you m-made last night,' said Antony, 'I should n-naturally want some unprejudiced person present, even if Mr Horton weren't m-my solicitor. As it is –' He broke off, seeming to notice Sykes's presence for the first time. 'I don't understand,' he said. 'I'm pleased to see you, of course, Chief Inspector, but offences under the Perjury Act are hardly your province, are they?'

'I'm afraid the matter has become a little more serious,' said Sykes in his quiet way. 'As investigating officer it now concerns me very closely.' There might or might not have been a warning note in his words.

'I don't see how it could be more serious for me,' Antony told him. 'Has the Chief Superintendent told you what passed between us last night?'

'He has.' He was about to go on when Briggs interrupted him, saying abruptly,

'We're wasting time. Where were you this morning, Mr Maitland?'

'I think,' said Geoffrey, 'that before we answer that question we should like to know the purpose of it. If Mr Maitland can give any help to the police,' (a slightly sardonic look appeared on Sykes's face), 'I'm sure he'll be glad to do so. But you've no earthly right to expect an answer to your questions unless you explain what lies behind them.'

'Murder,' snapped Briggs. 'As you might have inferred from Chief Inspector Sykes's presence here.'

'You'll forgive me, I know,' – this was Geoffrey at his blandest, a pose in which at any other time Antony might have found some amusement – 'but I still don't find that's sufficient explanation. If I am to advise my client to answer –'

'Vincent Gilchrist has been murdered,' said Briggs in a goaded tone. 'He was shot to death at point blank range in the flat he shares with his mother while she was out shopping this morning.'

III

Again Sir Nicholas went straight home from court, a little later than usual as the judge had postponed the adjournment until the jury had concluded their deliberations. He let himself into the hall at Kempenfeldt Square to find Gibbs waiting for him with a message instead of the usual greeting.

'Lady Harding asked me to tell you, Sir Nicholas, that she is upstairs with Mrs Maitland. Mr Maitland came in a few moments later with Mr Horton and they went upstairs together. I've instructed Mrs Stokes that you will not be dining this evening.'

'Shan't we indeed?' Sir Nicholas sounded a little taken aback but his mind was already racing ahead of him. 'Thank you, Gibbs,' he said and made for the staircase.

Antony met him in the upstairs hall. 'Sorry about this, Uncle Nick,' he said, 'but I thought we ought to have a council of war.'

117

Sir Nicholas looked at him keenly but decided that perhaps a show of normality was the best way to deal with the situation. 'As long as Mrs Stokes doesn't give in her notice because her dinner's been spurned,' he said.

'Vera says she can handle that,' Antony assured him. 'And Jenny had made a casserole in any case, and has just been throwing in everything she could find out of the refrigerator so I don't think any of us will go hungry. Come in and I'll tell you.'

Sir Nicholas discarded his coat, which he hadn't waited to take off downstairs, and laid it on one of the chairs. 'Some new development?' he asked.

'And how!' For once Sir Nicholas didn't even blink at the expression, let alone voice a protest. 'Vince Gilchrist has been murdered.'

'When?' asked Sir Nicholas sharply, following him into the living-room.

'Between ten and eleven o'clock this morning.'

Contrary to his usual habit, Sir Nicholas gave no greeting to the assembled company. 'Could they fix it so accurately?' he asked.

'His mother was out for an hour shopping. He was alive when she left, and dead when she came back. Unless she shot him herself before she left, of course, but that doesn't seem very likely. Some of the neighbours heard what they thought was a car backfiring, but none of them noticed the time.'

They had reached the fireside by now and Sir Nicholas sank into his usual chair. 'Stay me with flagons!' he requested. Jenny had already reached the writing-table and had the decanter in her hand but she wasn't to be deterred from voicing her grievance.

'I still don't see why that should make them rush immediately to ask Antony questions,' she said. 'Antony says Geoffrey was simply marvellous and made them tell what had happened –'

'Which he could quite well have done himself,' Geoffrey put in.

'And Inspector Sykes was doing his best to keep the peace, you know his way, but they both of them lost their tempers. Antony and that awful man Briggs, I mean.'

'You hardly need to tell me that, my dear,' said Sir Nicholas drily, not noticing that she had stepped outside her usual role of seeing the best in everybody. 'However, I think on the whole I should prefer to hear what happened from one of the people who

118

was present.'

'I only want to know why,' said Jenny, coming to his side with a glass that was a little overfull. 'You'd better drink some of that before you put it down, Uncle Nick,' she recommended.

'Thank you, Jenny. This question of yours: I'm sure any of the others could have explained it to you.'

'Yes, but they all did it at once,' Jenny complained. 'Please tell me, Uncle Nick, why should they think that Antony had anything to do with it?'

'He had the opportunity. At least I gather from what he told me at lunchtime that he hasn't an alibi.'

'I left Geoffrey at about a quarter to ten, and saw nobody else I knew until I joined you at Astroff's,' said Antony. He sounded almost cheerful about it, in fact he might have been said to have spoken with a sort of relish.

'Very well, then. That's what they wanted to find out, Jenny.'

'Why?' Jenny almost wailed.

'Don't you see, love,' – Antony took over the explanation – 'because he was the second witness against me. There's only Ned Bates now, and one person's evidence isn't enough for a conviction under the Perjury Act.'

'Why on earth didn't you say so before?'

'I did try to, but you see, love, it was so obvious to Vera and Geoffrey that they both wanted to help you understand.'

'But that's awful,' said Jenny.

'Not a bit of it! Don't you see, I didn't kill Gilchrist so it follows that somebody else did. That gives us something to get our teeth into. If we can find out who it was – '

'We still shan't have disposed of the other charge,' Geoffrey pointed out.

'Unless that was just a preliminary. Unless someone wanted to frame me for Vince Gilchrist's murder and thoughtfully provided me with a motive. In which case finding out what happened this morning will solve the whole thing.'

'Sounds a bit complicated,' said Vera doubtfully.

'It is, but – '

'You're postulating somebody with a motive for Gilchrist's murder,' said Sir Nicholas, 'but I have my own reasons for thinking the two charges may not be connected, at least not in that way.'

'You've thought of something, sir? Tell us,' said Antony

eagerly.

Sir Nicholas was not to be hurried. 'First I should like an account from you, or from Geoffrey if you prefer, of what happened when Briggs and Sykes visited you this afternoon.'

'I made them wait until Geoffrey got round to chambers. I didn't know then that Sykes was the second man, and I nearly had a fit when I found out. Obviously I couldn't understand it at all. But then, as Jenny told you, Geoffrey made sure Briggs told us exactly what had happened.'

'Can you let me have a little more detail about that?'

'Not really. Mrs Gilchrist, poor woman, found her son in their living-room shot through the chest. He obviously hadn't died quite immediately, there was rather a lot of blood; in fact he might not even have been dead when she found him, though she thought he was, and he was certainly dead by the time the doctor arrived. There was no sign of anyone breaking in, in fact it would be rather hard to do in the block of flats in mid-morning, so presumably Vince let his murderer in himself. I suppose inquiries among the neighbours as to whether anybody saw anything are still going on.'

'And then?'

'We went at length into the subject of my alibi or lack of one. I can't say I enjoyed the process particualry, but as I wasn't in Halkin Place nobody can possibly prove that I was. Briggs, of course, pointed out what I knew already as to motive. That was where I really lost my temper,' he added rather shame-facedly.

'Perhaps you may be forgiven for that,' said Sir Nicholas.

Antony stared at him rather blankly for a moment. Even after his uncle's forbearance the evening before, his words came as a surprise. 'I think it would have been more sensible not to,' he said.

'And that is where the matter rests?'

'It is, but of course I'm going to try to find out . . . I do know something about Vince Gilchrist, Uncle Nick, enough to give me a start at any rate. And if you're going to tell me I shouldn't meddle I can only say I'm sorry but I'm going to.'

'As it happens I was not going to say anything of the kind.'

'You've got something up your sleeve, Uncle Nick. An idea of some sort,' he added, seeing his learned relative's look of outrage. 'Won't you tell me?'

'I think I shall echo something that the Chief Superintendent said to you on one occasion, Antony. Something to the effect that because you were intent on proving a certain theory of yours, something would come up to support your view.'

'You're saying that perhaps a third witness . . . no really, Uncle Nick, that's too much to swallow. Two men willing to perjure themselves–'

Sir Nicholas sighed elaborately. 'Two men suffering simultaneously from the delusion that their lies could benefit them,' he said.

'I've heard of mass hysteria, but–'

Again his uncle didn't allow him to finish. 'I am unwilling to believe that you are being wilfully obtuse, Antony, but surely by now you must realize that Briggs's distrust of you amounts to an obsession. Your aunt and I have warned you often enough.'

'I know you have, but . . . you're not saying *he*'s responsible for everything that's happened.'

'Not the murder, though I shouldn't put it past him to take advantage of that now that it's happened. But all the rest of it–'

'I don't believe it. I know he dislikes me intensely. Well, I feel the same about him, so I can't blame him for that. But you see, sir, I've always thought he was quite honest about the things he accused me of, that he genuinely distrusted me. You're talking about manufacturing evidence.'

'I'm afraid you've caught the gift of charity from Jenny,' said Sir Nicholas, rather as though it was an infectious disease. 'I'm talking about an obsession and where it may have led him at last. Can you think of any other explanation, except your own guilt, that will cover what has happened? You made a great point last night of the fact that somebody who knew the details of the crime must have coached Ned Bates, and certainly Briggs is in a position to have got to know them if he made it his business.'

'Uncle Nick, if I propounded this theory to you you'd tell me I'd run mad.'

'It is merely the logical conclusion of what has been going on for years,' Sir Nicholas pointed out. 'What is more, I shouldn't be at all surprised to find that Chief Inspector Sykes agrees with me. It only occurred to me after we had talked at lunchtime, Antony, and I haven't had the opportunity of discussing it with your aunt yet. What do you think about it, Vera?'

'Hadn't occurred to me, but think you're right,' said Vera succinctly.

'Geoffrey?'

'It does sound improbable, but I've always told Antony he made too light of Briggs's attitude towards him. In the circumstances, Sir Nicholas, I agree with you too.'

'And I wouldn't put anything past that horrible man,' said Jenny, not to be left out of the discussion. Which second uncharacteristic remark made them all glance at her in awe, because it was only very rarely that she was heard to say anything uncharitable, however much she might be provoked.

'Very well then, the feeling of the meeting is against you, Antony. The question now is, how do we proceed? I have always heard,' he added reflectively, 'that attack is the best form of defence.'

Antony laughed suddenly, and Jenny's indignation vanished on the instant when she heard the real note of amusement. 'That ever I should live to hear you recommend my meddling,' he said. 'Do you really think that Briggs may try to introduce some more evidence against me?'

'I'm afraid it's only too likely. When I spoke of an obsession, Antony, I was trying to convey that he really believes – and has believed all these years – that you were guilty of at least some of the things that he's alleged against you. I think he is genuinely of the opinion that you prompted Ned Bates's evidence, and that now you have killed Gilchrist to save yourself from prosecution. In his mind it follows that he has every right to see that you suffer for what you've done.'

'You're saying he's gone off his rocker.'

'I trust I should not put it quite so crudely. However, I won't quarrel with the sentiment.'

'Then I think I'd better stick to my original plan, and try to find out who did kill Vince Gilchrist. If any more evidence turns up as you expect, Uncle Nick, that may give us a lead too, but I'm not counting on it. Meanwhile Geoffrey can get some inquiries made into Ned Bates's background. There may be something to help us there.'

'I'll get on to it first thing in the morning,' Geoffrey promised.

'And meanwhile,' said Sir Nicholas, draining his glass, 'I think we should all have a little more sherry. After which, my dear Jenny, we will sample what sounds from Antony's description to be this highly suspect concoction of yours.'

It was odd that the depression that had gripped them all the previous evening seemed to some degree to have lifted. Perhaps it was merely a reflection of Antony's mood, on whom the prospect of action seemed to have acted like a shot of adrenalin.

Thursday, October 24th

I

Before Geoffrey left the previous evening there had been some discussion as to whether he should accompany Antony on the various visits he meant to make. Because this scheme had to some extent Sir Nicholas's blessing he refrained from too much criticism, but it was quite obvious that he felt that only his sobering presence could restrain his friend from all manner of indiscretions. 'Besides,' he added, 'you'll need a witness.'

Antony, however, was adamant. 'I'm taking a chance,' he said, 'but it's worth it to me, especially if Uncle Nick's right about Briggs having gone round the bend.' (Sir Nicholas at this point had closed his eyes as though to shut out a world in which such vile turns of phrase existed.) 'Look at it this way, Geoffrey: I don't stand to lose anything, but I'm damned if I'm going to let you get into trouble with the Law Society because of me. It isn't as if we had a client.'

'If it comes to that, you are my client,' said Geoffrey stubbornly. But he conceded the point at last when Sir Nicholas lent his weight to the argument. 'Then I'd advise you to take Roger with you,' he said. 'Not that I think he'll have the slightest influence on your actions, but at least if anything comes of all this he'd be able to back up your story.'

'If that's your advice I'll probably take it,' said Maitland, who had intended in any case to do exactly that. Roger, having no ties with the legal fraternity, could hardly be harmed by doing a favour for a friend.

Sir Nicholas too had his own warning to give, and startled Jenny by coming upstairs at breakfast time to drink his second cup of coffee with them, a thing he had never done before. 'You don't really believe me, do you, that it's Chief Superintendent Briggs who is behind all this trouble you're in?' he asked when another chair had been brought to the table by the window and

125

they were all settled down again.

'I don't think,' said Antony cautiously, 'that I'm quite as convinced of it as you are.'

'Perhaps,' said Sir Nicholas, 'you underrate your own capacity as an irritant.'

'Perhaps I do,' Maitland agreed. 'You know, Uncle Nick,' he went on awkwardly, 'I'm tremendously grateful to you for backing me up like this.'

'Haven't I always backed you up?' asked Sir Nicholas, producing the phrase as though it left a bitter taste in his mouth.

'Yes, I know. I really meant without throwing up all my past indiscretions in my face.'

'The temptation was there,' his uncle admitted. 'Have you been in touch with Roger?'

'I phoned him half an hour ago.'

'And?'

'Like the good chap he is, he's quite willing to drop everything and lend me a hand.'

'Good. Then there is no need for you to come in to chambers. I'll talk to Mallory as I promised, and put your affairs in order for the moment.'.

'Thank you. I admit I –'

'You will have quite enough explaining to do to Roger, my dear boy,' Sir Nicholas reminded him. He drank some of his coffee, put his cup down carefully, and fixed his nephew with a compelling eye. 'I realize, Antony, that things cannot be left as they are, and I'm trusting to your ingenuity to find a way out of your difficulties. But I hope you won't take my endorsement of your activities as *carte blanche* to commit any imprudence that may occur to you.'

Antony laughed suddenly, and turned to look at Jenny to try to share his amusement with her. 'That's better!' he said. 'I've told you before, Uncle Nick, I find it positively unnerving when you adopt an attitude of gentle forbearance towards me. It generally means you think things are hopeless, and I've rather fallen into the habit of trusting your judgement.'

Roger arrived just as Sir Nicholas was leaving about a quarter of an hour later. Jenny had already made another pot of coffee, and poured some for him without finding out first whether he wanted it or not. Roger took the chair Sir Nicholas had vacated. 'I gather,' he said, looking from one of them to the other, 'that this is serious.'

'I've asked your help a hundred times, Roger,' Antony exaggerated, 'and it's always been serious. But this time it's different, because it's personal as well.' He plunged without further ado into an account of everything that had happened since Matthew Barlow brought Vince Gilchrist to see him. 'You and Meg were still away then, or I expect I'd have told you about it before.'

'You've always said you don't like coincidences,' said Roger slowly.

'Yes, I should have thought about that when Ned Bates's evidence turned up, and also of the fact that he gave in rather quickly to my advice. But I didn't, Roger, and . . . honestly if you'd heard him, you'd have believed him too. Geoffrey did, and you know what a sceptic he is.'

'Well, get on to the next bit, which I suppose is where the personal aspect comes in.'

Antony obliged with a detailed account of the last few days. 'Let me get this straight,' said Roger when he had finished. 'Sir Nicholas thinks that Briggs has finally gone round the bend and is responsible for this rather complicated plot to discredit you, though in the case of the murder he's just taking advantage of circumstances as he has done in the past. You, however, are inclined to the belief that everything is connected, the Gilchrist trial being merely a preliminary to framing you for murder. Have I got that right?'

'That's exactly what I thought before we talked it over last night; but now Uncle Nick's come up with this theory I frankly don't know what to think. Briggs is one of the few people who could have done it, you know. You said it was complicated, but he's no fool, and he had the knowledge to prime Ned Bates for the part he had to play. Only I'm still not sure—'

'So what are we going to do about it?' Roger demanded.

Sometimes Maitland thought that his friend was one of the most complicated people he knew, never pausing to reflect that Farrell might well feel the same about him, though in a different way as their characters were so dissimilar. It seemed to him, too, that Roger had gone into stockbrokering more or less by accident, merely following in his father's footsteps. He was an intensely practical man, never happier than when action was called for. Jenny had been known to say that he reminded her of the man

127

who never went into a room without ejaculating 'Boom!' and it is undeniable that any place he lived in always showed very distinct signs of his occupancy: a picture slightly askew on the wall, gaps in the bookshelves where volumes had been taken out and never replaced, a newspaper on the floor, a vase of flowers pushed aside to accommodate a pile of records on the same table . . . a pile which, far from being neat, always showed every sign of imminent collapse. But that was just one side of his character. He had a sensitivity to other people's feelings that would have surprised anyone who didn't know him well, and a capacity for self-effacement when he felt it desirable that was one of the things that made him most useful to his friend on an occasion like this. Maitland trusted him as he would himself, and Roger was one of the few people – perhaps the only person – from whom he would accept help without resentment in any matter that was physically beyond his capacity.

'We'll start with the people who might have had a motive for murdering Vince Gilchrist, from what little I know of him.'

'That's all well and good if you're right, and the two things are connected . . . the accusation against you for tampering with the witnesses, and the murder. But if Uncle Nick's got it right you may clear yourself of a murder charge that way, but not of the other one.'

'You're forgetting, Roger, Uncle Nick looked into his crystal ball and came up with a prediction that some further evidence against me might be forthcoming. That might apply to the murder as well as to the subornation of perjury. So whichever of us is right it won't do any harm to try and clear that up first.'

'Do you think we can?'

'I said try, and meanwhile Geoffrey will be looking into Ned Bates's background. It isn't hopeless, love,' he added to Jenny, who smiled back at him faintly and refilled his coffee cup.

'There's one thing I'm not clear about,' said Roger. 'Do you now believe that Vincent Gilchrist was guilty or not?'

'I think he must have been. I think the whole thing was carefully planned the moment he got himself into trouble the second time. But when we went to trial I was so convinced that Ned Bates was telling the truth that I even came to the conclusion that Gilchrist was innocent of the first accusation as well. And so was Geoffrey,' he added with a touch of defiance in his voice.

'You don't need to convince me,' said Roger. 'All right, take it from there. What do you know about possible motives?'

'Let's start with the family. Mrs Helen Gilchrist might have been tired of having him to live with her, and partly on her. And she might not have liked the scandals he kept on causing.'

'I just don't believe that,' said Jenny flatly. 'No mother could –'

'It's not altogether without precedent,' Antony pointed out. 'Still, though I'd like to see her, I'm not really considering that possibility seriously. Then there's the elder brother, Arthur, with or without the connivance of his wife Judy. His motive would be similar, dislike of scandal, and being rather fed-up with having to continue to pay an allowance to a brother who was bringing nothing but disgrace on the family. There again I'd like to go down to Hollyhurst and see them, but I don't think I have any really serious suspicions.'

'But surely –'

'I haven't finished yet, Roger. You remember Mandy Barnard came to see me, which was really a blessing, love,' he added in an aside to Jenny, 'because if she hadn't made such an impression on you I wouldn't have known the first thing about Vince's background.'

'You're thinking of Nigel Midwinter,' said Jenny in a troubled tone.

'Yes, of course I am. I liked the chap, but you can't deny he's very much in love with Mandy, and I did get the impression there'd been something between them before Vince came on the scene.'

'It was more than an impression, he told us so,' Jenny reminded him.

'So he did, and he referred to her feeling for Gilchrist as an infatuation, and quite obviously thought that if he was out of the way – though not languishing in prison – she'd return to her old love.'

'Yes, I can understand that,' said Jenny. 'You know I was hoping that would happen anyway. Vincent Gilchrist sounded far too old for her, and not as if he'd be at all reliable as a husband.'

'I have to agree with you there, love, though I very much doubt if there was any question of his marrying her. I've no doubt he led her on, she's an attractive little thing and a chap like that . . . how could he help it when she threw herself at his head? So that does give Nigel a motive.'

'Tell me a little about him,' said Roger.

'A nice chap, as I said. I liked him and I very much hope what I'm suggesting isn't true. He works in a bank and is trying to be a novelist in his spare time.'

'So I suppose we go to see him.'

'You're very impatient this morning, Roger. I've two more possibilities to mention yet. First of all there's Mervin Chalmers, whose wife Karen was the first person to be robbed by Vince as I must now suppose. I may be making a mistake by taking his – Vince's – word for anything, but he said he'd had an affair with Karen and that Mervin was tremendously jealous. I must say when I talked to them I got the impression that the latter part of that statement was true at least. In a way it's immaterial whether Vincent and Karen had actually been intimate, so long as Mervin Chalmers believed they had.'

'And the other suspect? You said two more,' Roger pointed out.

'Yes, and this one's a chap I haven't met, Colin Johnson. Vince said he was going to visit him the night Denise Thurlow's jewels were taken. His wife, Rosanna, turned up outside the court at lunchtime the first day of the trial, and told me what I even then took to be a string of lies about her husband being out of town the night of the burglary and Vince having spent the whole evening with her.'

'But you believed Gilchrist at that stage. Why didn't you believe her?' Roger asked.

'Because I don't think he'd have had the faintest hesitation about admitting the affair to Matthew Barlow and myself. He was explicit enough about his affair with Karen, implying that it was a chivalrous motive that had kept him from mentioning it. There was no reason he couldn't have done the same about Rosanna. Anyway, I was saved the dilemma of whether to call her or not. If the court had refused to accept Ned Bates's evidence I suppose I should have had to, but even someone as easy-going as Hawthorne would have been bound to make a fuss about my introducing an alibi at that late stage.'

'Yes, I see. The law's changed about that, hasn't it?'

'The Criminal Justice Act of 1967,' said Antony rather absent-mindedly. 'In any case the law on the point would have been explained to Vince fully in the Magistrate's Court, and though we might have got away with the explanation that he was far too much of a gentleman to say anything, if the court had rejected Ned Bates I doubt if they'd have swallowed Rosanna.'

'No, I see that.' Roger was silent for a full minute, but so obviously thinking hard that neither of his companions attempted to interrupt him. 'You know, Antony, I've a nasty feeling you're not thinking straight about this,' he said at last. 'Not that I blame you: that first accusation of interfering with the course of justice or whatever it is must have knocked you for a loop. But none of these people could have had the knowledge to set you up that way.'

'No, that's true,' said Jenny. 'You said yourself, Antony, that only the prosecution lawyers, or Mr Barlow who was your instructing solicitor, or Vince Gilchrist himself could have known enough to give Ned Bates the details that he obviously had at his fingertips.'

Maitland looked from his wife to his friend and smiled. 'Logic from you, Jenny, love?' he said. 'And a very clear exposition of your case too. I don't know that I can bear it. You're my one refuge in this tremendously legal-minded household.'

'I was only quoting you,' said Jenny, 'because you seem to have forgotten what you said and I think you need reminding. It's perfectly obvious that Uncle Nick is right and Superintendent Briggs stage-managed the whole thing. I don't suppose he actually went so far as to murder Mr Gilchrist, but he'll exploit what happened for all he's worth.'

'Even to the extent of manufacturing more evidence in that case?'

'Yes, I think so. I agree with Uncle Nick and Vera, you've become an obsession with him and he'd go to any lengths to incriminate you. I daresay he justifies it to himself by really believing that you've been getting away with all sorts of illegal activities all these years, but that doesn't make it any easier to cope with. I just think you should face up to the situation, that's all.'

'Is that what you think, Roger?'

'Jenny has expressed my sentiments very clearly indeed.' He gave his hostess an affectionate look. 'Tigress defending her young,' he said, 'and an eloquent one at that.'

'This needs some thinking about,' Antony said. But he didn't spend quite so much time in consideration as Roger had done.

'You see, I've known for a long time that he's perfectly ready to suspect me of every crime in the calendar, but I always thought him completely honest in his own way, quite incapable of manufacturing evidence.'

'Well, think again,' said Roger bluntly.

'I am, don't worry. Let's see how it would work out. Vince Gilchrist is arrested, and this time the crime is within Central's jurisdiction, and Briggs gets to hear about it and that I'm acting for him. He could have made it his business to find out the details without any difficulty at all, and certainly without arousing any suspicion, and I don't suppose there's a man on the force in London who doesn't know something about Ned Bates. That could have been arranged quite easily, as Uncle Nick pointed out. As for Vince Gilchrist, I think the approach must have been made quite early in the game, almost as soon as Briggs knew I was acting for him. If he said to him at that time: "I can arrange to get you off if you agree to make a statement after you've been acquitted to the effect that it was your counsel who made the suggestion" I think Vince might have agreed. After all, a conviction would have meant his spending a considerable time in prison. There's a slight snag, in that he might have turned stupid after the trial and refused to say anything more, but I daresay Briggs could have got round that by telling him he'd use his influence for or against him about the suspended sentence, depending on which way he played it. He wouldn't have had any influence, but Vince was unlikely to know that.'

'There you see,' said Jenny, 'it all fits in!'

'So it does, love, so it does. And then when Vince is murdered, by somebody quite unconnected with that particular plot, Briggs jumps to the conclusion that I've done it to remove the second witness against me, without whom he can't proceed.' He drained his cup suddenly and stood up in a purposeful way. 'Well, I'm not going to just sit here and wait to see what happens,' he said. 'Let's get on with it.'

'What are we going to do first?' asked Roger, getting to his feet in his turn.

'See Mrs Helen Gilchrist,' Antony replied. 'If she'll let us in, of course. I suppose you realize, Roger, that we've no shade of an excuse for talking to any of these people, and that any one of them would be justified in turning us out.' He paused on his way to the door to smile at Jenny. 'We must both exert all the charm of manner at our command,' he told her and vanished into the hall after his friend.

II

In spite of his doubts, Mrs Gilchrist was in and very ready to receive them. Which surprised Antony, until he realized that she could know nothing of Briggs's suspicions that he had had a hand in her son's death, but only saw him as the man who had successfully defended Vince against a quite unjustified charge. This was helpful in one way, in getting them into the flat, but it also tied his hands to a certain extent as he hadn't the heart to tell her that Vince's admission to the police made it almost certain— in his eyes at least—that her son was guilty. But on the whole he felt that just for the moment circumstances were playing into his hands. Arthur Gilchrist, accompanied by his wife, had come to town to be with his mother at this sad time, and her acceptance of the visitors made it rather easier to talk to them than might otherwise have been the case.

He introduced Roger as his associate, which in a way was true enough, but for the first few minutes they had great difficulty in getting a word in edgeways to express their sympathy. Helen Gilchrist fluttered at them, that was the only word Antony could think of, and he only hoped that she really took it for granted, as she seemed to, that their visit was purely a matter of courtesy. About Arthur Gilchrist he wasn't too sure. Probably he wasn't quite so ready as his mother to take his brother's innocence for granted, though in her presence at least he certainly paid lip service to it. And Judy Gilchrist followed his example, but that was only what Maitland would have expected. Everything he saw that morning confirmed his opinion that they were a self-sufficient couple, and that whatever grief they felt at Vince's death was mainly concerned with its effects on the older woman.

First, of course, they had to listen again to the story of yesterday morning, to the shock Mrs Gilchrist had had, and to her grief for her son. 'And just when everything seemed to be coming right for him, thanks to you, Mr Maitland,' she mourned. 'I rang the doctor straight away, though I was sure really that it wasn't any use. And then I rang dear Arthur even before I called the police and he said he and Judy would come on the next train and I was so thankful because I couldn't have stayed here alone but I didn't know where else to go. But the police were very kind and when they'd finished everything they had to do they said I could come back here – I'd been across the hall with a neighbour – and Judy helped me to clear everything up.' Just for a moment her eyes strayed to the carpet immediately in front of the television set, round which the room seemed to have been arranged. There was an oblong patch of carpet rather darker than the rest, so that Antony guessed immediately that there had been a rug there into which Vince's life-blood had soaked. He wondered for a moment how she could bear to stay in the place, even with her elder son and his wife for company. But probably there was some slight comfort to be found in the very familiarity of her surroundings, perhaps even in the memories they invoked.

'Have you any idea who could have done such a thing?' he asked, hoping that the question would be taken for simple if rather tactless curiosity.

'He hadn't an enemy in the world,' declared Helen Gilchrist.

But Arthur took it upon himself to give a rather more detailed reply. 'It was somebody Vince let in,' he said. 'It doesn't necessarily mean someone he knew, a salesman for instance . . . there are a hundred different stories he could have told to get admittance. Something my mother was interested in, for instance, but the puzzle about that is that there's no sign of a robbery having taken place. As for a personal motive, like my mother I can't conceive of one. But I know very little of Vince's friends in town, and I gather she knows even less, if that's possible.'

They talked for a while longer, and then took their leave. Arthur came with them to the door, closing it carefully behind him. There were three other doors on the landing, but each was tight shut. 'The police didn't tell my mother,' he said, 'and I'm grateful to you for not doing so, but Vince had made a statement to them the day before he died.'

'I know all about that,' said Antony a little stiffly. 'And quite frankly the implications are not ones I'd want to get about.'

'I can understand that. Candidly the Superintendent – Briggs, I think his name was – was far more explicit than I would have considered possible. But . . . when you first saw Vince, Mr Maitland, what did he tell you about the family's reaction to what had happened?'

'He said you all believed in him implicitly, as did his

134

friends . . . those who knew him well, at least.'

'This is difficult to say,' said Arthur, looking from one of them to the other, 'but in my case I think it would have been more accurate to put it that I gave him the benefit of the doubt. For mother's sake really, you can understand that, I'm sure. She wouldn't hear a word against him. But there's always been a wild streak in Vince, which is why my father left things as he did, and I find it very difficult to believe that a man like you would put yourself in jeopardy, whatever the police may think, for what must seem to you a very small matter –'

'You're quite right, I wouldn't. But that would apply to any charge, however serious.'

'Yes, I expressed myself badly. I only wanted to say that I've wondered what sort of company Vince got into since he came to live in town. It may be that one of his associates had a motive for killing him of which we know nothing.'

'Thank you, Mr Gilchrist, I'm grateful for the hint. And even more grateful,' he added, smiling at the other man, 'that you don't place too much reliance on the police theory about my activities.'

'And there goes your argument,' he said to Roger when they had reached the street again. 'I should have thought of it myself. I can only suppose Briggs's first visit rattled me even more than I supposed.'

'I don't quite see –'

'If Vince was guilty of those two thefts, as I now tend to believe (though we mustn't forget that Ned may have been telling the truth about his part in the second burglary and was only later induced to go back on his statement) he must have had some idea about disposing of his ill-gotten gains. If there was a falling out . . . that argument might lead us right back to my first idea.'

'I see that, but I still think . . . you know, Antony, it's just the logical culmination of Briggs's attitude towards you all these years.'

'More logic!' Maitland grumbled. 'Anyway, it's something we must bear in mind, and I think we'll add Father William to the list of people we're going to see. Do you remember Father William, Roger?'

'How could I forget? Do you think he might know who Vince disposed of the stuff to?'

'I think he might be able to find out. I set him on to the question, actually, when I was still in doubt as to whether Vince was guilty or not, and then called him off when Ned Bates came forward. It's worth a try, anyway.'

'Well, what do we do next? Apart from shaking your faith in my opinions, I don't see that we've done much good so far.'

'Don't you, Roger? We've provided Arthur Gilchrist with an alibi for one thing. If he answered the phone when his mother called him immediately on finding Vince's body, he couldn't conceivably have been up here shooting him and got back to Hollyhurst in time.'

'That's one thing out of the way, I suppose, but you weren't inclined to suspect him anyway.'

'True. Would you like to drive me down there now, Roger? We could get lunch in Haslemere and then visit Karen Chalmers. With any luck her husband will be in town.'

'Yes, I can see that there are questions you may want to ask her that could hardly be put if they were both present,' said Roger rather drily. 'I know the way to Haslemere but —'

'I can direct you from there. The Chalmers live just outside Hollyhurst, and I went there with Mr Barlow.'

'Shouldn't you phone first?'

'No, I don't think so. We've been lucky once today in finding all the Gilchrists together. Perhaps we'll be lucky again.'

And as it turned out they were. Over lunch it had been decided that for this interview at least Roger's presence should be dispensed with, his value as a witness being likely to be overset by the unlikelihood of Karen Chalmers being moved to confidences in the presence of a second man.

'You again?' she said when she saw Antony, but her tone wasn't altogether unfriendly. 'What on earth can you want with us this time?'

'You've heard what happened to Vince Gilchrist?'

'Yes, it was in the papers. But that can't have anything to do with — with the things he was accused of,' she protested.

'I've been to see Mrs Gilchrist this morning, and Arthur Gilchrist and his wife were with her,' said Antony, leaving the statement there and hoping for the best. Even in a good cause he had some scruples about an out and out falsehood, though he was only too well aware that it wasn't always possible to avoid one; in this case he hoped the half-truth would suffice. And rather to his astonishment it did.

'I see, they want you to look into the matter,' said Karen. 'I know you have a reputation for being very clever about things like that. But what can *we* do for you?'

'It was you I wanted to see, Mrs Chalmers, not your husband at the moment.'

'That's a good thing, because he's in town as usual. But why me?'

'Because Vince Gilchrist told me a certain story about your relationship when his solicitor first brought him to see me, and I wondered if it was true.'

'And why on earth should I tell you if it was?'

'You're full of questions this morning, Mrs Chalmers, as full as I am myself. I'd better explain a little further. Vince told me by way of explaining how your bracelet came into his possession. He said you'd given it to him to sell on your behalf because you were hard up and didn't want your husband to know that you were disposing of it. He said the reason for secrecy even in the face of the charge against him, was that Mr Chalmers already suspected your intimacy, and was intensely jealous.'

'Yes he was, but—' She broke off and sat staring at him for a moment. 'I think I'd better tell you the truth, Mr Maitland, because goodness knows what you're thinking. Mervin is a jealous man, he's jealous of all sorts of people besides Vince, though it was only in Vince's case that he really had cause to be. If he'd been certain what was happening he might have—have beaten Vince up, but he's got far too much instinct for self-preservation to have done anything as drastic as shoot him. Besides, the whole thing was over months ago, when Vince went back to London after the first trial in fact.'

'And the rest of his story?'

'Quite untrue. Even the fingerprints . . . it's quite true some of his might have been found in the bedroom, but he'd never had occasion to go to that drawer. I knew he'd stolen the bracelet, so I didn't feel under any obligation to try to make things sound better for him. Particularly at the expense of making Mervin angry. And you can quite see that I didn't want to have anything more to do with Vince—I didn't even know if that was the whole reason he'd pretended to want me. I don't think Mervin will ever get over being jealous, it's his nature, but we've been getting on pretty well these last months and he certainly had no further cause to be angry with Vince.'

Antony got to his feet. 'I'm more grateful than I can say, Mrs

137

Chalmers, for your being so frank with me, far more frank than I'd a right to expect.'

'Are you going to see Mervin?' she asked rather anxiously.

'So far as I can foresee at the moment, no. But in any case I shouldn't tell him of our conversation,' he added with a smile, and left her, he hoped, a little reassured.

III

On the way back to town he gave Roger a full account of the conversation. 'She'd hardly have been so frank with you if I'd been present,' Roger agreed.

'No, I think not.'

'Did you believe her that Vince Gilchrist was lying about the bracelet?'

'Yes, I think I did. There wouldn't have been much point in denying it now, when she was being so open about other things, much more intimate things. From my own observation,' he added thoughtfully, 'Mervin Chalmers is a man who could well be inclined to violence, though I didn't stress that point with his wife, of course.'

'Of course not,' Roger echoed. 'Where now?'

'Back to town and we'll see if we can be lucky a third time and catch Rosanna Johnson at home alone.' He added the address, and then fumbled in the glove compartment at Roger's instructions for a map of the relevant area. 'Off the Fulham Road,' he said after a moment, 'a little way east of the Fulham Broadway tube station. Head for that and I'll direct you.'

'If you find her alone, do you want me to wait for you again?' asked Roger.

'No, this time I'd like your company if you can find a parking space' He wasn't too worried about that, Roger's skill in that direction was legendary. 'She's talked to me once, and she wouldn't have minded repeating what she said in open court. I don't think she'll object to one other person's presence.'

'But you didn't believe her story.'

'No, but if the alibi wasn't true the part about their being lovers probably was. If so the affair may have been in full swing until the time he died. And she can't possibly know anything about his statement to the police, or if she did she wouldn't believe its implications anyway as far as Vince is concerned. I wonder though,' he added consideringly, 'what will happen at the inquest.'

'Have you been asked to attend?'

'No, and I don't intend to go. But I can't help wondering—'

'Keep your eye on the ball,' Roger advised. 'You've enough on your mind at the moment without worrying about something that may never happen.'

'I was only speculating about how far the police evidence might go,' said Antony meekly.

'I know you were. My advice still stands,' said Roger. And concentrated rather ostentatiously on his driving, as they grew nearer to town and the traffic grew thicker.

The parking place was duly found and Rosanna discovered in a rather ancient block of flats, which might lack some modern conveniences but had been well maintained. She led them into a cheerful living-room, furnished in rather too modern a style for Antony's taste and without the advantage of a single chair that looked comfortable. Not that it mattered: he introduced Roger again as his associate but neither of them was asked to sit down. Rosanna today had a peaked look, and there were some signs that she had been crying. All the same her manner was inclined to be belligerent as she faced them.

'I don't know what you want with me *now*,' she said, stressing the last word.

'I was hoping for your help,' said Antony gently. 'I can see you're upset by your friend's death and I'm really sorry to worry you at such a time. But I've been to see Mrs Gilchrist . . .' He repeated his half-truth in almost the same words that he had used to Karen Chalmers, and added, when Rosanna still looked uncertain, 'There is besides the natural concern one continues to feel for someone who has been your client.'

'I didn't think lawyers cared anything for the people they worked for, beyond getting their fee,' said Rosanna, obviously not much mollified. But at least she showed no signs of disbelieving the explanation of his activities that he was trying to convey.

'Don't be too hard on us, Mrs Johnson. We have to live, like everybody else.'

'I suppose so,' she said rather grudgingly, so that Antony muttered to himself, *Je n'en vois pas la nécessité*. 'You didn't use my evidence,' she added accusingly.

'You must have read about the end of the trial as it concerned you so nearly.'

'Yes, of course I did.'

'Then weren't you even a little relieved that I didn't have to call you? Or did you choose giving evidence as a rather oblique way of telling your husband what had been happening?'

She looked confused, and her eyes no longer met his. 'I don't know,' she admitted.

'Have you told him since?'

'No. No, I haven't.'

'Then will you tell me now – I'm sorry to add to your distress, Mrs Johnson – just how much truth there was in the story you told me that day?'

She closed her eyes for a moment, but when she opened them she was looking at him again. 'Vince wasn't with me that evening,' she said, 'though Colin *was* away. We've known Vince for a long time, you know, and all of us have been the best of friends. But the other . . . our falling in love . . . didn't ever arise until about three or four months ago.'

'Did you as his friend, or perhaps later in a more intimate relationship, ever know anything about his associates in London?'

'He was . . . he used to describe himself as rather a loner. I think Colin and I were his closest friends, and of course occasionally he met other people here, but he never mentioned having become further acquainted with any of them.' She broke off there, listening. 'That's Colin now,' she said and a moment later there was the sound of a key in the lock of the outer door. There was another short pause, during which they heard what might have been the door of the hall cupboard sliding open, and then Colin Johnson came in.

'Entertaining, my dear?' he said as he saw the visitors. And then he looked more closely at Antony. 'I know you,' he said. 'At least . . . I've seen your photograph.'

'Of course you have, Colin,' said Rosanna. 'It's Antony Maitland. I expect he knows you better by reputation than by sight,' she added to Antony rather as though an apology might be needed. 'And this is Mr Farrell, another lawyer. Mrs Gilchrist has asked Mr Maitland to look into the circumstances of Vince's death and as we were such close friends of his –'

'How did you know that?' The question sounded casual but it seemed to Antony that there was some keener interest behind it.

140

'That we were friends of Vince's, I mean.'

'He told me that he was on his way to see you the night Mrs Thurlow was robbed.'

'As it happens I was following a story down to Brighton,' said Colin, for some reason making Antony think of King Pelinore and the Questing Beast. 'But I don't suppose Vince knew that. Anyway he never got here. He told me later he'd been to the pictures instead.'

Colin was a rather sharp-featured man of about Roger's height – about two or three inches shorter than Maitland himself – with very fair hair and an attractive smile when he chose to use it, as he did now, saying, 'If we can help you in any way hadn't we better all sit down? Is it too early for a drink, or would you like me to ask Rosanna to make some tea?'

'Neither, thank you.' Though they had accomplished so little Antony felt suddenly as though the day had been going on for ever. The sooner they could finish this interview and get back to Kempenfeldt Square the better he'd like it, though at the same time he felt again the touch of panic that had swept over him when Briggs first approached him with Ned Bates's new story. Whether Uncle Nick was right about what had happened or whether his own interpretation was the true one made little difference: there was no time to lose. By rights they should have been working all night, but that was hardly practical. 'I shan't keep you a moment, Mr Johnson, as Mrs Johnson has already told us that you know nothing of Vince's other friends.'

'No, he was very much a chap who kept himself to himself. I met him because of the freelance work he did for my newspaper, though I think it was lucky for him he had an allowance as well: the amount of work he did was never going to make him a fortune. But you know, Mr Maitland, there's a story going around that he got off the charge you defended him on, on rigged evidence. Would you know anything about that?'

The question was slipped so casually into the conversation that for a moment Maitland, like a man who had been stabbed, hardly felt the pain of it. But before he could collect his wits Roger had come into the conversation with a question of his own.

'It would be interesting to know,' he said, 'exactly what Vince Gilchrist told you when he was arrested.'

'First time or second time? But it makes no difference, on each occasion he said he didn't do it.'

'Did you believe him?'

'Of course I did. It wouldn't have been the first time the police had made a mistake.'

'How did he explain the bracelet found in his possession?'

'By saying it had been given to him to sell. Rosanna and I don't know the Chalmers, from what Vince said they are rather a boring couple, and that was why he'd gone out that night when they were dining with Arthur and Judy. I don't know why Mrs Chalmers – Karen, isn't it? – should have chosen him as a suitable person to raise the wind for her, but Vince said the husband was a jealous man and would be bound to think there was something more than friendship between them if he found out. So he didn't want to get her into trouble.'

'And she hadn't the decency to come forward?'

'No, I must say I think that was a bit thick. But Vince was like that you know, always the gentleman.' Antony, for once a passive onlooker, thought he detected the faintest note of sarcasm in that remark. 'Not one to kiss and tell I mean, especially when there was nothing to tell.'

'Are you so sure about that?'

'He said – '

'Yes, Mr Johnson, what did he say?'

'That he and Karen were friends, nothing more.'

'She says, however, that she did not give him the bracelet.'

Colin glanced in a rather puzzled way from one of them to the other. 'You're confusing me, Mr Farrell. Are you telling me that Vince was lying about that?'

'I'm beginning to doubt whether he was capable of telling the truth about anything,' said Roger deliberately.

'Are you implying that his relationship with Karen – ?' Unaccountably, the idea seemed to trouble him.

'No, just that it might be as well to take everything he told you with a grain of salt.'

'He's dead,' said Rosanna in a stifled voice. 'I think that's a beastly thing to say.'

'You keep out of this!' Colin didn't turn to look at her as he spoke, his eyes were fixed on Roger's face. 'If I was mistaken about Vince – '

'So far as his honesty is concerned, I think you were.' Roger shrugged, as though it was a matter of complete indifference to him. 'Of course you might say that there are more kinds of dishonesty than purely financial ones.'

'If I thought that—'

'It can hardly be a matter of much concern to you, now that your friend is dead.'

'Oh, I don't know. There is always the question of being fair to his memory . . . isn't there, Rosanna?'

She was staring at him as though fascinated, but made no attempt to reply. 'What did Gilchrist tell you the second time he was arrested?' Roger asked when the silence had grown oppressive.

'His denial was good enough for me—at least, I thought it was. The only real evidence against him, except for the similarity to the other case, was from the chaps who said they'd seen him going in to the Thurlows' back yard, and as Vince said it's easy to be mistaken in a matter of identification.'

Antony shook himself out of his lethargy. 'And after he was acquitted?' he asked.

'He told me you'd been of the greatest help to him about that,' said Colin Johnson. And added, when he saw Maitland get to his feet and Roger follow his example, 'Shall I see you at the inquest tomorrow? There may be some interesting revelations about the motive for Vince's murder.' This time there was no mistaking the malice behind the words.

'Are you covering the story? I shouldn't have thought your editor would have asked you to,' said Roger, 'considering you were such a close friend.'

'I volunteered. It works both ways you know. I can't say I'm looking forward to all the gory details, but I do want to know who killed him.'

Five minutes later they were out in the street again and making their way towards the car. 'You heard what he said,' Antony remarked to Roger as they went. 'It's obvious that Fleet Street know everything that's been going on, and perhaps—in the way they have—a little bit more.'

'Don't worry about that now,' said Roger, but he stopped as they came up to the car and laid a hand on his friend's arm. 'No, that was a daft thing to say, of course you can't help worrying. I'm worried myself. Do you want to go on, or shall I take you home?'

'I shouldn't wonder if we find Meg there,' said Antony. 'Jenny said something about phoning her so that you could both have

143

dinner with us. I'll be grateful if you will. I daresay we shall just go over and over things, but Meg's always good for Jenny – she may cheer her up.'

Sir Nicholas had not got back from chambers when they arrived at the house at Kempenfeldt Square. Antony stuck his head into the study, while Roger preceded him up the stairs. He intended to say only, 'No progress, tell Uncle Nick,' but Vera put down her book and said urgently, 'Come in and shut the door.' It was only when he had obeyed her that she added, 'Got to tell you, house was searched this morning.'

Antony was still leaning against the door. 'So that was why Gibbs was looking even sourer than usual,' he said. But there was no use pretending to take the matter lightly, Vera knew him too well for that. 'Jenny?' he asked. 'It happened once before, and she said it didn't upset her, but – '

'Jenny's all right. Gibbs brought them to me first so I was able to look after her. Not a nice business,' said Vera 'but doesn't make things any worse really. Pointed that out to her.'

'Bless you,' said Antony with some fervour. 'But I ought to be apologizing to you, Vera. I'm really sorry – '

'Not your fault,' Vera interrupted him quickly. 'Went to chambers too, Nicholas phoned.'

'I can imagine his reaction to that.'

'Not pleased,' Vera conceded. 'Couldn't expect him to be really.'

'I didn't, you can be·sure of that.' There was perhaps in his voice the ghost of his usual humorous acceptance of life, and Vera nodded approvingly.

'Good boy,' she said. 'No use letting it get you down.'

Antony straightened and moved across the room towards her. Perhaps he no longer felt in need of the door's support. 'Did you get an inkling of what they were looking for?' he asked.

'Didn't say. But I can tell you one thing, Antony, they took Nicholas's automatic away with them. Gave me a receipt.'

'That means it was the murder weapon they were after. Well, at least we know that won't help them.'

'Didn't even know he had it,' said Vera going off on another tack. 'Never told me about it.'

'I daresay he'd forgotten, which probably means the licence has run out again,' said Antony rather ruefully. 'It had when I last had occasion to use it . . . well not to use it, to borrow it. But I daresay we can weather that storm, even though I expect he'll make me pay the fine again, and it was a lot more than I expected, I remember.'

'But why did he get it?' asked Vera, who was not without her share of curiosity, and who felt besides that if Antony was reduced to talking for the sake of talking any distraction might help.

'After a rather exciting night here when it might have come in useful,' Antony told her. 'Hasn't Uncle Nick told you about how we met Roger? It was while that business was going on.'

'Well, as you say, it won't do them any good,' said Vera with some satisfaction. 'Didn't seem interested in anything else, either here or in chambers so far as I can gather. Meg's with Jenny, you'd better go and join them, and I'll do my best to calm your uncle down before you see him. Might be as well though for you to come down later and have a word with him.'

'You're as bad as Jenny,' said Antony essaying a smile for the first time since he had come in.

'Don't quite know what you mean.' Vera seemed to be in an especially elliptical mood that evening.

'She's always telling me the one thing that gets Uncle Nick really riled is being kept in the dark about what's going on,' Antony explained.

'Think that goes for most people,' said Vera reflectively. 'What she means – as I think you know perfectly well, Antony – is not that he'll be angry but that he'll be hurt.'

'Yes, I do know,' said Antony soberly, and then added on an impulse, 'Vera, if anything happens to me, you'll look after Jenny won't you?'

'Don't need to ask.' Her tone was even more gruff than usual, which Maitland would have said was impossible. 'Besides, got some good friends. And now get along with you, I'll see you later.'

So he went up to his own quarters, and Jenny and Meg greeted him as if nothing had happened, though he was pretty sure that both the Farrells must have heard by now of the day's events, just as he hoped Roger had enlightened the others about what they had been doing. They talked studiously of everything except the matter that was uppermost in all of their minds: of Meg's new play . . . she was going back to Shakespeare ('anything for a change,' said Roger); the unsatisfactory result of the general election; the Watergate trial, and President Ford's pardon of Richard Nixon . . . in all of which matters they were at the moment supremely uninterested.

All the same, Antony for one would have been glad enough if the interlude could have continued uninterrupted, but just as Jenny was getting up to pour a second round of drinks there came a knock on the outer door which they all recognized from the bad old days when Gibbs, enjoying his martyrdom, had insisted on stomping upstairs every time there was a message. This time it was to the effect that a young lady and gentleman had called to see Mr Maitland. 'Miss Barnard and Mr Midwinter, and knowing you were engaged, Mr Maitland, and Sir Nicholas and Lady Harding are in the study, I wondered what I should do with them.'

Antony hesitated only for a moment. It would save time tomorrow, and neither Mandy nor Nigel had showed themselves in any way disinclined to talk in the presence of a third party. True, Roger and Meg were now added to their number, but somehow he didn't think it would make any difference. 'Ask them to come up, Gibbs,' he said, and remembered to add his thanks as the old man turned away looking as though this new errand was an intolerable burden.

He stayed where he was until these two new visitors reached the landing and then stood back to let them go past him into the hall. His own coat lay over the chair near the cloakroom door. Using a coat hanger was clumsy, though not impossible, especially where a heavy garment was concerned, and he avoided it whenever he could. 'Put your things down there,' he invited, 'and come and join us. Jenny and I have two friends here, so if you've anything particularly confidential to say perhaps you won't mind a conference round the kitchen table. Otherwise – '

Mandy and Nigel exchanged a quick look which was obviously a wordless consultation. 'Nothing at all confidential,' said Mandy. 'I think we should both like to meet your friends, Mr Maitland. It's only just that I was wondering . . . there are such terrible rumours going round.'

If it was possible for him to feel worse than he did already her words would have done it. Nevertheless, 'Come in,' he repeated, 'and tell me about it.' Tonight, more than at their previous meeting, he understood what Jenny had meant. There was an other-worldly quality about Mandy, as though however deep her

146

feelings – and he didn't discount the fact that they might run very deep indeed – she would somehow be able to rise above them. He opened the living-room door and she went ahead of him; there was a brief skirmish between Antony and Nigel as to who should first follow her, but finally they were all in the room and the introductions had been performed. A certain rearrangement of seats was necessary, but Antony took his own preferred place on the hearth-rug where he could indulge, if he wished, his instinct to take refuge from a difficult situation in movement. Jenny offered drinks and supplied them, and a short silence fell.

'I should have come before,' said Mandy, 'to thank you for all you did for Vince. I suppose after what has happened some people would say it didn't really matter, but I think it does very much. And even if it didn't, you were kind enough to listen to me and to take some action, and I'm very grateful to you.' It was obviously a carefully prepared little speech.

'There's no need for that,' Antony told her. 'It's true I . . . poked about a little, but it was none of my doing that Mr Gilchrist was acquitted. A witness came forward –'

'Didn't you find him?' This was getting near the bone for Maitland's taste and he contented himself with shaking his head but Mandy went on regardless. 'I'm sure you did really and you're just being modest. I told you, didn't I, that if you'd take some action everything would be all right?'

'Did you also foresee –' Antony began thoughtlessly, and then broke off appalled at his own ineptitude. Everything might be very far from all right as far as he was concerned, but that was another matter and he had no wish to hurt her.

'Did I know what was going to happen to Vince?' said Mandy. 'That was what you meant, wasn't it? No, of course I didn't or I'd have tried to stop it, but now I'm almost glad because he'd have been so terribly upset by all this.'

At that Jenny leaned forward. 'Mandy,' she said and the girl turned towards her. 'You're going to have to explain a little more clearly what you mean. You've got me confused, and I'm sure my husband feels just the same way.'

'Not to mention Mr and Mrs Farrell,' Nigel put in with an apologetic look in their direction.

'No, I'm sorry. We've come here and spoiled your nice evening together,' said Mandy. 'It's quite simple really,' she went on, taking Roger and Meg into her confidence. 'Vince Gilchrist was

147

accused of something he didn't do – you must have read about it in the papers – and Mr Maitland appeared for him in court and he was found Not Guilty. But now people are saying there was something wrong about the confession of the man who really robbed Aunt Denise, that now he's saying he didn't really do it at all.'

Antony moved then across to the nearer of the two windows, where in spite of the darkness the curtains had not yet been drawn. Roger looked after him with mingled sympathy and exasperation, glanced at Jenny to see if she had any more to say, and then took up the conversation himself. 'It would be interesting to know where you heard that,' he said.

'Tell them, Nigel,' said Mandy imperiously.

'It was Colin Johnson who told me,' said Nigel obediently. 'You know how these Fleet Street fellows get hold of every scrap of information that's flying around. That was all he said, just that there was this rumour, but it left me wondering . . . about Vince, you see.'

'That's really why we're here,' said Mandy as though that made everything plain. '*I* don't need any convincing that Vince was innocent, whatever people are saying now, but Nigel's been such a comfort to me all this time I can't bear for him not to understand the truth.'

Antony came back to the fire then but this time he made no attempt to appear relaxed by leaning his shoulder against the high mantel as he so often did. 'I don't think any of us know the truth now, Mandy,' he said, and only the three people in the room who knew him well recognized the raggedness of his tone. 'It's perfectly true what I told you, I did try to help and failed, and then Ned Bates's confession came up more or less out of the blue. I couldn't have been more surprised.'

'And is it true too,' asked Nigel, 'that he's now gone back on what he said?'

'Apparently.' No use denying it, it would be common knowledge soon enough, at the inquest tomorrow or he missed his guess. Briggs would hardly let the opportunity go by of suggesting a motive for Vince's murder, and the newspapers would be only too ready to jump on the bandwagon.

'Then where does that leave us?'

Antony nearly said 'In the soup,' as he might have done in the interest of annoying Sir Nicholas. Instead, 'Exactly where we

148

were before Ned Bates came forward,' he told them. 'One of his stories is true and the other's a lie, but I for one wouldn't take it upon myself to say which.'

'I thought perhaps, Mr Maitland, you'd try to find out for us.'

'For you, Mandy,' Nigel corrected her. 'As an intellectual exercise I'm more interested in who killed Vince and why.'

'That's another question I can't answer,' said Antony, 'though like you I wish I could. As for whether Ned Bates is telling the truth, in a way I am trying to find the answer to that and so are the police. But I'm pretty sure they think they've found it already.'

'What is it?' asked Mandy eagerly.

'That his second story is true.'

'That still wouldn't make it absolutely certain that Vince was guilty though,' Mandy persisted.

Antony glanced helplessly at Nigel. 'I'd be infinitely obliged to you,' said Nigel, speaking rather as though they were alone, 'if you'd tell her what you really think.'

'I don't know,' said Antony indecisively. This time he looked from Jenny to Meg, and Meg said encouragingly,

'Tell her, darling.'

'All right. I'm ninety-nine percent sure, Mandy, that Vince was guilty. I don't like having to tell you this, but I know now that some of the story he told to his solicitor and me to account for the evidence against him the first time he was charged just wasn't true.'

'You mean about the bracelet being given him to sell?' said Mandy in a small voice.

'Did he tell you that?'

'Yes, he said he couldn't tell anybody else because Mr Chalmers would be bound to think there'd been something between him and Mrs Chalmers when there wasn't really, it was just that she trusted him. You mean that wasn't true?'

'You seem to trust my judgement, Mandy. In my opinion, not one word of it.'

'Then when he said –' She was fumbling for a handkerchief, and Nigel produced a clean one promptly as though this wasn't the first time he had performed the office. Mandy blew her nose defiantly. 'You mean when he told me I was the only one . . . ever,' she said, 'he wasn't telling the truth?'

'That I can answer with more certainty,' said Antony. 'I'm

afraid he wasn't.'

'Oh Nigel!' They were both sitting on the sofa, and now she turned and hid her face against his shoulder. 'I'm sorry,' she added as a sort of polite afterthought to the assembled company, her voice muffled.

'I'd better take her home,' said Nigel, getting up and pulling her unceremoniously to her feet. For a moment his eyes met Antony's directly. 'It's good of you to take so much trouble about our problem,' he said, 'when you must have plenty of your own.' After that good-nights were said, rather tearful good-nights on Mandy's part, and Antony went downstairs with them to see them out.

When he got back all the good resolutions about keeping off an uncomfortable subject seemed to have gone by the board, and Meg – who must have found it agonizing to have kept silent for so long – was talking nineteen to the dozen. 'That's one of the men you think has a motive for murdering Vince Gilchrist, isn't it?' she demanded as Antony came in. 'Well, from what Jenny and Roger have been telling me, it sounds very much as though he deserved to be killed.'

'I daresay he did, but don't look at me when you say that,' said Antony.

'No, of course not, darling. You know I didn't mean anything like that. But what do you think of this Nigel Midwinter?'

'I think he'll marry Mandy as soon as she shows the first sign of getting over her infatuation for Gilchrist,' said Antony. 'As for what happens after that . . . he seems a little too inclined to oblige her, even when it creates an awkward situation.'

'He knows where to draw the line,' said Jenny positively.

'That's all very well, darlings.' Meg knew what she wanted and intended to get it. 'I meant as a possible murderer.'

Antony shrugged. 'There you have it. Possible,' he said.

'He seems a very nice young man.'

'You know better than that, Meg. You'll be telling me next he couldn't possibly have done a thing like that,' said Antony, allowing a rather savage inflection to creep into his sarcasm. 'Nice young men have been known to commit murder before now.'

'You said yourself the girl – Mandy – would probably turn to him now,' Meg insisted, 'and if he expected that . . . but Roger says there are other possibilities. Vincent Gilchrist seems to have been one of those men who go about spreading gloom and despondency among husbands and lovers wherever they go.'

'You're perfectly right, Meg.' Maitland sounded a little calmer now. 'As far as that goes Roger and I have three perfectly good suspects on our list. But surely he told you about our conversations today, and Arthur Gilchrist's suggestion that it might be one of his partners in crime that Vince Gilchrist fell out with?'

'His fence,' said Meg wisely. 'That's a perfectly logical idea, darling, but I like the jealousy motive best.'

'I told you how it would be,' said Roger, so gloomily that Antony burst out laughing.

'You mean because the new play's *Othello?*' He looked from one to the other of his companions, still smiling, and then flung himself down on to the sofa beside Jenny. 'I suppose we shall have to get used to her playing Desdemona, even on informal occasions, for at least the next year,' he said.

V

And that was that until the phone rang just as they were finishing dinner. Maitland, who was still restless, left his apple-pie unfinished and went to answer it, and when he heard Sykes's familiar voice at the other end of the line he hooked a chair towards himself with his foot and sat down to listen.

Again the Chief Inspector opened abruptly, without his usual inquiries as to the family's well-being. 'A couple of things you ought to know about, Mr Maitland,' he said, and the note of amusement that Antony had so often in the past heard in his voice was altogether absent. 'First about the question of your actions concerning Gilchrist's trial.'

'A second witness has turned up to supply what's lacking now that Vince Gilchrist is dead,' said Antony rather quickly.

'How did you know that?'

'Uncle Nick warned me it might happen.'

That silenced Sykes for a moment. 'You were going to tell me –' Antony prompted him.

'The man to whom Gilchrist sold Mrs Thurlow's jewels has come forward.'

'A buyer? But –'

'You'd better let me finish, Mr Maitland, then you'll be able to see what you're up against. This man, Joseph Carleton, is a perfectly respectable jeweller in a small way of business . . . that is, so far as we've ever been able to prove. He says he bought the stuff in the ordinary way of business. Vince Gilchrist looked perfectly respectable to him and he'd no reason to question his story that the stuff had belonged to his mother who was recently deceased, but as he was unmarried he wanted to dispose of it. Then, of course, Carleton got our circular about the stolen goods, but didn't have time to check it over immediately . . . so he says. When he did look at it he was just about to get in touch with us when a man answering your description and giving your name called to see him.'

'Of course, I always give my own name when I'm arranging for perjured evidence,' said Antony bitterly.

'I haven't quite finished, Mr Maitland,' said Sykes reprovingly. 'This man – and I think there's no doubt that Carleton would identify you if given the chance – '

'Sykes, you said – '

'I'm saying, Mr Maitland, that you've been photographed often enough so that there'd be no difficulty about his recognizing you, whether he's ever seen you in person or not. This man said to him that he was acting for a client who came from a very good family and who had previously had a blameless reputation . . . a sob story, in fact, about how upset his relations would be, and how just because he'd succumbed to a momentary temptation . . . you know the kind of thing.'

'I know exactly the kind of thing,' said Maitland harshly.

'Well, the long and the short of it is,' said Sykes as though there had been no interruption, 'that the suggestion was made that no report should be given to the police. And to satisfy Carleton's conscience – which I'm pretty sure is a commodity he doesn't possess – the jewellery should be packed up and returned anonymously to Mrs Thurlow, Mr Carleton, of course, being recompensed for the amount he'd paid for it – plus a little bit over I should imagine, though he didn't mention that. Mrs Thurlow received the package by messenger this morning, with everything intact, and Carleton came to Scotland Yard saying that his conscience had been troubling him and he wanted to make a clean breast of the whole thing.'

'Heaven and earth!' said Antony blankly. He couldn't think of any other comment.

'There's just one other thing that may be relevant when you

come to consider the matter,' Sykes's voice went on. 'I said that Joseph Carleton was respectable so far as we'd ever been able to prove, but my colleagues who deal with such things tell me that they think they've got the goods on him at last.'

'I see. Yes, I think that's extremely relevant, but at the moment I don't see what good it does. Unless they were going to make a move before my affair comes to trial, but even then the matter would be still *sub judice* and I don't see how we could use it. No, Briggs has got his second witness all right.' The conversation at the dining table had stilled long since, and he was quite aware that the three of them were listening unashamedly. Still he had to find out . . . 'When does he mean to act?' he asked.

'Not immediately. I don't know that this will be of much consolation to you, Mr Maitland, but I think he's holding out in the hope of being able to make the more serious charge stick.'

'Am I supposed to be grateful to him for that?' Antony wondered.

'Which brings me to my second point,' said Sykes, again ignoring the interpolation. Antony had the sudden feeling that for once in his life the detective's placidity had been shattered, that he was afraid of what he might be betrayed into saying if once he allowed himself to be distracted from the strict thread of his narrative. 'The weapon has been found.'

'Some of your minions borrowed Uncle Nick's automatic pistol today,' said Antony. 'I hope Briggs isn't counting on that being what he wants, because he's going to be disappointed.'

'That isn't what I meant. The one I meant is still with ballistics, but I think there's no doubt it's the right weapon. It had been pitched down the garbage chute at Halkin Place.'

'As I don't suppose many of the tenants number guns among their possessions, I think there's no doubt it's the right one,' Antony agreed.

'Mr Maitland, did you ever own such a weapon?'

'Not since I left the service which my uncle is pleased to refer to as "that gang of thugs in Whitehall",' said Antony precisely. He wondered for a moment if the question meant that the detective was beginning to doubt him, but even if that was the case he was almost past caring.

'I only asked because if you did, and there was any chance it might have been stolen . . . we have to face it, Mr Maitland, there's been a concerted attempt to incriminate you.'

'I thought we'd faced that long ago. The thing is, what the hell is going to turn up next?'

'What does Sir Nicholas think?'

'He thinks exactly as you do,' said Antony, 'and I can see now I should have believed him from the beginning. We'd better not talk about that over the telephone though.'

'I'm at home, and I picked the two men who executed the search warrant myself,' said Sykes. 'I can assure you they didn't take the opportunity to bug your telephone or anything of the sort.'

'I'd already checked on that,' Antony admitted. 'All the same, Chief Inspector . . . do you mean you could trust them to do a job for you and not go running to Briggs with the information?'

'Yes, Mr Maitland, I do. Have you something in mind?'

'Alibis,' said Antony, 'for the morning of Vince Gilchrist's murder. There are three men, any of whom might have been jealous enough to kill him.'

'Give me their names,' said Sykes. He was the kind of man who kept a pad and pencil conveniently beside the telephone, so that there was no need for him to go searching for something to write on.

'Mervin Chalmers. He lives in the country but comes to town every day. The other two are Colin Johnson and Nigel Midwinter.' He went on to add addresses, and what few particulars he knew of each of the men. 'I'm grateful for your help, Chief Inspector,' he said when he had finished, 'and even more grateful, if that were possible, for your keeping me up-to-date on developments.'

'That's all right, Mr Maitland, think nothing of it,' said Sykes, and replaced the receiver gently as though anxious to cut off any further expressions of appreciation.

The moment Maitland stood up and began to move rather stiffly away from the writing-table the others came to join him by the fire. It wasn't till later that he noticed that not one of them had bothered to finish the dessert. 'I didn't like the sound of that,' said Roger frankly. 'Are you going to tell us what it was all about?'

'It was Inspector Sykes, wasn't it?' asked Jenny.

'Chief Inspector,' he said, and thought as soon as he had spoken how foolish it was to be bothering about a small matter like that. He went on to tell them as exactly as he could remember what had been said. 'You see what it means, don't you?' he challenged them when he had finished.

'Darling, you know you're going to tell us, so why waste time with a question like that?' said Meg.

'It means I've come round absolutely to Uncle Nick's way of thinking. Briggs is rigging the evidence on a possible subornation of perjury charge.'

'I'm not saying I don't agree with you,' said Roger, 'in fact you know my opinion. But how did this talk with Sykes convince you of that?'

'For one thing, there are altogether too many things that only a few people could have known. But more important still, Sykes gave me the clearest hint that that's what he thinks himself. He'd never come right out into the open about it, he's a cautious chap and you can see what a difficult position it is for him, but he's warned me any number of times about Briggs's attitude towards me, and once he went so far as to say that it was intensifying.' He closed his eyes for a moment as though in an effort of recollection. 'I think I can give you his exact words. He said, "He gets an idea into his head and nothing in the world will convince him that he's wrong." It's only a step from that to the kind of obsession that Uncle Nick was talking about. Don't you see?' he added with a certain desperation in his voice. 'Again and again he's thought the worst of me, and again and again he hasn't been able to prove it. And this I suppose is the result.'   •

'You don't have to convince us,' Roger told him. 'After all, you were the only sceptic. But I'd be interested to know how Sykes hinted at his opinion.'

'When he told me that Carleton might be going to be arrested.'

'You mean that Briggs might again have offered to use his influence?'

'Something like that.'

'The question is then, what are we going to do about it?'

'Find out the truth of what's been going on and ram it down his throat,' said Maitland, suddenly sounding very determined. 'As to how—'

'Yes, how?' asked Meg.

'I'm going down now to see Uncle Nick and put him in the picture, as I promised Vera I'd do before any of this came up. Then in the morning, Roger, will you come with me first thing to see Father William?'

'Of course I will. What time would you like me to pick you up?'

'Why don't you both come round to breakfast? A bit early for you, Meg, but as you're resting—'

'It sounds a good idea to me,' said Meg decisively. 'As a matter of fact,' she admitted, 'I shall be just as glad of the company as Jenny will.'

VI

The interview with his uncle was just as unpleasant as Antony had expected, though in a rather different way. If Sir Nicholas had indeed needed placating after the day's events, Vera had succeeded only too well. He heard his nephew's story out almost without interruption, a thing quite unprecedented, and only said when he had finished, 'Something will have to be done!'

But Antony was still confused by Sykes's revelations, and by his own conversion to Sir Nicholas's way of thinking. 'I seem to be hurting all the people I – I think most about,' he said.

'Don't start feeling guilty,' his uncle adjured him. 'That's about the worst thing you can do at this stage. And if you think about it, my dear boy, the only difference between this case and the other times you've been up against the Chief Superintendent is that this time you're the person in jeopardy, not one of your clients.'

'It's all very well saying the only difference, Uncle Nick,' said Antony recovering his spirit a little. 'It alters everything, and I'm sure you know it.' But though they tossed the matter backwards and forwards between them for another quarter of an hour, Antony went upstairs at last with no other plan in his mind than the one he had outlined to Roger.

Later, when Roger and Meg had gone, he came back into the living-room to find Jenny on her knees before the fire. After a moment's hesitation he knelt down beside her, and she turned and put a hand on his arm.

'You're shivering, Antony,' she said. 'Shall I –?'

'No, leave it. I'm not cold.'

'It's like the last time,' she said, and turned her head to look across the room. 'You've left the door open.'

'Have I? I didn't realize it. Oh God, Jenny, what am I going to do?'

'You think some more evidence is going to turn up against you about the murder, don't you?'

'I'm sure it is. But even if it doesn't, Briggs has enough now to convict me on the other charge, and that means . . . I'm an officer of the court, love, the Judge will take the dimmest of dim views.' There was a pause, and then he added with difficulty, 'I ought to be thinking only of you, and what this is going to do to Uncle Nick and Vera. But you know what's wrong, Jenny, because I told you once. I'm desperately afraid—'

'Of being shut in.' Jenny finished the sentence for him when he broke off and seemed to have forgotten what he had been going to say. 'But I'm the only one that knows,' she said as though that might be of some comfort to him.

'Geoffrey's perfectly well aware how I feel about visiting a client in prison,' he told her, 'though there's no way he can guess how I feel every time I hear a door shut behind us and the key turning in the lock.'

'Even if he did realize it, it's nothing to be ashamed of. Lots of people feel like that, and you don't blame *them*.'

'The trouble is,' he said as though she hadn't spoken, 'I can't forget. I should have been able to put it all behind me by now, something to be talked about and laughed about when old comrades get together. And most of the time I can as long as nothing reminds me, but there are only too many things that do.'

'Do you remember what you said to me last time?' asked Jenny. 'The last time we thought . . . this . . . was going to happen. You said *it's a poor sort of memory that only works backwards.*'

'I seem to have talked an awful lot of nonsense,' said Antony, trying to speak more lightly. And suddenly as he looked at her the years rolled back. They were no longer in the comfortable, familiar room but in the far more formal drawing-room in Jenny's parents' house, where he had gone to her with his unhappiness and bitter self-distrust. Jenny had been seventeen (did she look so very different now? She must, he supposed, but he couldn't remember) and he himself not so very much older, but even then there had been the clear, serene look that he had come to think of over the years as his refuge, and even then she had given him comfort and a strength he hadn't known he possessed. 'It's so long ago,' he said, as though she could know his thoughts.

Perhaps she did, or perhaps she was just answering his great need of her. 'You've fought your demons before, Antony, and whether you realize it at this moment or not, I know you can do

157

so again.' And with her words the present came back into focus.

'As long as I know you're here, Jenny.'

'I'll always be here.'

'I know.'

'Besides, Antony, if—if what we're afraid of happens, do you think Uncle Nick would let it rest there? Or Inspector Sykes, if you're right about what he thinks. It would only be a matter of time.'

'Time?' said Antony, rather as though he had never heard the word before. Then he smiled and put up his left hand to gently touch her cheek. 'My dear and only love,' he said, 'I think perhaps those demons of mine know I've got an ally. They're probably cowards at heart.'

I

At ten o'clock the following morning Antony and Roger walked down Bedford Lane until they stood outside Father William's shop. There had been changes since the first time Antony visited it, the neat brass plate by the door said now only *Webster's*, but the narrow window was just as sparsely and just as artistically arranged. Antony hesitated a moment as though admiring it, though he was perhaps merely unwilling to embark on an interview that as far as he could see was the last useful step he could take towards vindicating himself. 'I wonder if there's anyone in the shop,' he said.

'The only way to find out is to go in and see,' said Roger practically, and when his friend still hesitated he pushed open the door.

The shop was just as free from clutter as the window had been, father William obviously did not keep all his wares on display. It was also, to Maitland's relief, free of customers, but before the bell above the door had stopped jangling a little white-haired man appeared through the door at the back. 'Mr Maitland!' he exclaimed in complete surprise. 'I didn't expect to see you again so soon.' He had blue eyes and an air of benevolent simplicity, the latter a façade, as Antony knew well enough, though he believed the benevolence was genuine so far as he was concerned.

'I always seem to come to you when I'm in trouble, Father William,' he said.

'I'm very sorry to hear that. Is it anything to do with the matter you discussed with me recently?'

'Everything,' said Antony. Father William's gaze had gone beyond him. 'And Mr – Mr Farrell, isn't it?' he said. 'I'm very pleased to see you again. A resourceful gentleman if my memory serves me rightly.'

'I'm glad to see you again too, Mr Webster,' said Roger,

concealing well enough his anxiety concerning his companion's intentions.

'You'll find I answer more readily to Father William from my friends,' said Mr Webster. His eyes going from one to the other of them were full of awareness, as though he saw, thought Roger rather resentfully, even more than he was intended to see. 'But come along, come along,' he added, beginning to move towards the back of the shop. 'My assistant is out today–flu she says, though I don't suppose it's anything more than the common cold–so we'll have to stay in the office where I can hear if anyone comes in. I'm afraid it's a little crowded,' he went on as they followed him into the tiny room. 'But I had the sofa re-sprung and re-upholstered,' he added in a self-congratulatory tone. 'I'm sure, Mr Maitland, you'll find it more comfortable than you did the first time you came here.'

'I'm sure I shall,' said Antony, seating himself and motioning Roger to join him.

Father William took the chair near the rather battered rolltop desk, and swung round to face them. 'This trouble of yours, Mr Maitland,' he said. 'One of your clients? The matter you consulted me about before . . . I'm sure I read somewhere that the client you were representing at the time had been murdered.'

'That's part of the trouble,' said Antony. 'The details aren't really important, but I'll give you the gist of it.' He proceeded to do so, omitting any mention of their suspicions concerning Briggs's part in the affair. 'So you see–' he concluded, and didn't attempt to finish the sentence.

'An extremely unpleasant situation,' Father William agreed, nodding. 'I don't need to tell you, Mr Maitland, that if there is anything I can do I shall be only too happy.'

'Yes, I know. I don't know if it will help or not, but what can you tell me about Joseph Carleton? If you know him at all, that is.'

'I know him slightly. We have on occasion done business together.' His eyes turned for a moment to Roger's impassive face. 'Am I to understand that Mr Farrell is in your confidence, Mr Maitland?'

'Fully in my confidence about my own affairs,' said Antony.

'Then I shall trust him too.' The old man smiled delightedly. 'Joe Carleton is in a small way of business, not so good a situation as this, but it's well known in the trade that the shop is merely what I believe is called a front.'

'Don't be a humbug, Father William,' Antony implored him. 'You know very well you mean he's a buyer.'

'A receiver of stolen goods,' Father William nodded, as though the other phrase were unfamiliar to him. 'As I said, when a client of mine has been looking for some particular thing there have been occasions when he has been able to supply it. But our acquaintance stops there.'

'In other words, he isn't in your class,' said Antony bluntly.

'Always so forthright, Mr Maitland,' William Webster rebuked him. 'And that, I'm afraid, is the sum of my own knowledge of the man. But there are rumours . . . do you want something that is merely hearsay?'

'I want anything you can tell me, however trivial it seems.'

'He has never been in trouble with the police, you understand. People in my line of business have to be so very careful,' he confided in Roger. 'The police I'm afraid – as Mr Maitland is finding to his cost – have nasty, suspicious minds. Joe has been lucky, there's no denying that, but rumour has it that at the moment he's very worried about a certain recent transaction.'

'You mean the police are on to him?'

'I'm afraid Joe has been very careless. To a person like myself who deals in such precious things, certain pieces of jewellery are easily recognizable. A lady who dealt always with Fenton & Son – she had a weakness for Daniel Fenton's designs, though I can't see their beauty myself – was burgled a couple of months ago. The proceeds of the robbery came into Joe's possession and he was incautious enough to try and sell one of the brooches without breaking it up. Fenton & Son, as you may know, have the highest reputation, and I'm afraid that with their evidence poor Joe has had it, as I believe the saying goes.'

'I see. That tallies with our information, Roger, but it doesn't really get us much further.'

'Don't despair yet, Mr Maitland. I haven't quite finished. When you told me you'd have no further need of my help in finding out where the Thurlow jewels had gone, out of pure curiosity, I'm afraid, I continued with my inquiries.'

'Heaven be praised! And you found something?' asked Antony eagerly.

'I did indeed, though not something that you would at that

161

time have been pleased to hear. They were sold to Joe Carleton.'

'But I've just told you he admits that.'

'So you have and he's quite right in saying that it was your deceased client who sold them to him. But I was going to put forward a theory –'

'Go on, man, go on!'

Father William was not to be hurried, but nor was the benevolence of his look in any way disturbed. 'This problem of yours, Mr Maitland,' he said delicately. 'I'm not telling you anything you don't know when I say it's a frame-up –'

'Of course it is!'

Roger put out a hand and touched his friend's arm warningly. 'Don't be so impatient, Antony,' he advised. 'Let Father William tell his story his own way. He may have got something.'

'Yes, of course, I'm sorry,' said Antony. 'You were saying –?'

'Part of the evidence against you is that Joe Carleton said it was at your instigation that he originally concealed Vince Gilchrist's part in the transaction, but that, overwhelmed by the wickedness of what he had done, he came forward later to make a clean breast of it.'

'I couldn't have put it better myself.'

'Well, there are two things about that. For one thing, Joe doesn't know the meaning of the word conscience, certainly not where business dealings are concerned.'

'I doubt if that's susceptible of proof,' said Maitland in a disappointed tone.

'Two things, I said. If his recent statement to the police is part of the frame-up –'

'Of course it is!'

'I was about to add, as of course it is. I am quite aware of your integrity, Mr Maitland.' (An integrity which, as Roger was beginning to understand, in his own peculiar way William Webster shared.)

'Thank you,' said Antony, already regretting his outburst.

'The point I was going to make is this. Over the years Joe has, I'm sure, amassed a fortune. I don't know where he keeps his money, a Swiss bank account perhaps, and he has made no secret of the fact that he intends to retire fairly soon. I don't think that his evidence could have been bought with money.'

'What then?'

'I told you, and you and Mr Farrell have obviously heard the

162

same thing, that the police are closing in on him. I think the only bribe he would have accepted would have been a promise of freedom from prosecution in this other matter. To a temptation like that he might very easily have succumbed, seeing the enjoyment of the fruits of years of labour being delayed by a long prison sentence. And that means, Mr Maitland, that your enemy is someone who is in a position to guarantee him immunity, or at the very least ensure that because of his co-operation in this matter he would get off with a much lighter sentence. I'm inclined myself to favour a member of the police force.'

Antony turned to look at Roger, and for a moment despair was written clearly on his face. 'It all fits in,' he said, 'but it's telling us something we already knew. And there's no proof at all.'

William Webster's eyes were intent. 'I'd hoped to give you a lead,' he said, 'but I see this is something you've already thought of for yourselves. As regards to proof, however –'

'I don't think you can help us there, Father William.' He smiled at his old friend suddenly. 'You've said yourself, Joseph Carleton wouldn't be susceptible to bribery in the ordinary way.'

'Nor would I attempt it,' said Father William with dignity. He got up himself, seeing the two younger men were already on their feet. 'Let me give you a word of advice before you go. Despair pays no dividends. You may think it's too late for anything else, and you may find yourself wrong.'

II

They were on foot that morning, the Jensen safely parked in a space Roger had found in Kempenfeldt Square, so it was not much before noon when they arrived back there again. Gibbs wasn't in the hall – of course at that hour he couldn't have been expecting them – but he popped out of the door from the servants' quarters almost before they were safely inside. 'Sir Nicholas wished me to tell you, Mr Maitland, that he would not be in chambers today. If you need him he's in the study with Lady Harding.'

'Thank you, Gibbs. Did he say he wanted to see me?'

'No, Mr Maitland.' (If you were listening I wouldn't have to

163

say everything twice, his tone implied.) 'He said quite clearly, if you needed him he'd be there.'

'Thank you,' said Antony again and began to move towards the staircase with Roger in close attendance. 'I don't think we need bother him with a report on our activities this morning,' he said. 'I have a sort of feeling . . . but I suppose I'm in the frame of mind to clutch at straws.'

'I rather liked the old boy,' said Roger, following him up the stairs.

'You should do. He and you between you saved Jenny's life once. And mine,' he added as an afterthought. (And a month from now, three months from now, shall I still be grateful to you for that?)

'Yes, but the events of that evening were . . . somewhat chaotic,' Roger reminded him. 'I didn't really get a chance to weigh him up, but at least he gave you an argument you can use.'

'Without involving Sykes, you mean? Oh, I shall use it, never fear, but I can't see that it will be the slightest use. In fact . . . I think I'll ring Geoffrey when we get in, Roger. I ought to bring him up-to-date, and there's always a chance he may have found something helpful in Ned Bates's background.'

But it was just as well that he hadn't really expected any help from that quarter. When he got through to Geoffrey's office he was informed that Mr Horton had been called away that morning on urgent business, and wasn't really expected back at work before the weekend.

'So that's that,' said Antony, turning from the phone. 'And you can look as disapproving as you like, Meg *darling*, but Roger and I both need a drink even if it isn't what you consider a suitable time of day for such indulgence.'

Jenny was already rummaging in the cupboard, the tray on the floor beside her. Antony had a sudden qualm that their conversation the evening before had embarrassed her; then she looked up and smiled at him and he knew the idea was a foolish one. 'I think it's a very good idea,' said Meg, 'and Jenny and I will join you. I gather,' she added, giving him a straight look, 'nothing came of this expedition of yours.'

'Am I so obvious?'

'Not just you, darling, but if you both come in with your tails between your legs you can't expect us not to draw our own

164

conclusions,' said Meg. 'I don't think it was a very good idea anyway. Haven't you a better one up your sleeve?'

'One only and it involves another talk with Sykes. And that had better wait until this evening when he's at home and none of his colleagues within earshot,' he said, and did not add 'if I have so much time,' though the thought was in all their minds.

After that the day wore on slowly. It was like, Antony thought, being seen off by friends at a railway station, when in the last moments you are awkwardly aware that there is nothing more to say. Roger created a slight diversion during the afternoon, when he thought the evening papers would be on the streets and went down to get one to see if there was a report of the inquest. There had been an adjournment with only evidence of identification and of the cause of the death provided. 'Very dull,' said Roger tossing the paper aside, which in its way was a relief, but they were none of them in a mood to take an interest in the rest of the daily ration of doom and gloom.

The afternoon was wearing on when Gibbs toiled upstairs with a message that two persons from the police were wishing to see Mr Maitland. Antony knew well enough that he was in the old man's black books, and half expected to see Briggs and Sykes coming up the stairs behind him. Perhaps Gibbs read his thoughts for he added, not quite so sourly, 'I did not wish to disturb Mrs Maitland so I instructed them to wait in the hall.'

'That was good of you. Is my uncle still in?'

'Sir Nicholas and Lady Harding are still in the study.'

'Then I'll come down as soon as I've told Jenny. Would you mind going ahead, Gibbs, and asking my uncle if the interview can take place there?'

'If that is what you wish, Mr Maitland,' said Gibbs repressively, and turned away.

All day this moment seemed to have been drawing inevitably nearer. At least there was no need for a long explanation. Jenny was already on her feet and came towards him. 'This is it, isn't it, Antony?'

'Two persons from the police,' he mimicked, trying to lighten the moment. 'I'll go down now and see them in the study with Uncle Nick's permission. I don't imagine he'll deny me it, I think that's why he stayed in today, to be on hand if he was needed.'

'All right, darling.' The endearment came strangely from

165

Jenny, who had given it up years ago when Meg started to use the word so indiscriminately. 'I was just going to make tea,' she added, 'so I hope you'll be back before it gets cold.'

When he got downstairs Gibbs had disappeared, Sir Nicholas was standing in the study doorway and Briggs and Sykes were crossing the hall towards him. Seeming to sense Antony's presence, Briggs stopped and motioned him to go into the room ahead of them. Once inside he greeted Vera smoothly – presumably he had already exchanged courtesies with Sir Nicholas – and turned to Antony, who noted with some trepidation that the familiar hectoring manner was for the moment in abeyance. On the contrary, Detective Chief Superintendent Briggs was looking self-satisfied, if not downright smug. 'Well, Mr Maitland,' he said.

Antony shot a quick glance at Sykes, and received in return a look that could only be construed as a warning. 'Well, Chief Superintendent,' he echoed, and the mimicry of Briggs's tone could hardly in this instance have been accidental.

'If you mean that as a statement rather than as a question,' said Briggs, 'I think I should tell you, Mr Maitland, that from your point of view things are very far from well. There are some matters I wish to put to you, but – '

'I trust you will have no objection to my presence and that of my wife,' said Sir Nicholas. His tone rivalled the detective's for smoothness.

'That is for Mr Maitland to say.'

'Of c-course I've no objection,' said Antony swiftly. The familiar stammer betrayed the fact that Briggs's attitude was already getting home to him.

'I'm very glad to hear it,' said Briggs, 'though you're showing more consideration for your relatives than I believed you capable of. You see, Sir Nicholas, there are things I feel you should know, about which I very much doubt that you are in your nephew's confidence. Perhaps it is better for you and Lady Harding to hear the truth now rather than later.'

'On the contrary, I am fully in my nephew's confidence,' said Sir Nicholas coldly. 'But if you are willing for us to hear what you have to say, hadn't we better all sit down? Do you wish to take notes, Chief Inspector?'

'I don't think there's any need for that, Sir Nicholas,' Sykes replied in his sedate way.

166

'Then we'll sit round the fire. You'd better take my chair, Antony.'

'If you think this is going to be an informal discussion, Sir Nicholas, I'm afraid I must inform you that it is nothing of the kind. I told you once that the day would come when your nephew would go too far—'

'And very rude about it you were too,' said Sir Nicholas pensively, so that Antony thought all at once that his uncle was finding Briggs's lack of bluster as unnerving as he was himself.

'If I was angry I had reason to be,' said Briggs. 'I was about to say that before we go any further I should warn you Mr Maitland that—'

'Thank you, I know the w-wording as well as you do,' said Antony. 'And as Chief Inspector Sykes is here to back up your s-statement that you proceeded with due propriety, there's no need for you to go any f-further. What are these m-matters that you wish to put to me?' Again the mimicry was very obvious, even if slightly marred by his stammer, and this time it seemed to get under Briggs's skin, and his colour began to rise.

'Wait a minute, Antony,' Sir Nicholas put in. 'Hadn't you better call Geoffrey?'

'He's out of town, Uncle Nick. In any case I think you and Vera between you will provide just as much protection, don't you? It isn't as if I have anything to say to the Chief Superintendent.'

'You'll answer my questions here or at Scotland Yard,' said Briggs harshly.

'Now w-where have I heard that b-before? Are you arresting me?' Antony wondered.

'That depends upon whether you have any explanation of the facts I'm about to put to you,' said Briggs. There was no doubt in Antony's mind now, the detective was enjoying himself. 'Unless you care to save everyone's time by making a voluntary statement.'

'About w-what?'

'There are two matters that concern us and about which *you* would do well to be concerned,' said Briggs. 'The first, as you very well know, concerns the arrangements you made for the acquittal of your client, Vincent Gilchrist. The second has to do with his subsequent murder.'

'Let's t-take everything in order. The alleged perversion of the 'c-course of justice came first.'

'As you wish.' For a moment his eyes turned to Sir Nicholas in a speculative way as though he were wondering why there was no objection from that quarter to his nephew answering any questions at all. But Sir Nicholas and Vera would be hoping to learn as much as they could about the police's case, as Antony was himself, so to him at least their silence came as no surprise. 'We have already discussed Edward Bates's evidence –'

'Which was a p-pack of lies.'

'So you say. There was also Vincent Gilchrist's statement, though after his murder it would have been impossible to proceed on Bates's evidence alone. However a man has come forward . . . how long have you known Joseph Carleton, Mr Maitland?'

'I don't know him.' It would have been more satisfactory to say, I never heard of him, but almost against his will that innate dislike of lying framed his answer for him.

'That's odd, Mr Maitland. He says you called on him not very long after Vincent Gilchrist's arrest.'

'Wait a bit! Did he give you the exact date?'

'During the second week in September. I'm perfectly well aware that you spent the long vacation in the country, but I hope you are not going to deny the fact that you came up to town during that period for an urgent conference with Mr Bellerby and a client of his, and spent a couple of nights here.'

'No, I won't d-deny it, but I wonder how you found out, C-Chief Superintendent.'

'It wasn't difficult.' Briggs shrugged the question aside. 'And as you are so well acquainted with Mr Bellerby, no doubt he mentioned to you that he had given your name to a friend of his, Vincent Gilchrist's solicitor.'

'He t-told me nothing of the kind.'

'The matter would be unimportant to him, and has no doubt slipped his mind. But to get back to Joseph Carleton –'

'Yes, that does interest me. Why should I have visited him?'

'Because you had seen Vincent Gilchrist on that same trip to town and he had confided in you that Carleton was the man to whom he had sold Mrs Thurlow's jewels.'

'Come n-now, I can't see any man giving himself away to you as you say Carleton did.'

'He had bought the jewels in good faith, but foolishly he

listened to the rather pathetic story you told him concerning Gilchrist's widowed mother and the distress to his family in general if he were found guilty. He agreed to return the jewels, upon being compensated for the sum he had paid for them, but later he realized his own responsibility in the matter and came forward with a statement.'

'Well, I shouldn't b-believe a word of it if I were you. But I don't s-suppose you do for a moment.'

'What do you mean by that, Mr Maitland?' For the second time he had shaken Briggs's complacency.

'I went to see Mr William Webster this morning,' said Antony, in the tone he might have used if he'd been changing the subject.

'I'm very well aware of that.'

'Yes, that's something I forgot to tell you, Uncle Nick, that I've had a detective constable on my heels for the last couple of days. I didn't tell Roger, as a matter of fact: I was afraid it might make him self-conscious. We shook him off when we went to the country, but that was sheer accident. There was no secret about our activities.'

'We know all about Mr Webster,' said Briggs ominously.

'Do you really? I doubt if anyone can honestly say that about anyone else. Anyway, what do you think you know?'

'That he's a receiver of stolen goods.'

'Really, Chief Superintendent, you m-mustn't go in for slander with three lawyers present. Who knows where it might lead?'

Briggs ignored this. 'I should be interested to know why you introduced this person's name,' he said.

'Because he told me a rather interesting story about this Joseph Carleton you mentioned.'

'You said you'd never heard of him.'

'I said I didn't know him, which is rather different.' (And what a good thing, after all, that I put it that way.) 'I'd asked Mr Webster, you see, whether he could get any line on the person to whom the jewels had been sold, and he had rather an interesting story to tell me about this Joseph Carleton.'

'And this . . . gentleman is, I believe, a friend of yours?'

'If you mean William Webster, c-certainly he is. He saved Jenny's life, as you must very well remember.'

'The powers that be,' said Briggs, 'knowing rather less than I do about your activities, decided that—although his action was rather drastic, resulting as it did in the death of another man—there was no case for him to answer.'

'To kill in d-defence of another is very little different from k-killing in self-defence.' His stammer was very evident now. 'But you h-haven't asked me w-what it was he told me.'

'Perhaps because I don't wish to know.'

'I think in all fairness you must hear what Mr Maitland has to say,' Sykes put in quietly.

'Very well. What is this story?' asked Briggs scornfully.

'Nothing very exciting, b-but I found it enlightening,' said Antony. 'Because you see I know, and I believe you know too, Chief Superintendent, that all this evidence you're trotting out against me is completely false.'

'We'll see what the court has to say about that.'

'Indeed I'm afraid we shall. But you're f-forgetting William Webster. What he t-told me was that Joseph Carleton, after a long and successful career as a b-buyer, was getting ready to retire. But there was some gossip going about that the police were at last about to c-catch up with him.'

'I don't see the significance of that, I'm afraid.'

'Don't you?' His tone was mocking, but where was this getting them, after all? He might find out the strength of the case against him but Briggs had mentioned the murder, and there seemed no doubt that the further evidence Sir Nicholas had predicted had come to light in that case too. But there was no going back now. 'I asked Mr Webster what c-consideration Joseph Carleton would have needed to induce him to make this lying statement to the police. Not money he told me, because the man had plenty already. But if someone was in a position to offer him immunity, or to promise to use his influence to get him a lighter sentence, then he might have been induced to agree.' He paused deliberately, letting the silence lengthen. 'I'm t-talking about you, Detective Chief Superintendent Briggs.'

'You . . . you . . . you have the impudence to suggest that I—?' Briggs broke off there as if words failed him. 'I think your nephew's run mad, Sir Nicholas,' he said roughly.

'On the contrary, Chief Superintendent, he seems at last to have come round to a way of thinking that I've been urging on him for years.'

'Let him try to prove it! And there is still the murder of

170

Vincent Gilchrist to be explained. You haven't an alibi, Maitland, and we're now in a position to prove motive, and . . . did you know that we'd found the weapon?' Antony didn't answer but Briggs didn't seem to notice his silence. 'Well, it makes no matter. It was thrown down the garbage chute at Halkin Place, and the ballistics team say it was the one used. A gun that you bought less than a week ago in a shop in a side street off Ludgate Hill. We have the owner's statement to that effect.'

'He's admitting he s-sold it to me without a certificate? How d-did you persuade him to do that?'

'There was no question of persuasion.' The familiar hectoring tone was back in Briggs's voice now. 'He knows you quite well by sight, he says, and knowing you're a legal gentleman, as he put it, he thought your assurance that you had the document was sufficient. I don't think anyone will be likely to come down too hard on him in the circumstances.'

'And just how was this witness turned up?' He couldn't delay matters much longer, and he knew it. With this evidence Briggs could have proceeded to an arrest without any further ado; the only explanation for this game of cat and mouse was that he couldn't resist the temptation to humiliate as far as he possibly could a man whom he had come to regard as an enemy.

'Inquiries were made of registered firearms dealers, starting with those in the vicinity of the Temple.'

'At your instigation no d-doubt.'

'We're wasting time,' said Briggs impatiently.

'On the contrary, we've all the time in the world. I have a f-feeling of my own about Vince Gilchrist's death.'

'I'm sure your counsel will be interested to hear it.'

'Yes, but we w-won't wait for him. This was your idea, Briggs, that we should talk the m-matter over. It might look a little odd if you refuse n-now to hear what I have to say . . . don't you think?'

'It won't make any difference to the outcome.'

And that was true, but the instinct to delay was still strong in him. 'Vince Gilchrist, as you may or may not know, was a man who seems not to have been able to keep his hands off women. *I* say that jealousy was the motive for his murder, and I could name three men to you without any difficulty who had such a motive.'

171

'Name them!' Briggs challenged.

'Very well then.' He did so, just as he had done to Sykes the night before. 'They may not be the only ones, of course.'

'And one of these three, I suppose, borrowed the gun you had bought –'

'I was never near the s-shop, as you very well know. But –'

'We're wasting time,' said Briggs again.

'One moment, sir,' Sykes intervened quietly. 'I should be interested to know, Mr Maitland, which of these three men you think most likely to be the guilty party.'

'Colin Johnson. That's partly because he's a journalist –'

'And you don't like newspaper men,' Briggs sneered.

'I don't particularly, but that wasn't my reason. The other two men both work in offices, and are much more likely to have alibis. Of course, that's something I can't check. But a journalist has a ready-made excuse to be anywhere he likes at any given time.' His eyes were on Sykes as he spoke, and Sykes responded with the merest inclination of his head, too slight to attract Briggs's notice. 'The other reason I suspect him,' said Antony, too intent on getting his message over to the Chief Inspector for his stammer to trouble him, 'is his rather odd behaviour when Roger and I talked to him, and it's possible that his wife –'

'That's enough!' This was Briggs's moment of triumph and he was savouring it to the full. 'I might have known you'd have some fantastic story ready, Maitland,' he said. 'But this time I'm afraid the evidence is just too strong.'

Just for a second Antony closed his eyes. His instinct about Colin Johnson was nothing like proof, his only hope was that what he had said would provide a basis on which Sykes could build. But that would take time, and even if anything came of it the other charge would still remain, and even if they didn't proceed with it, once the whole thing became public knowledge that was the end of him professionally. So now there was the immediate future to get through, his arrest and all that followed it, with what rags of dignity he could manage to maintain. He raised his head and looked Briggs full in the face.

'You were saying, Chief Superintendent?' he asked.

'That I think we won't waste any more time –' Briggs began, but at that moment the study door opened and Gibbs came into their midst again like a malignant ghost.

'Mr Horton is here, Sir Nicholas,' he said, and for once he

172

sounded completely at a loss. 'And there are a number of other persons –'

Sir Nicholas started to say, 'Show Mr Horton in,' but Geoffrey was already in the room, having slipped past Gibbs's elbow. There was a moment's pause while he took in the fact that there were two police officers among those present, and then (drawing his professional manner round him like a cloak, as Antony put it later) said severely,

'What's going on here?' rather as though he suspected that some clandestine plotting had been going on behind his back.

Sir Nicholas took it upon himself to answer. 'I suspect that Antony is about to be arrested,' he said. 'Of course, I suggested sending for you when these two gentlemen arrived, but I was assured you were out of town.'

'On what charge?' said Geoffrey, swinging round to face Briggs directly.

'For the murder of Vincent Gilchrist.'

'And the alleged motive? Am I right in thinking that you will say that it was to remove the second witness necessary for a conviction under the Perjury Act?'

'Quite right, Mr Horton,' said Sykes. Then placatingly, to his superior officer, 'Mr Maitland's solicitor has the right to this information, sir.'

'Then I think it's high time I got here,' said Horton.

Antony found his voice. 'For heaven's sake, Geoffrey, who have you got outside?' he demanded.

'The reason I was out of town is that I went to see Mrs Bobbin who lives out Windlesham way,' said Horton, addressing his remarks indiscriminately to the assembled company.

'Who the devil is Mrs Bobbin?'

'Ned Bates's widow. The woman he wants to marry,' Geoffrey amplified. 'I have her with me, and we picked Mr Bates up on the way here.'

'Gibbs said –'

'Yes, I know. I can't tell you who the other people are. When we got out of the car your friend Father – Mr Webster – was walking along from the cab rank on Avery Street. He seemed pleased to see me, and told me he too was calling on you. And while we were waiting for the door to be opened a woman I've never seen before arrived from the opposite direction, and came up and joined us. She didn't say anything, except to Gibbs when he opened the door . . . that she wanted to see you as well!'

'Is this an invasion?' inquired Sir Nicholas in an overwrought tone.

'Something like that,' Geoffrey agreed.

'I might have known it! Nothing – you will agree with me in this, Vera – nothing is ever done in a normal and orderly fashion where my nephew is concerned.' Except for Vera, they had been on their feet all this time, but now Sir Nicholas staggered to his usual chair and sank into it. 'We're in your hands, Geoffrey,' he said in a despairing way.

'Another witness has come forward to take Vince Gilchrist's place,' Antony told Horton. 'And yet another one who says I bought the weapon from him that was used in the murder. They're both lying, of course, but you might as well know the worst straight away.'

'Is that all?' said Geoffrey. 'I still think, Chief Superintendent, that you'd be well advised to hear what Mr Bates and Mrs Bobbin have to say.'

Briggs's colour had risen alarmingly and was now the rather violent shade of purple that was his most familiar reaction to his meetings with Maitland. 'If these people have evidence to give,' he snapped, 'it can surely wait until the trial.'

'I think,' said Geoffrey, 'you should consider that a little, Chief Superintendent. Quite frankly I believe it's something you'll regret all your life if you don't hear them out now.' Without waiting for a reply he turned to Gibbs. 'Will you please ask Mr Bates and Mrs Bobbin to come in?'

Gibbs, who had been standing all this time in the doorway, listening to what was going on with his most supercilious look, glanced inquiringly at Sir Nicholas, who aroused himself to nod his agreement.

'And Gibbs, please ask the other members of the – the invading army to wait,' he said. 'I think they would be most comfortable in the dining-room.'

It seemed that Mrs Bobbin at least could only have been awaiting her cue. She was a small, round woman whose name Antony thought suited her very well. She had rosy cheeks and a face that seemed to be formed more for smiling than for frowning, but at the moment she was belligerent. Ned Bates followed her willy-nilly, she had a firm grip on his wrist. For a moment she surveyed the assembled company, and then turned

174

her eyes on Geoffrey. 'All right, Mr Horton?' she said on a note of enquiry.

'*Lafayette we are here!*' murmured Antony irrepressibly. Something in Geoffrey's confidence seemed to have communicated itself to him, so that his spirits, in the depths a moment before, were rising quite unreasonably.

Horton ignored him and maintained his strictly professional air. 'Yes, Mrs Bobbin. Perhaps I should make some introductions. Sir Nicholas and Lady Harding,' (Sir Nicholas heaved himself out of his chair) 'and these two other gentlemen are police officers. Also my client, Mr Maitland.'

'Pleased to meet you, I'm sure,' said Mrs Bobbin indiscriminately. 'I'm Sue Bobbin and this is Ned Bates, my intended.'

There was a murmur of greeting. Sir Nicholas bowed, but kept a tight grip on the back of his chair as though he needed its support. For a moment his eyes met his nephew's, a long, assessing look as though he were asking, Is this your doing? 'We are much obliged to you for coming here, Mrs Bobbin,' he said gravely.

'Right's right and fair's fair, and I'm willing to overlook things as is over and done with, but lying I will not have!' said Sue Bobbin, still in warlike mood.

'I'm sure that does you great credit, madam,' Sir Nicholas told her.

'So when Mr Horton here tells me what Ned's been up to I comes up to town and I says to him you tell the truth now or it's all over between us. Saying he robbed that woman indeed, when he was down at the Queen's Garter with me that very night – that's me pub that me late husband left me – and there's at least a dozen people can tell you the same thing.'

'Thank you, Mrs Bobbin,' said Geoffrey. 'I think we should let Ned speak for himself now.'

'Yes, you tell them the truth, Ned Bates, and no more nonsense,' she admonished him.

Ned looked round sheepishly. 'Well it went against the grain,' he said, 'Mr Maitland being a reasonable sort of bloke even if he does speak his mind rather open-like at times. But it couldn't do me any harm as I could see. It was true what I told you, Mr Maitland: I mean to go straight and I wanted to clear the slate first. But it didn't seem as admitting to one extra thing could make much difference, and when he told me that if I did very likely he could get the court to go easier on me . . . well, I know I didn't ought to have done it, but I gave in to temptation as they say.'

Horton opened his mouth to speak but Maitland was before him. 'That's all right, Ned, no hard feelings,' he said. 'But who told you this, who put you up to it?'

For a moment there was no reply, then Ned Bates turned and looked at Sue Bobbin, and she nodded at him vigorously. 'All right, Mr Maitland, it was him,' he said pointing at Briggs. 'I knew he was in the police because I've seen him in court when we was both younger, so when he said he was a high ranking officer with plenty of influence I'd no reason to disbelieve him.'

'You've no doubt at all about this identification?'

'I'd know him anywhere,' said Ned confidently.

'Thank you.' He might have been addressing a witness in court. 'Now then, Chief Superintendent, what have you to say to that?'

'If you think you're going to escape this charge with more perjured evidence –' Briggs started.

'If I were, wouldn't that be fair? Fighting fire with fire, as they say. And though a jury might find Ned a little on the shifty side, I'll bet you anything you like they'd believe Mrs Bobbin without question, and as she and some of her friends can swear to his alibi . . . there goes your case against me for subverting the course of justice.'

'As to that,' said Briggs, 'we shall see!'

'We shall, shan't we?' For the moment Antony had taken charge of the proceedings. 'Uncle Nick, may I ask Geoffrey to show Mrs Bobbin and Mr Bates into the dining-room, and ask Mr Webster to join us here?'

'If you must,' said Sir Nicholas in a goaded tone.

'Thank you, sir. Will you do that, Geoffrey? And say something nice to the lady who's in there. I don't want her to get tired of waiting.'

'Do you know who this woman is, Mr Maitland?' asked Sykes, when Geoffrey had gone on his errand.

'I don't *know*, and my uncle doesn't like guesses,' said Antony.

'Pray do not consider my feelings, my dear boy,' said Sir Nicholas plaintively. He had gone back to his chair since Sue Bobbin left the room. 'If you wish to add your share to the afternoon's entertainment –'

176

'Thank you, sir. I think Chief Inspector, I just think it might be Rosanna Johnson.'

'The wife of this Colin Johnson you mentioned earlier?'

'Ever since I have known him,' said Briggs, suddenly asserting himself again, 'Mr Maitland has had a genius for muddying what would otherwise be quite a clear trail.'

'In this instance,' Antony pointed out, 'there is obviously no evidence that I killed Vince Gilchrist, except perhaps the lack of an alibi which is hardly incriminating in itself, and a vague suggestion as to motive which cannot now be substantiated.'

'I should still like to know why you think it might be Mrs Johnson who is waiting to see us,' Sykes persisted.

Antony glanced round, but Geoffrey was taking his time. 'It's a long story,' he said, 'but to be as brief as possible she offered to give Vince Gilchrist an alibi, admitting at the same time that they had been lovers. As you know, it wasn't necessary to call her evidence, which relieved me because, though I had no proof of the fact, I very much doubted its truth, at least as far as the alibi was concerned. Later, when I talked to her she confirmed the affair, but on both occasions I had the distinct impression that her offer to give evidence had been partly prompted by self-interest, and that she regretted the fact that she had not been called upon to do so.'

'That sounds a rather complicated state of mind,' said Sykes.

'What I'm trying to say is that I think she wanted her husband to know that Vince Gilchrist had been her lover without actually having to tell him. It *is* complicated, as you say, Inspector. Perhaps she thought that would precipitate the breakup of her marriage, perhaps she valued the family home and hoped her husband would leave her in possession. I could think of a dozen reasons . . . but one thing I'm sure of, whatever she thought her husband already knew—'

At that moment Geoffrey erupted back into the room followed closely by Father William. 'I don't know who the woman in there is,' he said. 'I've never seen her before today, but she's got an absolute beauty of a black eye.'

'Does that fit in with your theory, Mr Maitland?' asked Sykes. Antony could almost have imagined that some of the underlying amusement was back in his tone, and in spite of the fact that he was pretty sure where the detective's sympathies lay, the present situation must be a difficult, if not an agonizing one for him.

'It's not exactly a necessary part of it. Come in, Mr Webster. I think you know everybody here except perhaps my aunt, Lady Harding.'

It was only too obvious that the situation was meat and drink to Father William. He spent some time crossing the room and bowing politely over Vera's hand, before he turned to Sir Nicholas who waved at him feebly in response to his greeting. Sykes he saluted like an old friend. 'But I don't know this gentleman,' he added.

'Detective Chief Superintendent Briggs,' said Antony.

'Good afternoon, Chief Superintendent.' Briggs growled something, but it was obviously not in the nature of a welcome. 'I came to give you a piece of information, Mr Maitland,' Father William went on. 'Do you wish me to speak before all these people?'

Antony looked at him for a moment, and the guileless blue eyes met his reassuringly. 'Yes, I do,' he said firmly.

'It is merely that I received a communication from a gentleman who is in the same line of business as myself. A jeweller,' he explained with a bow in Vera's direction. 'Unfortunately I believe he combines this perfectly legitimate business with certain illegal activities, in connection with the purchase of goods which he knows to be stolen. This man has now admitted to me that he bought Mrs Thurlow's jewels from Vincent Gilchrist. Do I interest you, gentlemen?'

'You're telling us something we all knew perfectly well already,' said Briggs. 'If that is all Mr – Mr Webster – '

'Very far from all. The next part of my information I think will be of particular interest to you two gentlemen as police officers. It concerns an attempt to bribe a prospective witness.'

'Please go on, Mr Webster,' said Sykes politely.

'Joe – I'm speaking of Joseph Carleton – tells me that he bought the jewels in good faith. And here I rather doubt his statement, but I will come to that in a moment.'

'You needn't bother to go into too much detail, Father William, I've already told them our theory,' said Antony.

'Then you mentioned that you visited me this morning? I wonder if that was wise of you. Ah well, it makes no matter. In brief then, gentlemen,' – he was addressing the two Scotland Yard detectives directly now – 'Joe wishes to revise his statement. He was certainly approached about giving false witness in

178

this affair, but not by Mr Maitland. The perjured evidence was intended to incriminate him, and the consideration he was to receive for so doing was not monetary, but in the form of behind-the-scenes assistance if he should ever come to trial.' He paused (he's enjoying this, the old humbug, thought Antony with some affection) and allowed his eyes to travel slowly from Sykes's face to Briggs's. 'It's an odd thing, Chief Superintendent,' he said then. 'Joe gave me a very detailed description of the man who had actually approached him. A big man, he said, balding and growing stout. A description, my dear sir, that would fit you very well, if that is any help to you in your inquiries.'

And at that Briggs came to life. 'So that's your game, is it, Mr Maitland?' he said. 'I don't think much of your witnesses, if you don't mind my saying so. What kind of a showing do you think they'll make in court?'

'A respectable jeweller,' – Briggs made a scornful noise – 'and an equally respectable lady who happens to be a publican. We'll leave Ned Bates out of it if you like. His story to me was obviously a lie, but it deceived me as it also deceived my instructing solicitor, Matthew Barlow – who come to think of it is even more respectable than all the others put together.'

'There is still – need I remind you again, Mr Maitland? – the fact that you purchased the gun that killed Vincent Gilchrist.'

For the first time since Gibbs had announced that there were visitors Sir Nicholas seemed to rouse himself. 'Do you not think, Chief Superintendent,' he asked silkily, 'that the explanation of that bit of evidence may prove to be precisely the same as the explanation of the evidence we have just disposed of. I think the Chief Inspector here will agree with me that there is every reason to think that my nephew has been the victim of a plot.'

Briggs turned on him rather as if that were the last quarter from which he'd expected an attack. 'What precisely do you mean, Sir Nicholas?'

'What I say, no more than that. At the moment I make no accusation. But I think before we go any further we had better hear what our other caller has to say. Whoever she may be.' And when Briggs made no reply he turned to Father William. 'We're all grateful to you for coming here, Mr Webster,' he said . . . a slight exaggeration for which he might be forgiven. 'But may I ask you now to wait in the other room? Geoffrey, will

179

you play messenger again and ask the lady who is waiting there to come in?'

There was a dead silence while Horton was gone, except for Briggs's heavy breathing. And Antony had time for yet another change of emotion. The anger he had felt at Briggs's accusation, which had prompted him to a certain almost vicious pleasure when it seemed that the tables had been turned, had all drained away now. Whoever the woman outside might be, there was no question that the warrant for his arrest would never be served. The long years of anxiety that Briggs's animosity had caused him were surely over; there was relief in the thought, but no pleasure. He was conscious only of a deep weariness, and the feeling – which any of his family or friends could have told him was perfectly in character – that somehow or other the whole thing was his fault.

Geoffrey came back, and it was in fact Rosanna Johnson whom he was ushering before him; nor had he been exaggerating when he said that she had a black eye. She stood a moment surveying the assembly. 'It was Mr Maitland I wanted to see,' she said doubtfully.

Sir Nicholas, having gauged his nephew's mood well enough, exchanged a glance with Vera and came forward to greet the newcomer. 'Mrs Johnson?' he asked.

'Yes, I'm Rosanna Johnson. How did you know?'

'My nephew – I have what I sometimes feel to be the misfortune of being Mr Maitland's uncle – informed us that you might be coming.'

'How could he know?'

'If you knew him better, Mrs Johnson, you would know that he has a habit of jumping to conclusions with an agility that leaves most of us panting in his wake.'

'It was Mr Maitland that I came to see,' she repeated, eyeing Sir Nicholas with all the fascination that a rabbit might feel for a snake.

'I should be very much obliged to you, madam, and so I think would Mr Maitland, if you would say what you have to say in front of all these people. As to that he will, of course, speak for himself –'

'I should like it very much if you would, Mrs Johnson,' said Antony, finding his voice.

'But first I should introduce my companions to you, so that

you can make your own decision. This is my wife, Lady
Harding; the gentleman who summoned you from the outer
room is Mr Geoffrey Horton, a solicitor; and the two gentlemen
on your right are police officers, Detective Chief Superintendent
Briggs and Detective Chief Inspector Sykes, both of the
Criminal Investigation Department at Scotland Yard. They
appear to have come here to arrest Mr Maitland for the murder
of Vincent Gilchrist.'

'Oh, but they mustn't do that! I can't see why they should
want to, I can't see what reason he would have had, but that's
what I came to tell him . . . who had done it. I thought he'd tell
me what to do.'

'Do you still want to see him alone?'

'No . . . it doesn't matter . . . not if that's the way it is. I never
thought, I never dreamed that he was under suspicion himself,
but I came to tell him that it was Colin who did it. My
husband.'

Briggs took one lumbering step towards her. 'A wife cannot
be compelled to give evidence against her husband, Mrs
Johnson.'

Sir Nicholas and Geoffrey started to speak together, then
Horton fell silent and let the older man continue. 'It is hardly
necessary for me to point out to a man of your rank, Chief
Superintendent, that if you proceed with this preposterous
charge against my nephew there is nothing to stop us from
calling Mrs Johnson as a witness in his defence.'

'Anyway, I'm not being compelled, I want to,' said Rosanna
firmly.

'It might be as well to get clear at the outset, madam, exactly
why you wish to make this statement.'

'Because it's only right.'

'And because, perhaps, you have been the recipient of some
violence,' said Sir Nicholas gently.

'I suppose that's part of it,' she admitted. She was speaking
directly to him now, her fear of him gone. 'You see Colin and
I – I suppose we got used to each other. We'd known Vince for
years, he was a good friend of ours, but then suddenly it was
more than that and we were very much in love. I thought if I
gave him an alibi for the robbery Colin couldn't help knowing
about it and would divorce me, and then Vince and I could be
married. I knew of course . . . I'm afraid he didn't care for me as

I did for him, but I thought he'd be so grateful and that might make all the difference, and once we were married he'd see we were right for each other.'

'Why didn't you wish to tell your husband outright, Mrs Johnson?'

'All sorts of reasons, I suppose. I didn't want to hurt him . . . does that sound foolish when I was breaking faith with him anyway? And in the beginning I thought he might turn on Vince if he knew, and then after Vince was killed nothing seemed to matter. Until Mr Maitland and another man came to see us, a Mr Farrell, I think, he asked a lot of questions. And he made it obvious, heartbreakingly obvious, that I wasn't the only one Vince had had an affair with. Karen Chalmers, for instance, and if there was one there must have been others, in spite of what he'd told me. But you see it was equally obvious to Colin, too, and I didn't realize till then that he'd known about us all the time, and that's why he shot Vince. He thought then we could go on together, and I'd get over it in time. But somehow – I don't understand it at all – when he knew about Vince's other affairs it seemed to drive him into a fury. He called me a whore and a slut and that's when he hit me, and he told me to get out and never go back. I spent the night with a friend, but she went to work this morning and I've just been walking about ever since trying to get up nerve to come here.'

'To make an accusation against your husband which is apparently purely activated by malice,' said Briggs. 'I'm afraid, Mrs Johnson, there's still the little matter of proof.'

'I only know what he told me during that last quarrel. He was furiously angry, far too angry to think of the consequences of what he was saying. And I can give you this. I found it in one of Colin's pockets a week or so ago, but even when I knew Vince had been shot it didn't occur to me . . . not until Colin admitted to me yesterday what he'd done. You don't think of people you know in connection with murder and I'd got it fixed in my mind that perhaps he felt safer being armed on some of his assignments.' She had opened her handbag as she spoke and now produced a sheet of paper. Briggs took a step forward, but Sykes was before him, almost snatching it out of her hand.

'A receipt from the gunsmith who said he sold the weapon to Mr Maitland,' he said. 'Thank you very much, Mrs Johnson, I wouldn't be surprised if this clinches things.' He tucked the slip of paper into his pocket, and very deliberately removed what none of his companions except Mrs Johnson had any difficulty in recognizing as a warrant. 'I don't think we shall be needing this after all, Mr Maitland,' he said, and tore it across and across.

Again there was a prolonged moment of deathly silence, broken only by Briggs's heavy breathing. 'I wonder, Mr Horton, if you would take charge of the witnesses for me,' said Sykes, 'and see that they all get down to the Yard to make their statements.' He turned his eyes on Antony. 'Mr Maitland—?'

Antony looked up, but it was not at his old friend the Chief Inspector but directly at Briggs. Even now, even when he had admitted the truth to himself let alone had it proved to him, he was shaken by the venom in the other man's eyes. He turned to Sykes. 'Just get him out of here,' he implored. 'And there's no need for any witnesses except Mrs Johnson, Geoffrey. I shan't press charges.'

'That decision may not rest with you,' Sykes pointed out. But before Antony could reply Briggs had taken a quick step in his direction, his head thrust forward so that he looked rather like a bull about to charge.

'Am I supposed to admire your magnanimity?' he asked. 'I say you daren't take action because you're afraid of what might come out. You know and I know that it would only have been justice—' He broke off there, looking round contemptuously at his companions. 'To hell with justice!' he said. 'I've served the law all my life and it has to end like this.' He looked again at Maitland for one long, bitter moment and then turned on his heel. They heard his footsteps crossing the hall and then the slam of the front door.

The room seemed very quiet after everyone had gone. After a moment Maitland roused himself. 'I should have seen them all,' he said.

'Never mind that! Geoffrey, you may be sure, will do everything that is proper,' Sir Nicholas told him. 'Besides there are a few things I should like to say to you.'

'I'm sure there are, sir.'

'I have never in my life been subjected to such intrusion on my privacy,' said Sir Nicholas. 'And may I remind you, Antony—'

'Nicholas!' said Vera.

'No, my dear, for once I will have my say,' said her husband as though this was something quite out of the ordinary. 'I must remind you, Antony, that if you had shown any discretion at all in your dealings with Briggs from the beginning of your acquaintance, all this might have never happened.'

'That's all very well, Nicholas, but it will wait,' said Vera firmly. 'Merely about to point out to you that Antony's going to be sick at any moment.'

'Then my remarks must wait,' said Sir Nicholas, but his voice followed Antony as he made a dash for the door. 'Don't think, however, that I have not still several things to say to you on the subject.'

Sunday to Tuesday, October 27th to 29th

When Antony had gone upstairs on Friday evening he could not, of course, escape altogether from making some explanation of what had happened, but once he had seen that Jenny was reassured he seemed strangely disinclined to discuss the matter further. Jenny, knowing and perhaps even understanding his mood, let him have his head, but Meg was inclined to be indignant at his silence. It wasn't until Roger assured her, 'Uncle Nick will fill us in on the details, Meg,' that she consented to let the matter lie for the present, but on Sunday at tea-time, when they were all together, she had demanded and received a statement from Sir Nicholas as to exactly what had happened.

Antony still seemed disinclined to add anything to the narrative, only rousing himself to protest when his uncle again expressed his dissatisfaction with the handling of the affair, 'But none of it was anything to do with me, Uncle Nick. Except perhaps Father William's intervention,' he added thoughtfully. 'Geoffrey produced that delightful Mrs Bobbin, and it was Roger's questions that led to the rumpus between Colin Johnson and his wife, which finally brought her to us.'

'I am a little puzzled,' said Sir Nicholas, 'as to how Mr Webster obtained Joseph Carleton's co-operation. It appears that money was not a consideration.'

'I asked him that, Uncle Nick.' For the first time for several days Maitland spoke with the humour that came more naturally to him. 'Father William has a client called Michael O'Keefe, a burglar (Father William's story is that he's trying to help him go straight) who is apparently a bit of a bruiser. Carleton seems to have preferred the prospect of jail to a few broken bones.'

'The company you keep!' said Sir Nicholas in a fading voice. 'And while we're on the subject, what exactly *did* Roger say to the Johnsons?'

'I thought I was helping the wretched woman to see Vince Gilchrist as he really was,' Roger explained. 'I didn't realize, of course, that Colin Johnson . . . and I still don't know what makes him tick.'

'A streak of unexpected puritanism,' said Sir Nicholas, for once not taking up the cudgels on behalf of the purity of the English language. 'Not completely logical, but human motives rarely are. Apparently he could bear his wife's infidelity so long as he thought the feeling between her and her lover was a serious commitment on both sides, but once he knew she had been only one of many . . . at least, that is how I read his actions.'

'He may have been resigned to Rosanna's actions but he still killed her lover.'

'I said it wasn't logical. Mrs Johnson said they had grown apart, but it may be that he wished to restore the status quo.'

But it wasn't until the following Tuesday evening that the last word about the affair was spoken. Jenny's dinner party was larger than usual that evening, as Meg and Roger would be with them as well as Sir Nicholas and Vera, and when Vera came up to help with the preparations it was to inform her hostess that Sir Nicholas had also invited Geoffrey Horton to be of their number. 'Knew it would be all right, knowing you, Jenny,' she said. 'Always prepared to feed an army at a moment's notice. But Nicholas should have given us a bit more warning.'

'It doesn't matter,' said Jenny. 'He usually has some reason of his own when he does something like this.' And when Geoffrey arrived a few minutes after Roger and Meg she greeted him warmly.

Antony and his uncle came back from chambers together. It had been a busy two days, reorganizing all the matters that Sir Nicholas had disorganized the week before. Antony was tired and the nagging pain in his shoulder seemed worse than usual. Uncle Nick had hardly spoken to him on anything but professional matters for days, with that brief exception on Sunday, so that he thought rather wearily it might have been better if Vera had allowed Sir Nicholas to speak his mind at once and get it over with.

He was a little surprised to see Geoffrey Horton on that particular evening, even though he was quite a frequent visitor.

But for once Sir Nicholas condescended to come to his point without delay, as soon in fact as the whole assembly was supplied with sherry, or in Meg's case the Dubonnet she preferred. 'I have been talking to Chief Inspector Sykes,' he said, leaning back in his chair and sipping his sherry as though there was very little else on his mind besides the pleasure it gave him. 'I thought it was time that somebody found out exactly what was being done in this matter, and as you seem disinclined to take any further action, Antony –'

'Uncle Nick!' Antony had been seated in the chair opposite his uncle's, but now he came to his feet and began to move restlessly about the room. 'What have you been up to?' he inquired.

'I have not been up to anything, as you call it,' said Sir Nicholas rather coldly, 'other than tying up the loose ends to which you should have attended yourself.'

'You haven't . . . look here, sir, you know I didn't want –'

'Let me finish, Antony. I believe our friends have some small interest in the matter even though you yourself seem to have none. And as Roger and Geoffrey must both bear some responsibility for the mishandling of the affair, along with your own actions, of course, I felt that they should both hear what I have to say.'

'They did it all practically and I'm grateful to them,' said Maitland.

'Yes, my dear boy, as you have told us *ad nauseam*, and so are your aunt and I,' said Sir Nicholas cordially. 'But I am trying to tell you what I learned from Sykes. Joseph Carleton has gone back on his story so far as it concerns you, and described the Chief Superintendent quite unmistakeably, though it has not been thought necessary to put him through an identification parade. Further, the gunsmith has identified Colin Johnson as the person to whom he sold the weapon, saying that as it was a police matter he was only too willing to oblige with his original story. I take it he meant that his operation isn't completely legal in all respects, and that Briggs had found some irregularity to threaten him with if he didn't co-operate.'

'Yes but, Uncle Nick,' – Maitland came back to the fireside again – 'you can't just leave it there.'

Sir Nicholas, who had picked up his glass, put it down carefully again. 'What else is there to say?' he inquired.

'Well—'

'Think we should all like to know what is happening about that man, Briggs,' said Vera, voicing the question that was in all their minds, and particularly, as she knew, in Maitland's.

'Oh that! What do you suppose has happened?'

'Uncle Nick!' Antony's vagueness of the last few days seemed to have vanished. 'You've told me often enough, year after year if we must have it, that Briggs's feelings towards me were largely my own fault. Do you think I want to see him broken for what's happened?'

'If I have spoken somewhat intemperately upon occasion, I'm sorry for it,' said Sir Nicholas, not sounding in the least contrite. 'But you must realize, Antony, that having engaged in this very complicated plot against you he could hardly retain his present position.'

'He really believed me guilty. He's believed me guilty of one thing after another for years now, and never been completely satisfied with the explanations that we provided. You say he was obsessed by his dislike for me, but I really don't think he'd have done what he did finally if he hadn't persuaded himself that he was somehow serving the cause of justice. You heard what he said.'

'I find myself quite unable to agree with you, my dear boy, except insofar as this obsession of his finally drove him round the bend, as you so imaginatively put it.'

'*What's going to happen to him?*'

'The police don't want a scandal any more than you do,' said Sir Nicholas, relenting. 'They're even grateful to you for not wishing to press the matter, which considering everything I find strange. However, the Chief Superintendent will take an early retirement, on full pension. He was due to retire in two years in any event I understand.'

'Thank heaven for that!' said Antony. He came back to his chair, settled down, and picked up his glass. Across its rim his eyes met Jenny's and they exchanged a look of complete understanding. 'So much behind us, and this time for good and all,' he said, and raised his glass in a sort of salute to her and to their guests. 'To all my partners in crime,' he said. 'And now let's forget about the whole beastly matter.'

'There's just one thing I should like to add,' said his uncle.

'What's that, Uncle Nick?' asked Antony warily.

188

'You've told me often enough, my dear boy, that you don't like coincidences.'

'I don't.'

'Yet what but coincidence was in operation when it brought four different witnesses, with three different sets of information, to my doorstep on Friday afternoon? I only ask for information,' he added and looked all around him blandly.

All Papermac Crime File titles can be obtained through your usual bookseller. In case of difficulty, you may send your order to:

John Darvill,
Macmillan Distribution Limited,
Houndmills, Basingstoke,
Hampshire RG21 2XS

quoting author, title and ISBN.

Prices are £3.95 per title plus £1.00 postage and packing. Please send cheque/Postal Order for total amount made payable to Macmillan Distribution Limited, or your Access/Visa/Diner's Club/American Express credit card can be charged by quoting your credit card account number and expiry date. Please remember to enclose clearly printed name and address.